I0670044

Princes of Air

ALSO INCLUDES "THE ICE RAVEN"

Elizabeth Schechter

Princes of Air ©2022 Elizabeth Schechter

All Rights Reserved. No part of this book may be reproduced or transmitted in any form or by any means, electronic or mechanical, including photocopying, without permission in writing from the publisher.

This is a work of fiction. Names, characters, places and incidents are the product of the author's imagination or are used fictitiously. Any resemblance to actual events, locales or persons, living or dead, is coincidental.

For more information contact:
Riverdale Avenue Books
Circlet Books Imprint
5676 Riverdale Avenue
Riverdale, NY 10471
www.riverdaleavebooks.com

Design by www.formatting4U.com
Cover by Scott Carpenter

Digital ISBN: 9781626016309
Print ISBN: 9781626016316
First Edition, Circlet Books 2012
Second Edition September 2022

Dedication (2011)

To the ERA Storytime crew,
the best crit partners the world has ever known,
To the wonderful ladies of the CFRWA chapter,
who welcomed me with open arms (and chocolate)
To Dan, Janet, and Gemma
my wondrous, wonderful beta readers
To Sasquatch,
because it's all your fault.
To my darling Boo,
for letting Mommy write.
To Michael, always and forever,
just because.
(You knew the job was dangerous when you took it!)

Dedication (2022)

To Cecilia, who took a chance on a new writer and said,
"So, do you have anything longer?"

Introduction

In 2011, I was a new writer, and had four short story sales under my belt. At least, I think it was four. Something between four and six perhaps. I was still fairly green. I'd been playing with longer work, and had written something about a shapeshifter, a raven-boy named Niall, who was the youngest son of the Celtic goddess, The Morrigan. *Prince of Air* was an odd length—just 12,000 words. Too long for a short story, not long enough for a novella. But Cecilia Tan had asked if I had anything longer, so I told her about it, and sent it off to her. Her response?

"Where's the rest?"

She pointed out that there was more story than could be encompassed in 12K words and encouraged me to expand on the story and on the universe. So I went back to work, and found the rest of the story, and a little over a year later, Circlet Press offered me a contract on the newly expanded *Princes of Air.*

It's been a very full ten years. This 10th anniversary of my first novel brings with it the release of novel number 19, and there are seven other completed novels in various places. Including, I might add, a sequel to *Princes of Air* that brings me back to my Celtic fantasy universe and takes a look at the next generation of the Morrigan's blood. *The White Raven: Morrigan's Heir* is coming, and there will be one more book after that. For now, though let's visit some old friends and go back to the beginning.

In ages past, the gods and goddesses of ancient Eire walked the wide world, dallying with mortals and meddling in their affairs, causing wars and ending them, making alliances and breaking them, playing fidchell *with living pieces. Some of these immortals, for amusement or out of boredom, chose to procreate with their especially favored mortals. Thus there came to be in Eire a race of demigods, who lived as part of the world and yet apart from it.*

Such it was with the Morrigan, the Great Queen, Goddess of War and of Fertility. Nine Princes of Air there were, nine sons of the Morrigan, each gifted by their mother with the mortal magics of their unknown fathers, and with the power to take on human form or a raven's wings, as it pleased them. When they took on their human guises, they walked as princes among men, each one a warrior, and each wearing a cloak of raven feathers that clearly marked them as Other. The Raven Boys, the old folks called them, those who remembered the days when the Morrigan brought the first of her sons to live in their mountain home. They remembered, and they warned the foolhardy against testing the mettle of the children of the gods.

Despite the warnings, there were those who never listened...

Part One
Raven Boy

My name is Niall. I am called Niall Gobha, Niall the smith, and I am the youngest of the Raven Boys, having seen only 19 summers come and go. Youngest and most foolish, I admit that now. I'm told that there are others like my brothers and me, other children of foreign gods, who also wear their seemings in their skins, and who can take those skins off and walk among men as we do. There are swan girls, I've heard, daughters of some river god whose name is unknown to me, who live far to the south and west, and who act as guardians for some treasure hidden beneath the waters. To the north, there are the great gray seals who live in the wild northern sea and only come on land once every seven years to mate with mortal kind, and with whom my oldest brother Diarmuid claims to have spoken in his travels. I wonder now if any of them have fallen as I have done?

As I said, I was a fool. Never did it occur to me that the men who live in the lands that surround Dun-Morrigan, our mountain baile, would learn there was a secret we hid in the folds of our raven-feather cloaks. Never did I dream there could be anyone even half so clever as one of the Morrigan's sons. Never did I ever think there would be a mortal so daring, or perhaps so foolish, that they would think they could challenge the child of a goddess and win. And if my brothers, older than I and wise in their years, had ever thought to warn me of such things, then that warning was lost in the reckless arrogance of youth.

Yes, I was arrogant as well as foolish. I admit that, too. I will also admit to being blind, but for that blindness, there was a reason that had its roots in more than my age and my inexperience. Ravens dally where they will, but when they mate, they mate for life, and the woman who would have been my mate had died two years before. It was a harsh thing, to know at 17 that you were doomed to spend the rest of your life alone, with neither wife nor children to warm your autumn years. The pain of that loss still haunted me, for I'd lived with Sorcha and her father, the smith Cormac, for three years while I'd learned the smith's craft and the ways of forge magic. Somehow, in all that time, I never realized what Sorcha meant to me, never knew that somehow, some instinct had pinned all of my future happiness on her crooked smile. It was half a year before I understood the meanings behind the ever-increasing erotic dreams that had kept me from sleeping since I'd left Cormac's forge, before I took wing to return to my red-haired beauty and make her my own.

But by then, it was too late; when I landed on the hill overlooking Cormac's forge, the ashes had already been cold for weeks. To this day, I've no memory of how I returned to Dun-Morrigan. All I know is that I spent the next six days hiding in the rafters of my forge, refusing to take my human form, barely eating, sleeping only when I could no longer keep my eyes open. My brothers eventually puzzled out what had happened, and I heard them whispering as they watched me, murmuring "inadvertent mating" and "pining away" in tones that made me want to scream. Somewhere in the middle of the sixth night, I slipped from my feathers and slept as a human in my own bed for the first time in a week; and woke the next morning howling with pain and sorrow, my dreams haunted by the image of Sorcha dying in flames.

There are, I've found, benefits to taking my human form over my raven one. Thumbs, for one. And that morning, I discovered another: ravens cannot cry. I wept for what felt like hours in Diarmuid's arms, until at last there was nothing left inside me, save only an emptiness that I knew would never be filled.

Some, faced with that emptiness, try to fill it with their craft, but working at my forge brought me no peace. There were too many memories there, memories of my lessons with Cormac, and of Sorcha working at my side. She had not a drop of forge-magic, but her skill at fine-work, at delicate filigree and the excruciatingly pains-taking art of granulation that I never mastered, was unsurpassed. After a month of seeing ghosts in the shadows, I cleaned my forge and then left it to gather dust, moving to sleep on the floor of the house belonging to my next oldest brother, Maelan.

It was he who first brought me down to Scath, the village below Dun-Morrigan, and to the tavern there. There, I learned that mortal men sometimes attempt to fill the void with wine or strong ale, but I also soon found that ravens have no head for drink. I succeeded only in making myself shamefully ill, and in losing my virginity to a sweet girl named Bride, who listened to my ravings, heard the pain beneath them, and tried to offer healing the best way she knew. In her arms, I found something approaching the peace that I craved, and she and I were lovers for months.

She taught me with a gentle hand, urged me to tell her about Sorcha, and helped me mourn. When she eventually married the miller's son, I fired my forge and gifted her and her new husband with every piece of metalwork that they could possibly need for their new home. They named their first son Niall, an honor I wish I deserved.

After Bride came Maeve, a bard as wild and intoxicating as the warrior queen for whom she was named. From her I relearned passion, and I learned again how to laugh. She knew I would never truly love her, and she didn't care—she lived for the moment, and when she tired of me, she left, leaving me with a kiss, a song that she had written for me, and a lighter heart than I'd had in a very long while. And yet, as the snow faded to a memory and the trees all turned to green, I could feel the old, familiar despair start to creep back into my soul. That was what drove me into the skies, and into the arms of the woman who would prove to be my downfall.

* * *

It was a spring so new that it was still raw around the edges, and I had taken wing to dance among the clouds, once again trying to flee from my memories. I hoped to find a maiden in the fields, one whom I could entice into my arms for an afternoon with promises of pleasure and a golden trinket or two, and who might find me pleasing enough to want more than an afternoon. In one of the hidden pools that dot the hills, I thought I found what I was seeking: a woman, bathing in the cold, clear water. She was graceful as a willow, with full breasts and long, nut-brown hair that streamed past her waist. Not as beautiful as Sorcha had been, but pretty in her own way.

I perched on a branch above the pool and watched her, trying to decide how best to approach her without causing her any alarm. That was when I saw a man creeping through the high grass towards the water's edge. I saw the sunlight shining off the blade in his hand, and called a low warning to the woman in the water. She looked up at me and laughed, then turned and waded towards the shore, where I could see her clothing waiting. As she reached the water's edge, the man rose, a cruel look on his scarred face, his knife ready. I forsook discretion and was on the wing before the woman had a chance to scream, changing forms in mid-air and landing in front of her with my sword bared and ready. The would-be rapist gaped at me for a moment, then took to his heels and ran.

At any other time, I'd have followed him, done more than simply frighten him into flight, but I was unwilling to leave the woman alone after her fright. My lust cooled, my thoughts turned instead to protecting an innocent, and I sheathed my sword and turned to face her. Up close, she was prettier than I'd previously thought, with a spray of freckles like gold dust across her nose, and rich, hazel eyes. And, to my surprise and amusement, she was a full three fingers taller than I was.

She stared at me for a moment, then her eyes flickered over my shoulder towards the distant mountain and she sank gracefully to her knees. "My lord, thank you," she said as she slowly looked up; I was startled to see her gaze lingering just below my belt. When she finally met my eyes again, she smiled. "May I know the name of my rescuer, oh Prince of Air?"

Intrigued, I held my hand out to help her to stand. "Niall. Niall Gobha mac Morrigan. What's your name? And where do you live?"

Her smile grew wider as she took my hand. As she got to her feet, she ran one hand up my arm in a firm caress that left goose flesh in its wake. "A smith. I should have guessed that," she murmured. "You're so strong. My name is Arlaith inghean Eochada." She gestured towards the south, "My home is on the other side of that hill. It's not far."

I nodded and stepped back, feeling the heat of her touch as sharply as if it was the flames of my own forge, and trying very hard to ignore it. She'd nearly been attacked—the last thing she would want was my attentions. I stooped, picked up her gown, and held it out to her, "Here, dress yourself. I'll see you safely home." She took the gown, and I turned away to allow her privacy to dress.

"You were watching me," she said, and I couldn't tell if she was amused or angry.

"Yes, I was. I apologize," I admitted, feeling a flush of embarrassment. I'd never been caught spying on someone before.

To my surprise, she took my arm again, turning me to face her. I could see her gown abandoned on the ground behind her. "You saved my life. How can I offer any complaint?" She moved closer to me, a small smile on her face, a flush growing on her cheeks. "Tell me, my hero. Is there no way I can repay your kindness?" She took another step, pressed her body against mine, wrapped her arms around my neck, and kissed me.

I swear, by Mother's tail feathers, until that moment I had put aside all thoughts of a tryst. I was fully intending to bring this woman back to her home and then take wing back to Dun-Morrigan. That was before I found myself with a lovely naked woman in my arms, her lips on mine, her hands sliding down my chest to work at my belt. Her skin was cool from the waters of the pool, warming under my touch as I ran my hands down her back, pulling her closer, feeling her wet hair tangling through my fingers. With quick motions she stripped me of my cloak of feathers and my leather jerkin, loosened the waist of my trews, and drew me down to lie with her, hidden in the sun-warmed grass. Arlaith knew what she was about, her long fingers dancing over my skin, pushing my trews down past my hips so that my cock sprang free. She laughed at the sight and mounted me, her hands on my chest, pinning me onto my back as she slowly lowered herself onto me, taking me into her an inch at a time until she was seated firmly against my hips. I reached for her, and she caught my hands in hers, lacing her fingers into mine and balancing like that as she rode me; I could feel the brush of her hair against my legs as she tipped her head back and moaned her pleasures to the wind, her cries sounding in sharp counterpoint to my own as her slow, deliberate rocking attempted to drive me insane with desire.

I hadn't expected it, but this woman was every bit as wild as Maeve had been, and it was incredibly exciting to me how completely Arlaith took command of our lovemaking. She knew what to do with a man's body, how to get the responses that she wanted; she stretched out over me and kissed me deeply, then slowly straightened, her hair falling in a curtain around us as she ran her hands over my chest, finding my nipples with her fingertips and toying with them until I moaned and grabbed her hips. I wanted her underneath me, wanted to lave her breasts with my tongue, drive into her until she screamed, but when I bucked underneath her and tried to roll her over, she laughed and pushed me back down. Her movements grew more erratic and her breathing grew faster; I could feel her tightening around me and I knew that neither of us would last much longer. She came first, drawing me over the edge with her, and our mingled cries echoed from the surrounding hills.

* * *

I woke, dizzy and confused, to find Arlaith leaning over me, tracing patterns on my chest with her nails. "I was wondering when you'd wake," she murmured softly as she smiled down at me. Then she moved away, sitting so that she could comb through her hair with her fingers.

I watched her, fascinated, thinking her the most beautiful woman in the world. I sat up and reached for her, shaking my head slightly to try and dispel the feeling that my head was in a fog. As I did, I noticed also the streaks of crimson to the west, the darkening purples to the east. Sunset. I grimaced, forgetting the idea of anymore love-play, scrambling to my feet and pulling my trews back up as I did. She stared at me, and I held my hand out to her, "It's late. I should get you home."

She looked up at me and pouted, turning away from my outstretched hand, "Is that all you have to say to me? Did I not please you, Niall?"

I stopped, silently cursed myself for a fool, and dropped to my knees in front of her, pulling her into my arms and kissing her deeply. When I pulled back, she was smiling. "I apologize, Arlaith," I said. "Yes, you did please me. Very much so. But it is getting late. The sun will set soon…"

Arlaith looked at the sky, then back at me, "Oh, I see! Ravens don't fly at night!"

I nodded. "If I'm to get back to Dun-Morrigan tonight, I'll need to be on the wing soon."

She nodded and stood up, walking over to where her gown lay near the water's edge, "You need not rush, Niall. You're welcome in my home." She dressed quickly, then picked up my cloak and smiled, swinging it around to rest on her own shoulders.

"Is this where you hide your magic?" she asked, laughing. "If I wear it, will I be able to become a raven, too?"

"Magic?" I repeated, caught completely off guard by her question. I'd had it drummed into me from the day I was old enough to leave the baile by myself that protecting my cloak was vital to my own safety. My brothers and I kept the fact that we needed our cloaks to make the change from man to raven a closely guarded secret; without our cloaks, we were as human men. Despite that, there was no magic in the cloak—the secret to the change was inside me. I shook my head, "No, the cloak doesn't have any magic."

I pulled on my sleeveless jerkin, tightened my sword-belt around my waist, and held my hand out for the cloak. She pouted again, draped the cloak over her arm and stroked the feathers, then handed it to me. I pulled it over my shoulders, then held my hand out to Arlaith. She took my hand in hers, and we walked towards the hill and her home.

"I don't want to be a burden on you, Arlaith," I said as we walked. "I should still be able to make the flight home once I leave you."

"You won't be a burden," she answered, her voice coaxing and warm in the growing chill. "You'll bring honor to my house if you'll accept my hospitality." She looked at me and smiled slowly, making my blood warm. "My bed is very large, Niall."

At her words, the tempting thought of spending the night in her bed suddenly turned to sharp need. "Is it?" I asked, trying not to sound too eager.

"Piled with furs and with cushions soft as a cloud. Spend the night with me. You'll have the hero's portion at my table tonight, guest right until the dawn, and a night in my arms."

I smiled, dizzy in love and with not a thought in my head of the worry my absence would cause, "With an offer like that, how can I refuse?"

* * *

In hindsight, I should have realized that something was amiss. As we walked, Arlaith told me that she lived alone, that her father was long dead, and that she had no husband. And yet, when we arrived at the fortified baile that Arlaith called her home, there was a meal laid and waiting that would have fed everyone at Dun-Morrigan, with enough left over for another meal. There was clothing laid out for my use as well, a man's robe that had obviously never been worn before, made from the finest silk from over the seas. If I'd been thinking, I would have asked the questions: why so much food for a woman who lived alone? Where did the robe come from, and why? And in all the years that I and my brothers had flown over this land, how was it that I had never seen or heard of this baile before, or known of the woman who lived here alone? If I'd been thinking, I would have been alarmed. But I was addled by Arlaith, enraptured by her attentions and by her touch, and I followed her without question.

We arrived in her home, and Arlaith formally granted me guest-right under her roof from dusk 'til dawn. Then she led me through the grand feasting chamber and into her bedchamber, where there was a large bath waiting. Again, she undressed me, waving off her servants so that she could attend me in the bath herself. She was the perfect bath-servant as she scrubbed my body and unbraided my shoulder-length hair, working through the tangles with a heavy horn comb. She held a warmed drying sheet for me when I stepped from the bath and sat with me before the fire so that she could comb my hair again and rebraid it, threading carved amber-and-gold beads worth a king's ransom into my hair. When I protested, she silenced me with a kiss, coaxing me to my feet so that she could dress me in the silken robe that was worth even more than the beads. She dressed herself in a similar garment, and led me back out into the feast-hall, where we reclined on silken couches as the Romans did.

Our meal was served on golden plates, with snow-chilled wine poured into jeweled goblets. I ate and drank without noting what passed through my lips, my eyes on Arlaith, my thoughts already ranging ahead to the promised night in her arms. In the firelight, the robes that we wore were sheer enough that I could see the rose-pink of Arlaith's nipples, and the hint of darkness betwixt her thighs, and I was certain that she could see my own arousal clearly. Indeed, she gave me a long, appraising look, and then laughed and set her goblet down on the low table next to her couch.

"Shall we retire, my hero?" she asked, standing and holding her hand out to me. I needed no further encouragement, getting to my feet and then, impulsively, scooping Arlaith up in my arms. She laughed, putting her arms around my neck and nuzzling my ear as I carried her into her bedchamber.

Her bed was everything that she had promised; I laid her down amidst the cushions, thinking only that I was the luckiest man in the world, to find favor with such a woman. She rose up on her knees and drew me onto the bed to kneel in front of her, her warm hands pushing the silken robe from my shoulders.

"You're so young. Are you as young as you seem, Niall? Or is it your magic that makes you so?"

I smiled, running my fingers over her shoulder, teasing the edges of her robe away from her skin, "It's no magic. I've 19 summers."

"Have you had many lovers?" Arlaith asked, not meeting my eyes.

I stopped, surprised by the question and by the inexplicable wave of sadness that rose in me in answer. Then I shook my head, "No one serious."

She slid the silk down my arms and let it puddle around me, "No one? And you so lovely? I find that very hard to believe."

"No one," I repeated, trying to ignore the feeling that I was missing something. I reached out and pulled her to me, "Until now, I think."

Arlaith laughed and pushed me away, then guided me to lie on my back amongst the furs and cushions. She knelt astride my legs and ran her fingers down my thighs, "I think you'll enjoy this, then. I know that I will."

I propped myself up on my elbows so that I could better see her, but before I could ask what she meant, Arlaith had stretched out over my legs and was slowly lowering her mouth over my erection. I yelped in shock—Maelan and Ronan had both told me that there were women who would do this kind of thing, but I'd never expected to have it done to me! She laughed, something that felt incredible through my cock, then she started doing something extraordinary with her tongue. Moaning, I fell back on the bed, stunned by sheer pleasure. I reached towards Arlaith, wanting to touch her, run my fingers through her hair, but she caught my wrist in her hand and pulled it down to my side. Then she did the same to my other wrist, holding me fast with a strength I wouldn't have expected, her nails digging painfully into my skin. If I wanted to, I could have broken her grip, but I didn't want to hurt her. So I lay there, captive in her hands, as she did the most wondrously profane things that made me moan and squirm under her. Her teeth scraped lightly along the length of my shaft, making me buck and yowl like a scalded cat; she laughed again and raised her head, propping herself up on her elbows before slowly swirling her tongue over the head of my cock, then moving down my length until she was licking my balls. I could feel my orgasm building, and strained under her, wanting her mouth on my cock again.

"Arlaith…" I groaned. She laughed and swallowed me again, taking me deeper than she had before, then starting to hum. It was the humming that did it, driving me completely out of my senses and leaving me screaming and writhing in her grasp as I came. She drank me dry, then released me and rolled to lie next to me on the bed.

"Did you enjoy that, my raven?" she asked, running her nails up and down my chest.

I caught my breath and rolled towards her, pulling her to me. "Did I leave any doubt?" I asked as I kissed her, tasting salt on her lips. I licked her lower lip and smiled, "Is that what I taste like?"

She smiled and licked her own lips, a tantalizing sight, "Delightful."

"I'm glad you think so," I said, running my hand down her back. "What would you like me to do for you?"

She pushed me back down onto the bed and stretched out on top of me. "Lie there and let me adore you, my beautiful hero," she murmured, leaning down and kissing me deeply. I wrapped my arms around her, running my fingers through her silky hair, then kissing my way down her neck. Her skin was warm, tasting of honey, salt, and the herbs that she had strewn in our bath, all at the same time. Before I reached her collarbone, she pushed me back down.

"Roll over, my hero. I have plans for you."

Curious, excited by the prospects of what she could have planned, I did what she asked, resting on my stomach while Arlaith poured something warm and heavily scented onto my back. Then she started to knead there with her hands, strong fingers finding every knot and every muscle and easing them loose, working down my back, over my arse, then down my legs. The spicy scent of the oil that she used was heavier than I liked and it made my head spin. Or perhaps it was what she was doing to me that was the cause. I could no longer tell. All I knew, as she urged me to roll onto my back, was that I wanted her again. She noticed—how could she not—and her ministrations took on a more erotic tone as she rubbed down my chest and belly, letting the head of my cock graze over her skin as she leaned over me. Finally, I could stand it no longer, taking her into my arms and pulling her close for another kiss before pushing her onto her back. She welcomed me with open arms, and I finally had my wish of having her legs tight around my waist as I entered her, feeling her tighten around me as I plunged into her depths again and again, and then hearing her cries ringing in my ears as I came once more . Completely spent, I lay down next to her, thinking to hold her close while we slept. But she smiled and pushed away from me, leaving me alone in the bed and returning with a cup that she handed to me without a word. Sated and sleepy, I drank, tasting richly spiced wine, heavy with honey, but with an odd under-taste, as though the wine were going sour. She lay down next to me, and I drew her into my arms, kissing her once more. Before I succumbed to darkness, I remembered hearing the muffled sound of the songbirds in the thatch roof above me, welcoming the dawn.

I was such a fool.

* * * *

Diarmuid made his way across the urla, the cold morning dew on the grass soaking into his shoes as he headed towards the feast-hall to share his morning meal with his brothers. The bright spring sunshine was warm on his shoulders, but not yet warm enough to chase the chill out of the air, and he hoped to find both a blazing fire and something warm to eat. Entering the hall, he stopped just inside the door to allow his eyes to adjust to the gloom, smiling at the sound of his younger brothers bickering. When he could see again, he looked around. The twins Ronan and Petran sat across from each other at the table, playing fidchell *and arguing quietly over which of them was cheating. Diarmuid was amused to see that it looked like both of them were; he turned to look at the rest of the room, and at the other young men scattered around it. Cuanu and Cathal were near the fire, both of them super-*

vising childlike Fergus with his meal. And reclusive Oscar sat in the far corner, ignoring the rest of them, as usual. Diarmuid smiled. Then he stopped and looked again.

"Where are Maelan and Niall?" he called out.

"Maelan's sleeping off his excesses," Petran called back without turning. "He was at the tavern again last night."

Diarmuid shook his head and walked over to help himself to a bowl of the grain porridge that steamed in a kettle over the fire, "And did Niall go with him?" Silence was his answer, and he turned to look the others. "Well?"

It was Cathal who answered, a frown marring his usually merry face, "Niall... was in a mood yesterday. He flew off in the afternoon. I stood the sunset watch last night, and unless he came back very late, I haven't seen him since."

"That's not like him at all," Diarmuid said slowly as he ate. "Even at his worst, he's never gone off without telling one of us."

"I wouldn't worry about him, Diarmuid," Ronan said. "He's probably found himself a nice little female to keep him warm. The boy is turning into a..." He stopped abruptly, and Diarmuid could tell that Petran had kicked his twin under the table.

"When you've finally found yourself a mate and lost her, Ronan an Dana, then you'll be able to speak to what your little brother may or may not have become," Petran scolded coldly. "Until then, you keep your sharp tongue where it will cut no one but yourself." Ronan grumbled and nodded once, then shrugged and stood, leaving the game behind.

"Perhaps he told Maelen?" Petran offered.

"Who told me what?" Maelan asked, wincing as he came into the hall.

"Maelan, have you seen Niall?" Diarmuid asked.

Maelan shook his head slowly, "No. His pallet wasn't even unrolled last night. I thought he might have gone back to his forge, but I didn't check. Why?"

"Because he never came home last night," Diarmuid said. He scowled and set his half-empty bowl aside, walking back out into the sun so that he could scan the empty skies. There was a soft footfall behind him; he turned and was surprised to see Oscar standing at his shoulder.

"What are you thinking, brother?"

Diarmuid looked back up at the clear, cloudless sky, then turned. "I don't know. There's something unquiet in the air. Tell the others to keep a watch. I'm going out." Without waiting for a response, Diarmuid shifted, taking to the air, riding the winds out and away from Dun-Morrigan.

* * *

I woke from dreams of flame-red hair and a fetchingly crooked smile to find myself alone, cold, and confused. I was sitting propped against one of the roof supports, and when I moved, the rattle of chain rang in my ears. I tried to move my hands and could not, my wrists caught in heavy shackles that were separated by a bar of iron. There was a chain running from the bar to similar shackles on my ankles, and from there to wrap around the support pole that I was leaning against.

I closed my eyes and took a deep breath, feeling something tight around my throat as I did so. What had happened? The last thing I remembered was being with Arlaith in her bed.

"Arlaith?" I called, growing alarmed and noticing more about my situation. I was not naked, but what I was wearing was even worse. Around my waist was a brief kilt made of coarse white wool. I raised my hands to feel my throat, and found not my gold torc, but a heavy leather collar. I could barely raise my hands high enough to touch my head, but by ducking my head and shoulders I was able to confirm that my hair had been shorn down to stubble. Someone had marked me as a slave. I looked around, trying to see where I was. No longer in the hall where we'd dined the previous night. This was a ruin, with gaping holes in the thatch, wet, rotting rushes underfoot, and the smell of decay everywhere. I tried to get to my feet and could not—the chain between my hands and feet was too short for me to stand upright. So I settled back down onto my haunches and tried to clear my head. What had happened?

In the quiet, I heard footsteps coming towards me. Turning, I saw two people came into the hall; one remained in the shadows, and the other came towards me. As she passed through a patch of light, I saw that it was Arlaith. She looked at me, a satisfied smile on her face, and I knew then that she'd done this to me. And with a sudden cold clarity, I knew how.

"You bespelled me," I accused.

"True. While you slept at the pool. Oh, and then there were potions in the oil and in the wine. But I hardly had need of any of them," she answered. "It was ridiculously simple to lure you here."

The truth erased the pleasure I'd found in her bed, and I wondered how I'd ever thought myself in love with her. Was that part of the spell? The idea that I'd betrayed Sorcha's memory made me feel ill. "You granted me guest-right," I said coldly.

"From dusk 'til dawn," she agreed. "It's well past dawn, raven boy. You're mine now."

"For what purpose? Ransom?" I sniffed. "Do you think you'd live long enough to enjoy it?"

She smiled wider, "You think your brothers will find you?" She raised one hand, and I could see her fingers glowing in the dim light. "You're hidden from them, boy, until I decide to release you. Which I will, if you give me what I want."

I scowled, stung by how easily I'd been trapped. "What do you want, woman?"

"The magic in the raven-feather cloak."

I turned to stare at her, "You took me hostage for that? I told you at the pool, there's no magic in my cloak."

"Do you think that I believe you?" She crossed her arms. "There's never been a sorcerer who could change their form for even a moment. We're taught that it's impossible. Yet you change your shape. I saw you do it. I examined you very closely while you slept, and you've no great gift, so the magic must be in the cloak. Give that power to me, teach me to use it, and I will free you to return to your mountain."

This time, I laughed. "*Power*? Woman, there is no power in that cloak. The only power I could possibly teach you is forge-craft. I know the charms to sing over iron and bronze. I can whistle the edge onto a blade, and I know the sacrifices to keep the thousand little forge gods happy and bring luck to my hammer. If you want that, and if you have the gift, then I can teach you. There is *nothing* in the cloak."

She took two great steps forward and slapped me across the face, "Liar! I will have your magic, raven boy. You will give it to me, or you will stay like this, chained in this hovel, for the rest of your days."

I spat at her, giving in to my temper and starting to sing the charm that would shatter the chain that bound me. It was short, as such things went. Six words, a simple melody. But I'd forgotten about the other figure in the doorway. Before I'd gotten a full word out, someone grabbed me from behind, clamping a large, heavy hand over my mouth to cut off my voice.

"You'd best silence this one, sister," a man said in my ear as I struggled and fought in his grip.

"Yes, I think that's best." Arlaith came towards me, her hands glowing softly. She rested her hands on my throat and sang a dissonant chant; her power sank into my skin, as tainted as the wine that she'd bid me drink in her bed. When she released me, so did the man, leaving me unsteady on my knees. In haste I tried to finish the chant, and was met with only silence. I caught my breath and stared at Arlaith with wide eyes, suddenly frightened beyond measure.

"Not a word will you say or a note will you sing until you give to me the magic of your feather cloak," she said, her words ringing with her magic, sealing the spell on me. Then her eyes narrowed. "You have two days, Niall Gobha. If you have not told me your secret by sunset on the second day, I will burn your cloak and keep you as my silent slave, chained to the foot of my bed for the rest of your days." As she spoke, the man came around to stand with her; I recognized the scarred man immediately as the attacker from the pool. He grinned when he saw that I knew him, and Arlaith laughed.

"Oh, yes. It was a trap. We've been hunting ravens for quite some time." And with that, she and the man turned and left, leaving me alone in the ruin.

I'd been overly hasty, using the charm in my anger

when I should have saved it and used it when I was alone. Now I had to think, had to try and find a way to escape. Or else the rest of my days would be very short indeed.

The sons of the Morrigan guard our secrets well, and Arlaith's words told me clearly enough that she really didn't know anything about us. But she was convinced that she knew the truth; she truly believed there was some kind of magic woven into my cloak, and anything that I told her otherwise would be counted as a lie. She would never believe me if I told her that the sons of the Morrigan are not born human.

That is the simple truth. We are born as ravens, and we learn the trick of the change when we're old enough to walk the world. My feather cloak is simply the skin that I had been born wearing. If I did not give Arlaith magic that did not exist, then she would destroy my skin, and that was what frightened me to my bones. What she didn't know, what she would never believe even if I could tell her, was that if she burned my cloak, I would die with it.

There had to be a way for me to escape!

* * *

I spent hours studying the chain that bound me, examining each and every link, searching for some kind of flaw. I was forced to stop before I was finished—it was too dark for me to see, and my hands were shaking from cold and hunger. But by then, I knew that most of the chain was flawless, and I was certain that I knew who had made it; there was a painfully familiar ring to the charms that lingered in the metal. I knew these charms as well as I knew my own, and I had reason to: they were created by the man who taught me everything I knew of forge-craft.

If this was indeed Cormac's work, there was no chance of me breaking free; he had been the best smith under the sky. But this chain was recent work, the edges of the shackles still sharp and bright, and Cormac was two years dead. It was impossible, and yet the chain and the shackles were his work, I was certain of it.

Cold, hungry, and mistrusting of the darkness around me, I shifted around, trying to find some comfort. Ravens are communal beasts—we don't live alone if we can help it. I'd never truly been alone for any length of time in my life, and now, captive and silent, I couldn't stop the feeling that the quiet dark was pressing down on me. I doubted that I would be able to sleep, but I knew that I needed rest, or I'd risk making a worse mistake than simply losing my temper. Without thinking, I lay down on my side, drawing my knees up to my chest. The cold rose from the ground and sank into my bones, making me ache and shiver. I tried to get back up, only to find myself stuck—the chain between my hands and feet was too short to allow me the leverage to rise. I cursed silently and struggled for a long time, rolling in the rushes as I tried to fight my way upright. When I finally fell still, I was exhausted and shivering hard enough that I could hear my teeth rattling. That was when I heard something else, the soft sound of footsteps in the rushes, a soft metallic jingling. I assumed it was Arlaith, come back to taunt me again. I closed my eyes, the better to ignore her. The steps grow closer, and I heard a gasp.

"Niall?"

I jerked at the sound of my name, craning my neck to see over my shoulder. The voice was not Arlaith's, but it was somehow tantalizingly familiar. All I could make out in the darkness was a woman standing a few feet away, one who wore the short white tunic of a slave, her ankles bound with a length of chain. She put down the tiny lamp she was carrying, dropped something else out of my line of sight, and helped me to sit back up. Then a rough blanket that smelled of horses was draped round my shoulders, and she knelt in front of me, taking both my hands in hers and holding on as if she were afraid I would disappear. I stared at her in the dim light, not willing to believe my own eyes as I realized who she was.

Sorcha. My own Sorcha. For a moment, I thought I was delirious and dreaming, but then I realized I couldn't be. In my dreams, Sorcha was still and forever16. This Sorcha was older, different. I knew her though, even though she'd changed, grown taller, more slender. More beautiful, even with the collar around her neck and her once waist-length hair shorn as close as mine was now. The day I'd returned to the forge and found it destroyed had been the worst of my life. To see her alive, even as a slave, was astounding. She looked at me, her blue-green eyes full of tears.

"It is you. I was so afraid… Arlaith is in the hall," she whispered, leaning towards me so that I could hear. "She's boasting that she's bested one of the Princes of Air, that she's taken your cloak and that she's going to keep you a slave." She looked down, and I felt one of her tears splash on the back of my hand, burning hot against the cold. "Niall, I'm sorry. This is all my fault."

Her fault? How could this be *Sorcha's* fault? I looked at my chains and realized that if I stretched one hand out hard against the shackle, I could reach her; I caught her chin and raised her head, letting her see my confusion.

"Niall?" she whispered. "What is it?"

I shook my head and shrugged my shoulders, then gestured to my throat and shook my head again. She looked at me, a confused look on her face. I grimaced, opened my mouth, closed it again and shook my head. Her eyes went wide.

"You can't speak?" she asked. I nodded and jerked my head backwards, towards the door. Sorcha looked puzzled for a moment, then gasped, "Arlaith? She did this to you?" I nodded again, relieved that she understood. I gestured for her to continue, and she nodded, taking my hands again.

"You're so cold," she murmured. She opened the blanket and slipped in next to me, wrapping the blanket tightly around the both of us and curling up against my side. She rested her head on my shoulder, the way she used to do when we would sit up together and watch the stars at night. Fighting back tears, I turned my head and buried my nose in her short hair, breathing in her soft scent like a balm. Sorcha, alive and whole. It was too much to believe.

"It's my fault, Niall," she repeated. "Arlaith came to the forge about a month after you left. She claimed that her baile was being threatened by a neighboring king, and she wanted to arm her men. She paid in gold, and because she claimed it was too far for her to travel, we granted her guest-right. She stayed with us for a month while Da worked in the forge, and made much of me, treated me like a daughter. We would talk… it was like my mother was still alive." Sorcha rubbed her cheek on my arm and then looked up at me. "I told her about you. How much I missed you. I showed your feather to her, the one you gave to me that last Midsummer. She was so interested that I told her everything." She took a long breath and let

24

it out before she continued. "She left with her weapons, and a month later she came back. This time, she brought Ailill with her. They wanted more weapons, and they wanted us to come with them and swear fealty to Arlaith. I don't know what made Da suspicious, but he put her off. He told her that he had another commission, and to come back in a month. Then he went to Dun-Righ to speak to the High King."

I blinked, surprised. I'd never known Cormac to go to the High King's fortress willingly, despite the fact that he answered to the High King Eogan alone, and by rights his forge should have been at Dun-Righ. Cormac hated the court, often railing at length over our evening meals at the petty bickering that the court was prone to fostering among those who lived there. At the time, it had amused me greatly; I'd noticed the same things the few times I'd been to court with my brothers, and I heartily agreed with Cormac that court was for nobles, druids, and sorcerers. Looking back on those nights, the idea of Cormac leaving his forge to go to court was chilling; he would never have gone unless he thought there was something truly wrong.

Sorcha shifted, loosening her hold on my arm. "While Da was at court, he found out that everything that Arlaith told us was a lie. The tale that Da was told was that Eogan's father kept Arlaith and Ailill's mother as his concubine, until he found the woman in another man's bed. He cast her out of Dun-Righ, and refused to acknowledge Arlaith and Ailill as his children. Arlaith thinks that she is the rightful High Queen, and she's planning to overthrow Eogan."

I nodded, understanding a little more why Arlaith was so power-hungry. If she was going to challenge Eogan for the throne, she'd need powerful magic—Eogan had the entire college of druids and sorcerers at his beck and call. It still didn't explain why she thought I had power she could steal.

"Da came back furious at how he'd been used, and when Arlaith returned, he told her to leave, that he wouldn't betray his oath or his king." Sorcha had started shivering, and I didn't think it was from cold. "They attacked the forge the next night. When Ailill brought us to Arlaith, she told Da that if he wouldn't serve her willingly, then he'd serve as a slave. They brought us here, and I've been here ever since."

I noticed with a gut-sinking wrench how she'd started talking about herself and her father, and then spoke only of herself. She must have seen the question in my eyes, because she nodded.

"He's dead, Niall. He died a few days after he finished that monstrosity." She tapped the shackle on my wrist. "He knew what she meant this for, because he was there when she made me tell them about you." Sorcha dropped her head, and without warning, started to cry again, deep, wracking sobs of heart-wrenching sorrow and loss. She clung to me, and I was helpless to do anything to console her. When finally she could speak again, she didn't look up at me.

"They tortured him, Niall," she said, her voice a mere whisper. "They put hot irons on my Da's back, to make me tell them about you. And in between the irons, he was crying, telling me not to help them, not to betray you. He loved you, you know. Like his own son. But I didn't think they'd be able to catch one of you, and I couldn't let them hurt him. So I… I lied. I told her wild tales about you and your brothers, and the power you wielded. I thought it would warn her off of trying." She sniffled and continued, "And then Da took sick, from the burns. They just let him suffer. And when he refused to work, they… threatened to do to me what they'd done to him. So he finished the chain. Then he took to his bed, and he never left it."

I sighed, deep in my chest, finally understanding where Arlaith's strange information had come from. Sorcha had always been gifted at spinning tales, a legacy she had inherited from her mother, who had been a bard. This would have been one of Sorcha's better tales if I didn't already know that my death was at the end of it.

"Niall?" she whispered. "I'm so sorry. Can you ever forgive me?"

I wanted to tell her that there was nothing to forgive, that she'd done nothing wrong by trying to protect her father, that the blame and fault all lay in the lap of the witch who sat laughing in her hall. I had to settle for rubbing my cheek against her hair and then kissing the top of her head. She looked up at me and smiled weakly.

"Thank you," she said. She sniffled and shook her head. "Are you hungry? I didn't think she would feed you. She starves her prisoners to make them easier to control. I brought something." She slipped out of the blanket and felt around in the rushes, coming up with a dusty chunk of bread. "It isn't much, but it's all I could get."

I rolled my eyes at Sorcha, and she made a face at me, "I know you don't like bread. I'd have brought meat if I could, but this is all I could get. It's all that the slaves are given. Now eat." She tore a small chunk off the bread and fed it to me, and I chewed it with distaste. Given my own choice, I preferred meat and boiled roots, or grain porridge and fruit. I truly disliked bread, and this was barely even fit to be called bread. It was rough and gritty, full of chaff and ashes, and it took an effort for me to swallow it. I forced down as much as I could, and when I was done, Sorcha held a clay bottle of water to my lips so that I could drink.

She glanced past me as she set the bottle down, then met my eyes, "You should sleep. Do you want me to stay? I can. No one will miss me, so long as I'm back to the kitchens before dawn."

Without hesitation, I nodded. Sorcha stood, taking the blanket and spreading it on the ground in front of me. She helped me to lie down on the blanket, then lay down next to me, pressed up against my back, drawing the other end of the blanket up to cover us both. She slid one arm tightly around my waist and pressed her cheek against my shoulder.

"Niall," she whispered. "Arlaith won't keep you for long. Your brothers will find you."

I nodded, certain of that. My brothers had probably searched all day for me, and would be out with the dawn to search again. By tomorrow sunset, I'd be back at Dun-Morrigan, with Sorcha by my side, where she belonged. It was that thought, and the feel of Sorcha's soft breathing, warm on my back, that lulled me into sleep.

* * *

I woke in the gray before true dawn to see Sorcha kneeling next to me. She smiled as I blinked up at her.

"I was about to wake you," she whispered. "I need to go. I'll need to take the blanket."

I nodded and let her unwrap the blanket and help me to move back against the post. She folded the blanket around the bottle and the now-empty lamp, then came over and knelt down next to me

"I'll come back if I can, and bring something for you to eat." She rested her hands on my arm, met my eyes, then leaned forward and kissed me, catching the back of my neck with one hand. The last time she had kissed me was on the morning I left her father's forge, and this kiss was even better than I remembered it; I groaned silently when she pulled away. She touched my cheek, then got to her feet, grabbed the bundle, and hurried away. I listened until I could not hear her anymore, then turned back to the chains that bound me. If Cormac had known that this chain would be used to bind me or one of my brothers, then perhaps he had crafted a flaw into it, something that I missed in my hasty first inspection. Slowly, I squinted in the growing light as I bent to examine my bonds once more.

* * *

My second examination of the chain was as fruitless as the first. Cormac had always been a perfectionist, and the chain was definitely up to his high standards. Frustrated, I settled myself with my shoulder against the post, watching the slow track of the sunlight as it moved across the floor, feeling hunger and thirst growing until I was lightheaded. Slowly, I drifted into an uneasy sleep. And I dreamed…

I was in Dun-Morrigan, running past small houses that were familiar, yet disturbingly wrong. There was a threat within our baile, something hunting me and my brothers, and I couldn't take wing and fly to find them because, for some reason, Diarmuid had my cloak. I could hear him nearby, calling to me, but I couldn't find him. When I opened my mouth to call back to him, there was no sound. I kept on running, only to realize that the

29

halls were shrinking, collapsing in on me. The hunter was close, and Diarmuid was still calling…

I woke with a start, disoriented, and with Diarmuid's harsh voice still ringing in my ears. It took me a moment to clear my head enough to realize that the voice I was hearing was *not* a dream. Diarmuid was in his raven form and, from the sound of his call, he was above me, in the thatch. If I could somehow let him know I was here…

I struggled to my feet, feeling the shackles cutting into my wrists as I tried to stand, feeling the blood flowing over my fingers as I hobbled away from the post, silently screaming my brother's name, willing him to look inside the hall, to see me. To save me.

I reached the end of my chain abruptly, overbalanced, and fell. With no way to catch myself, I landed hard, face-first in the dirt, bringing the taste of blood to my mouth and knocking the breath out of my body; I ignored it, writhing until I had struggled onto my side, just in time to see, through one of the holes in the thatch, a small black shape flying away, still mournfully calling my name. I watched until Diarmuid vanished from my sight, then closed my eyes against the tears that threatened and lay there, heedless of the blood still flowing from my badly lacerated hands, giving in to despair. There was no way for me to save myself from Arlaith's plots, and no rescue coming from my brothers. For the first time, I understood that I was going to die.

That was how Arlaith found me. I had no idea how much time had passed, nor did I care. I heard her coming towards me, softly calling my name in a teasing sing-song voice. When I didn't move, her footsteps quickened; she prodded my shoulder with one foot, then came around to stand in front of me. She must have panicked when she saw the blood, because I heard her running away, calling for Ailill. It was Ailill who examined me, his big hands surprisingly gentle as he poked at my wrists and prodded my bleeding nose.

"He's done himself some damage, but you found him in time. He'll live," he pronounced. "What should I do with him?"

Arlaith paced in front of me, "Clean him up. Make certain that he can't do this again. I won't be robbed of my prize. I'll make certain he doesn't fight you." I felt her fingers brush my forehead, heard her whispered charm, and then sleep rushed up and dragged me down into dreamless dark.

* * *

I opened my eyes to darkness and cold, with the smell of blood in the dirt under my cheek—my blood, I assumed. Whatever Ailill had done to me, it apparently hadn't involved moving me from the spot where I'd fallen. What he *had* done was strike my bonds, tend to my wounds, and then secure me again, this time with my wrists bound behind my back. I could feel tightness around my wrists that spoke of bandages, and the pressure of the shackles through wrappings. I shifted, rolling onto my side, hearing the jingle of chain that told me I was still tethered in place. Without warning, I was struck with the panic of an animal trapped out in the open. I needed to move, needed to get back to the closest thing to shelter I had: the post.

I somehow made my way across the floor without a clear thought in my head, reaching the shelter of the post and huddling against it, shaking from cold and fear and exertion, desperately fighting back the panic. Finally, I was calm enough that I could assess the damage that I'd done to myself. My head ached, I could barely breathe through my nose, and any small movement sent bolts of pain up both of my arms. My legs, sides, and arms were scraped and bruised from my panic-stricken scramble, my ankles rubbed raw and bleeding from the shackles. The kilt that I wore was torn, and had ridden so far up over my hips that I might not have been wearing anything at all. I closed my eyes, feeling myself again at the edges of despair, and steeled myself for a long night in the dark.

I wasn't sure how much time had passed when I heard the rattle of chains coming closer. That was when I realized that, in my despair, I'd forgotten about Sorcha. If I died tomorrow, what would happen to her? I somehow didn't think Arlaith would let her live, not once she knew everything that Sorcha had told her was a lie. I took a deep breath, then another, shook myself hard and told myself sternly that I was a son of the Morrigan, and that I was *not* going to die at the hands of some arrogant, power-hungry human witch!

Just like that, the barest glimmering of a plan formed in my mind; Sorcha was the key, but it would only work if I could make her understand what I needed her to do. After all, I might be chained and tethered in this ruin, but Sorcha was not. As a test, I whistled, very low, just to see if I could; the sound was swallowed up in the vast feast-hall. But I'd heard it, and I smiled.

Sorcha knelt next to me and put her tiny lamp down. In the dim light, I could see the traces of tears on her cheeks. "Niall? Are you all right?" she asked, her hands running down my arms. "Ailill told everyone that you'd gone mad." She shifted so that she could see the bandages on my wrists, then looked at my face. "He says you tried to kill yourself, that you tried to cut your own hands off on the chains." I shook my head and she nodded. "I knew that you wouldn't. I wish you could tell me what did happen."

Time to try it. I started to whistle, and Sorcha stared at me. I knew she'd know the melody. It was one that I'd taught her, and that we'd used to sing together when she'd help me clean her father's forge.

"Niall, that's 'Prince Raven's Hunt.' Why…?" She stopped, a furrow appearing between her brows. She looked up at the distant, unseen roof. "I thought I heard a raven today."

I nodded like a madman, silently willing her to make the connection. She studied my face, then understanding dawned. "It was one of your brothers, wasn't it? The raven I heard was one of your brothers!"

I nodded again, then threw back my head and laughed for sheer delight. She understood!

"That was your brother," she repeated. "I know why he couldn't see anything. Arlaith is a blood-witch. She has this entire baile bespelled so that no one can see it as it really is, or see the people who live here, and so that the slaves can't escape. She made us all watch when she renewed the spells after they caught you. Her newest victims are buried under the cornerstones."

I felt my blood run cold at that news, but I shouldn't have been surprised. Dark magic like blood-witchery was forbidden, anyone caught using it doomed to be buried alive in the bogs for the crime. According to my brother Oscar, who was a sorcerer, it was also an easy path to power. Of course Arlaith would have taken it. I pushed Sorcha's news aside to deal with once we were free. Knowledge like this would do no one any good if we were dead before we could reveal it. I looked at Sorcha, and found her watching me curiously, so I started whistling again, a charm that Cormac used to use in the forge to find misplaced tools.

"That's Da's finding charm. What do you want to find?" Sorcha asked. I shook my head and then nodded at her. "You want me to find something?" I nodded again, and again whistled 'Prince Raven's Hunt.' Her eyes shot open wide, and she looked frightened. "You want *me* to find your brothers?"

I nodded, grinning like an idiot, elated that I'd found a way to let her know the way to save us both. She just looked at me as if I'd told her to fly to the moon.

"Niall, I can't! I'd never make it past the walls. I just told you, the baile is bespelled! The slave chains are linked into the spells. If I try to go past the walls, I'll be caught."

I nodded and started whistling the charm that I'd tried to use and that had cost me my voice. Sorcha looked startled.

"I'm not a smith, Niall. I can't use forge-craft. I don't have the gift."

I nodded and smiled slightly. It took her a minute for put the pieces together, and then she was skeptical. "You want me to sing the charms for you? Niall, would that even work?"

I shrugged. How would I know? I'd never tried it before. But we needed to make it work now. I jerked my head over my shoulder to tell her that she needed to stand behind me. Sorcha took a deep breath and moved behind me, putting her hands on my shoulders. I reached with one hand and found the shackle around her ankle, found the chain with my other hand, and nodded sharply. Above me, Sorcha started to sing.

As I said, the charm was a simple thing. Six words, a simple melody. And before Sorcha was finished, the shackle around her ankle crumbled like day-old bread. Sorcha gasped, and when she sang the charm again so I could get rid of the other shackle, her voice shook slightly. Then she tapped my shoulder, "Try it on yours. We can both get out."

I nodded and reached down, catching the bar between my ankles in one hand. As Sorcha sang, I felt the metal start to bend. Then something else flared; I felt heat pulsing through my fingers and pulled my hand away before the trap spell could take effect. The charm wasn't one of Cormac's; Arlaith must have set it into the metal, just in case.

"It didn't work?" Sorcha asked.

I shook my head, and Sorcha sighed, "I'd hoped…" Her voice faded, and she picked her chain up and flung it violently off into the darkness. Then she knelt next to me, quiet for a long time. Finally, she turned to me and said softly, "The guards change shifts at dawn. If I go just before dawn, the night guards will be dozing. I should be able to get through without being seen."

It sounded like a good plan, and she knew more about what happened outside these walls than I did, so I nodded in agreement. In silence, Sorcha arranged the blanket and helped me shift around so that I was sitting with my back to the post and her next to me, the blanket wrapped around both of us. She rested her head on my shoulder and said, "Niall? If she burns your cloak, what will happen to you?"

There's something useful about counting among your brothers both a harper and a poet. Your knowledge of song fragments can be immense. I whistled a scrap of an old air, one that told the story of a woman mourning her dead lover. Sorcha nodded.

"I was afraid that would be your answer. So, we might both die tomorrow?" She looked up at me, and I nodded again, wishing I could tell her how much I loved her, how much I'd wanted her for my mate. I couldn't even take her in my arms! Sorcha must have seen something in my face, because she smiled slightly and shifted under the blanket, twisting around and straddling my legs. She rested her hands on my chest and whispered, "I love you, Niall." Then she kissed me, a kiss like none I'd ever had before, one that was full of hope and promise, and just a tinge of sadness, that told me without words that she knew what I felt, and that she felt the same. I closed my eyes, wanting nothing more than to disappear into that kiss. So engrossed was I in the kiss that I didn't notice where Sorcha's hands were, or what else she was doing, until she started to rock against me. I pulled back, shocked, and she smiled, not ceasing her movements.

Irrationally, my first thought was 'Cormac is going to murder me.' Then Sorcha leaned in and kissed me again, running her hands down my arms. "I love you, Niall," she whispered again. "I don't want to die without loving you." She leaned back slightly, stripped the slave tunic over her head and tossed it away, then pressed herself against me, holding me close for a moment. Then she took a deep breath and lifted her hips until my cock brushed her nether-lips, lowering herself slowly onto me until she settled against my hips. She moaned softly, and the sound made my blood race. I strained forward to kiss her, and she wrapped her arms around my neck and clung to me, her hips never falling still, instinct more than making up for the experience that she lacked.

It was maddening, having the woman I loved touching me, loving me, and not being able to hold her. I couldn't move with her, couldn't tell her anything, couldn't do anything but let her discover the steps of the dance in her own way and in her own time. Maddening, and yet so, so very intoxicating, to watch Sorcha find herself in my body, watch her discover her own pleasures in ways that I could never have taught her, even had I been free. She seemed to know just how to move against me as she ground her hips into mine, her movements growing more and more bold as she discovered the pleasure in them. Her hands trailed down my chest, her fingertips brushing over my nipples and making me gasp and arch my back, wanting more of her touch. She noticed and ran her short nails back over my nipples, watching my reaction.

"Do you like that, Niall?" she whispered. I nodded and she leaned forward, kissing me deeply while her fingers played over my chest and her hips moved in achingly slow circles against mine. I whimpered silently against her tongue, straining forward for more, and succeeding only in tipping the both of us over. Sorcha landed half-on, half-off me, giggling softly.

"I think I like this better," she whispered, resettling herself and resting her hands on my chest. She started to move against me again and moaned softly. "Oh, yes. I like this much better."

In truth, so did I. I was still helpless under her, but I had one thing that I didn't have before: leverage. Sorcha bit down on a squeal as I thrust up from beneath her, ending up with her nose barely an inch from mine as she fell over my chest. I couldn't help it; I grinned at her.

"Oh, you like that, do you?" she whispered. I nodded

and thrust up again, making her gasp. She put her hands on my shoulders and pushed herself upright; this time, when she moved, I moved with her, trying to forget the danger, forget the pain, forget that neither of us might live to see another sunset. For this moment, we were one, as one we soared to touch the stars, as one we burned with the heat of the sun, as one we tumbled back to earth, spent and exhausted. Sorcha dragged the blanket over us, then rested on my chest, staying with her arms around me, her cheek against my pounding heart, until we both fell asleep.

* * *

Sorcha woke me with a kiss. "It's time. I have to go now."

I nodded, wanting to say so much, and unable to utter a word. I finally settled for mouthing the words "I love you," but I had no idea if she could see me in the gloom. She touched my face, tucked the blanket around me, then kissed me again and was gone. With the plan in motion, I could do nothing now but wait, so I curled on my side under the blanket and let the warmth and Sorcha's lingering scent lull me back to sleep.

I woke again when Ailill kicked me in the ribs, hard enough to send me tumbling across the floor. Before I'd stopped moving, he kicked me again. Then he grabbed me and dragged me to my knees.

"Where is she?" he demanded.

I wasn't sure what was stronger, the relief that Sorcha had gotten away, or the sheer absurdity that he actually expected me to answer. I shook my head, and he cursed and punched me in the face, knocking me back to the ground. The pain was excruciating; the world faded to gray for a moment, and I tasted blood. When my ears stopped ringing, I heard Arlaith.

"Ailill, what are you doing?"

He turned on her, snarling, "You promised the smith's girl to me when this was over. She's gone. She never went to the kitchens today, and no one has seen her since last night. And the blanket I gave to her is here." Ailill pointed at the blanket that was somehow still wrapped around my legs.

"Impossible. She couldn't have gotten past the walls," Arlaith snapped.

Ailill scowled at her, then shoved me to the ground. "Call the chain," he ordered.

Arlaith narrowed her eyes and uttered a short chant. In response, there was a chime from the far reaches of the ruin. Ailill stalked towards it and came back with Sorcha's shattered chain, throwing it at Arlaith's feet.

"I told you. She's gone. She's gotten away. And she knows where the other ravens are."

Arlaith's eyes went wide, and she snarled a soft curse as she turned on me, "You freed her? How?"

I shook my head again, wincing as the motion made my head ache. Ailill kicked me again, and I stopped with a jerk when I reached the end of my chain. Gasping in pain, I looked up to see Arlaith looking down at me, her eyes cold.

"Ailill, go and wait by the door. I need… to talk with Niall."

Ailill grumbled and walked away, leaving Arlaith standing over me. A slow smile spread over her face, and she knelt next to me.

"Poor Niall. Ailill does have a temper, I'm afraid. I've kept him leashed this long by promising that he could have the girl once I'm High Queen. Now… now it will be nigh impossible to control him." She shrugged, then met my eyes and rested one hand on my chest. "I could send for a healer. Free you. Give me what I want, and I will give you what you want." Her hand trailed lower, down over my stomach. "Everything you want. You could rule at my side, Niall. Just let me have the power I need."

If I'd needed any confirmation that the uncontrolled desire that I had felt for this woman after I'd woken on the shores of the pool had been the result of a spell, this was it. There was no desire for her in me anymore, no arousal at her touch. In truth, I wanted nothing more than to pull away from her questing fingers, but I couldn't move. I settled instead for turning my head away and closing my eyes. She continued for a moment, until even she could not deny that she was having no effect on me. Then her hand fell away, and I turned to see her rise, her eyes cold.

"Ailill, I need a bonfire on the urla. Now." She swept away, and Ailill laughed as he followed her out of the ruin.

* * *

Diarmuid paced back and forth across the feast-hall throughout the night, snarling at anyone who dared cross his path. Yesterday morning, they had each gone off to search, and each of them had come back at sunset to report the same thing: no signs of Niall anywhere within a day's flight. Now they gathered in the feast-hall and waited for Diarmuid to tell them what to do next. He stopped and turned to look at them, noticing that Oscar was missing.

"Who saw Niall last?" he asked.

"I did," Cathal answered. "He seemed fine."

"You don't think he tried to do himself damage, do you?" Maelan asked.

Diarmuid shook his head, "I'm more worried that he's finally decided to renounce the change and flew off to live as a raven."

Maelan looked shocked, "Do you think he would?"

"How can I know? None of us really know what he's going through. None of us has taken a mate yet," Diarmuid answered. He rubbed his face and started to pace again, catching sight of Oscar in the doorway. "Brother, where have you been?"

"Hunting. You need to hear this, Diarmuid," Oscar answered, his voice cold and serious. He turned and gestured, and a young woman in a white slave's tunic followed him into the hall, shivering from either fear or cold. Diarmuid frowned and stepped forward, then gasped as he recognized the girl.

"Sorcha!"

"Hear her out, brother," Oscar said. "Quickly. We need to fly."

* * *

I lay where they left me, trying not to move. I could feel my ribs grating against each other, and even the smallest breath sent bolts of pain shooting through my side. Through the haze of pain, I could hear distant shouting, and I could taste the smoke in the air long before Ailill and a pair of guards came for me. The guards held me while Ailill unfettered my ankles, then they dragged me to my feet and half-shoved, half-carried me out of the hall and onto the weedy, half-dead urla. There, they forced me to my knees in front of the blazing bonfire. Arlaith was there, my cloak thrown over her arm, a look of triumph on her face.

"Now, raven boy, give me the secrets of the cloak," she demanded.

I looked at her, tired to my bones, and not even bothering to show the contempt I felt for her. There was nothing that Arlaith could do to me now that mattered. Even if I died, Sorcha was alive, she was free, and she knew that I loved her. She would find my brothers and tell them what had happened to me, and they would see that Arlaith paid for my death. So I smiled slowly and shook my head. Arlaith stared at me for a moment, then shrilled, "I will burn this unless you tell me!"

"You will not."

Arlaith went pale, and she turned to look to the other side of the bonfire, at the men who stood there, who had seemingly appeared from out of nowhere. I looked up and saw six dark shapes on the roof one of the halls, relaxing slightly at the sight of them. My brothers had come.

They were as dark as I, my two oldest brothers, Diarmuid carrying himself like a king, his braided hair more than a little silver at the temples. Behind him was Oscar, the sorcerer, who stood staring at Arlaith, a look of distaste on his narrow face.

Arlaith met Oscar's glare and tossed her head, "You unmade my spells. That was unkind." Oscar just smiled at her, that cold, mocking smile of his that so infuriates people, the one that tells them without a word that he is only suffering their presence because it would be too much effort to turn them into toads.

Diarmuid stepped forward, his hand on his sword hilt. "Release my brother, witch."

Arlaith laughed and gestured; someone grabbed me

from behind. I felt cold metal biting into my throat, felt a trickle of warmth over my skin, heard Ailill snarl in my ear, "Come and take him."

"You have something I want, and I have something you want," Arlaith said sweetly. "Give me the secrets of the feather cloak, or I kill the fool and burn this." She held my cloak out to the flames, close enough that I could smell scorching feathers and feel my skin prickling from the heat. I winced, reflexively trying to move away from the flames.

Oscar barked out his rusty-sounding laugh, "Foolish human, there's no magic in that thing. Give it here." He muttered something, then held his hand out; the cloak jerked from Arlaith's fingers and sailed above the flames and across the urla into Oscar's waiting hand. Without turning, he handed it to a small figure I hadn't seen behind them. My heart leapt when I realized that it was Sorcha who was standing in Diarmuid's shadow. She took my cloak in her arms and held it tightly, her features pinched with worry and fear.

Arlaith scowled when she saw Sorcha, and she spoke to Ailill without turning, "Ailill, give the fool to his brothers."

The knife across my throat was removed, and the guards pulled me to my feet and shoved me forward, towards the bonfire. I stumbled, unable to catch myself, but before I could fall into the flames, I was caught, and I looked up to see two more of my brothers, the twins Ronan and Petran. Petran shook his head at me as he helped me to stand. "Having a bad day, Niall?"

I grinned slightly and let them lead me towards Diarmuid. Halfway across the urla, I heard Arlaith start to chant, and Ailill's cruel laugh. Then something tightened around my throat, cutting off my breath. Ahead of me, I saw Sorcha grab at her throat and fall, Diarmuid going to his knee next to her. My knees buckled and I fell, my vision blurring as I twisted and fought to draw breath. Someone grabbed my arm, and I heard Ronan asking what was wrong, but I couldn't answer. I felt someone fumbling at the collar around my neck, heard Diarmuid shouting for someone to *stop that damned witch!* Then... my breath rushed back into my chest; I kicked away from the hands holding me, rolling onto my knees to curl up with my face almost buried in the grass, taking long, shaky, excruciatingly painful breaths. Somewhere, I heard the sounds of a fight, and the sound of Sorcha crying.

"Niall?" I looked up to see Maelan, closest to me in age, and my closest friend, kneeling next to me. He sighed and took my chin in his hand, turning my head this way and that, "Well, that nose is never going to be straight again, boyo. We know about the spell, Niall. Your girl told us. Brave little thing, that one. Don't move, now. Let me get this mischief off you." Quickly, he cut through the heavy leather collar and threw it into the fire, then studied the shackles for a moment before he called out, "Someone find the keys!"

"Why waste time?" Oscar asked, coming over to look seriously down at me. He rested his hand on my shoulder, and I closed my eyes and let him work, feeling the rush of his magic through me, destroying the trap spell and turning the shackles into dust. I raised my stiff arms, feeling the abused muscles pull and ache, and was immediately almost bowled over by Sorcha, who rushed into my arms. I closed my eyes, ignored the pain, and just held her for what seemed like forever, then kissed her gently and stood up. Without a word, she handed me my feather cloak, and

I swung it over my shoulders. Battered and bruised as I was, broken ribs and broken nose, half-naked in a slave's kilt, I finally felt complete. I pulled Sorcha to my side and kissed her again, and heard Oscar cough.

"Time to get rid of the rest of this foulness," he said, reaching out to touch my throat. I felt a moment of warmth, and then Oscar frowned and opened his eyes. He turned and shouted, "Where is the woman?"

"Ah…" Ronan mumbled, then gestured towards the bonfire. There, I could see Arlaith lying in the dirt, her eyes open and staring, the hem of her gown actually in the flames and already starting to smolder. Standing over her was Fergus, who we called Big Fergus for his size, and who had the mind of a child. He looked at us, his face colored with shame, and whispered, "I broke her. She was hurting Niall, and Diarmuid said that she need to stop and… I broke her. I didn't mean to…"

Oscar stalked over the body, then looked at me. "Who else would know? Was there anyone else there when she cast the spell?" he demanded.

Diarmuid joined him and asked, "Oscar, what is it?"

"She used a very specific spell on Niall. I need to know what it is so that I can craft a counter-spell," Oscar answered.

I snapped my fingers to get Oscar's attention, then pointed at Ailill, who glared back at me, his face battered and bloody. He was bound tightly and being guarded by four of my brothers. Oscar looked at me and asked, "He was there?"

I nodded. Oscar spoke quietly to our brothers, and then disappeared into the ruined feast-hall with Cathal and Cuanu dragging Ailill between them.

Diarmuid watched them go, then turned to the twins,

Fergus, and Maelan, "You lot search the place. Bring anyone you find here. I don't care if they're noble or slave. Bring them. Sorcha, see if you can find Niall something to wear."

He studied me for a moment, then ran gentle fingers over my ribs. "You're bruising here, Niall. Did he kick you?" I nodded, and Diarmuid scowled, "I'd never trust a healer we found here. We'll have to get you back to the baile. Sorcha, wrap these ribs, too. As tight as you can."

"Yes, sir," Sorcha said, taking my arm. She led me through the proper feast-hall and into to a room I immediately recognized as Arlaith's bedchamber, then settled me to sit on the bed while she tore Arlaith's fine linen sheets into strips that she used to bind my ribs tightly. Once that was done, she searched through the chests until she uncovered my clothing and my torc, helping me to dress, and claiming a fine green linen gown for herself. While we dressed, she told me about being found by Oscar and being taken to Dun-Morrigan. Finally, dressed and feeling more myself than I had in days, we returned to the urla.

When we got there, we found two small groups of people gathered under the watchful eyes of my brothers: a cluster of frightened-looking slaves, and a smaller group of men in fine clothing, Ailill's two guards among them. I didn't see Ailill anywhere. Nor did I see Oscar. I did notice that both Cathal and Cuanu looked pale, and decided that it was probably better not to know.

Diarmuid nodded as we approached, then raised his voice, "All of you who were slaves are now free. If you wish to return to your homes, we will see you given an appropriate blood-price for your losses. The rest of you will be taken to Dun-Righ to face the High King's justice." As he finished speaking, I saw Oscar come out of the ruined feast-hall. He was alone.

"I'll go to Dun-Righ with the prisoners. Just in case. I wish to speak to the druids there, in any case. Someone had the training of that witch, and I will find them out," he said to Diarmuid as he walked past us.

"Where's the man?" Diarmuid asked.

Oscar stopped walking and gave him a look of wry humor. "Do you really want to know?"

Diarmuid glared at him, and Oscar shrugged, turning towards the group of prisoners.

"Wait," Sorcha called out. Oscar stopped again and turned to look at her, annoyance clear on his face. Sorcha took an involuntary step back, looked up at me, then drew herself up and asked, "What about Niall? Can you give him his voice back?"

Oscar frowned for a moment, and then shook his head. "No. The spell was specific. Niall would be without his voice until he gave Arlaith the power of the feather cloak. Since she is dead, there's no way to undo the spell." He shook his head and looked at me. "I am sorry, brother."

I couldn't believe what I'd heard. Oscar couldn't undo the spells? I'd *never* speak again? Oscar murmured another apology, then walked away, leaving Sorcha and me alone. Sorcha said something, her voice soft and gentle. It was probably something meant to comfort, but I ignored her. I ignored everything until Diarmuid snapped his fingers under my nose. I jumped and stared at him, seeing sympathy and concern in his gold eyes.

"Niall, are you fit to fly?" he asked gently. "I want to get you home and see to your injuries properly."

I nodded dully, then tightened my arm around Sorcha and looked up at Diarmuid, suddenly frightened that he would insist that I leave her behind or send her to Dun-Righ. He looked at me and shook his head.

"Ah, Niall. I should have told you sooner. If you'd known, we might have avoided this." He smiled gently at Sorcha, and then looked back at me. "There *is* a magic in the cloak. One specific spell, albeit a minor one. The others all know of it, even though we've never used it. I didn't tell you about it before you left to apprentice with Cormac because you were too young to take a mate, and then… well, we all knew you'd chosen your mate in Sorcha. I didn't think you would welcome the knowledge of the cloak with your intended mate gone. My mistake, and it's cost you dearly."

I frowned, confused. Take a mate? What did my cloak have to do with taking a mate? Diarmuid nodded and continued.

"Our mother didn't wish to see us spend our lives apart from those we love, Niall. When we take a mate, we can grant her the power of the change and a share of our immortality. That's the only magic to the cloak." He sighed. "If you'd known that…"

I shook my head violently, wincing slightly at the pain the sharp movement caused me. I'd sooner live mute than have that witch as a wife, especially now that I knew that my Sorcha lived. Diarmuid nodded as if he could read my thoughts, then folded his arms over his chest and smiled. "So, are we finally welcoming a sister into the baile?"

I smiled broadly and looked at Sorcha. Her eyes were huge.

"Niall? Are you asking…?"

I didn't let her finish, pulling her into my arms and

kissing her. She returned the kiss warmly, and I knew her answer when I felt the magic flow, enveloping the two of us in warmth, then rushing through me to settle over Sorcha like a cloak. When I opened my eyes, I wasn't surprised to see a raven-feather cloak similar to mine draped over her shoulders.

Diarmuid rested his hand on my shoulder, "Let's go home."

* * *

And that is the story of how a Prince of Air lost his voice and gained a wife. I am called Niall an Adh now, Niall the Silent, and I no longer fly over the fields that surround Dun-Morrigan. I am vulnerable, I know that, and I will not put my brothers or my wife in danger. So I remain in my forge, and Sorcha sings the charms over our work. And each month, Oscar comes to the forge, offering new charms and spells and potions, and glowering at his failure to discover the way to break Arlaith's spells. I humor him, and I will continue to do so, but I have resigned myself to being silent to the end of my days.

Oddly enough, I find that I am content. I have my work, and I have my mate, and, soon, we will have the child that we created between us on that long, lonely night that we both thought would be our last.

It is enough. I am happy. And for that happiness, the loss of my voice was a very small price to pay.

Part Two

Courtship of the Raven King

I've missed the sound of the voices of children in Dun-Morrigan. The last time I heard it was nearly 20 years ago, when Maelan and Niall were both young. They grew, and the halls of Dun-Morrigan filled instead with the sounds of men, talking and fighting, as men are wont to do. Now, though, I come out onto the urla to hear children's laughter, and I find that the sound stirs something in me. I will see my 45th year this summer, and for the first time in my life, I find myself wondering what it would be like to have a mate, to have children of my own.

It's been five years since Niall brought Sorcha to our halls as his wife. His son, Cormac, is nearly four, a tiny terror of a child with his father's dark hair and his mother's blue-green eyes, and not a drop of fear in him. The boy ran before he walked, flew before he could speak, and seemed to wake every morning with the desire to find some new mischief against which to do battle. His sister Niamh, just a year-and-a-half old and as fire-haired as her mother, is thankfully milder by nature, more willing to cuddle with an adoring uncle and listen to another uncle sing songs or tell stories.

I know I'm not the only one among us to have these

thoughts. I've caught the same wondering look on the faces of several of my brothers in turn as they watch Niall playing with his children, working alongside his wife in the forge, or simply sitting in the great feast-hall at night, his arm around Sorcha, his son leaning against his knee, his daughter asleep in her mother's lap. Even though he'll never speak again, Niall is content, and happier than I've ever seen him before.

Late in the evenings, lying alone in my bed, I find myself jealous of that contentedness.

It's time, and past time, that I took a mate.

* * *

It was a bright summer afternoon, and I was in my raven-form, sitting on my accustomed perch. We each of us had one; mine was a ledge high over Dun-Morrigan, from which I could see the entire baile, and the village below. From this vantage point, I could see Maelan and Niall practicing swordplay on the urla, to the delight of Cormac, who watched from a safe distance. The boy had a stick clutched in one hand and was mimicking his father's movements. I heard his clear laughter as he saw his mother coming towards them, saw him run towards her and hug her enthusiastically. She knelt and said something to him, and he ran off towards the feast-hall. Maelan must have seen her, too, because he signaled for the bout to end. Niall fell back, picked up the feather cloak that was never far from his side, and walked off to claim a kiss from his wife. Their passion was clear even at this distance, and I felt as if I was intruding on something private. It was uncomfortable enough that I took wing and flew off to spend a few quiet hours alone with my thoughts. As usual, the thinking I did turned to marriage, and I wondered if there was a mate for me anywhere in the world. I wondered how I'd know, and resolved to ask Niall how he'd known Sorcha was the one.

By the time the sun was setting, I'd actually decided on one thing. My mate was out there, and since she wasn't going to come to me, I'd have to go looking for her. I knew where my search would start.

* * *

"I'm going to spend some time at Dun-Righ," I announced as the servants cleared away the remains our evening meal that night. "A month, perhaps two."

Conversation stopped, and my brothers stared at me.

"This is sudden, Diarmuid," Oscar murmured from his place at my left.

I'd actually given some thought to my supposed reason, wanting to save myself from the inevitable teasing from my brothers. "I've been doing some thinking," I answered. "We've been remiss in our duty to the High King. I should remedy that lapse before people start to forget who and what we are."

Oscar leaned back and smiled mockingly at me. "Oh? And is that the only reason?"

Damn the sorcerer! I looked away, and was surprised to see amusement on all the faces around our table. Niall was actually grinning at me.

"Diarmuid, you've been a little... obvious. We all know," Petran said gently. "You're going to the High King's fortress to hunt for a mate."

"There's something in the air," Ronan added. "All this marrying going on."

I frowned, "What marrying? Ronan, did you actually find someone who'd put up with you?"

Ronan snorted as the others laughed. Oscar was the one who answered, "There was a messenger this evening. Eogan's marrying in a month's time. We're all invited. This might turn out well for you, brother."

I nodded, seeing what he meant. This very well might at that. When the High King wed, every high-born woman in the kingdom would be in attendance. My chances of finding my mate would be better than I previously hoped.

"We were debating this afternoon, who was going to go on ahead with the messenger, to guard the wedding gifts and the luggage," Cuanu told me. "If you're the one to go ahead, then you'll be there when most of the guests arrive. It will give you more time."

I nodded. "That makes sense. When would you join me?"

"It's not that long a flight. Say… three weeks' time?" Oscar said.

Niall coughed, looking oddly tense. He looked at Sorcha, who nodded and smiled at him. He didn't smile back at her, instead drawing out of his pouch a metal case. It was a cunning device—inside the case were a stylus and a hollow space that he'd filled with beeswax. Niall might not have a voice, but he could still let us know what he was thinking. He wrote something, closed the case and passed it to Maelan, who opened it, coughed once, then passed the case down the table to me. I looked at Niall, then opened the case and read: *Sorcha is pregnant and doesn't want to fly so far right now. We'll be staying here.*

I burst out laughing. "Congratulations! We've another nestling on the way, brothers."

When the waves of congratulations were over, Maelan yawned and rested his elbows on the table. "I'm thinking I don't really want to make the flight either. The High King's hall bores me to tears. If it's all right with you, brother, I'll stay behind as well, and we'll keep Fergus here with us."

"If that's what you want, Maelan. Try to stay out of the tavern," I answered lightly, pretending not to see the tension in Niall's shoulders ease or Sorcha take his hand and run her thumb over his fingers in a comforting gesture. The others ignored it as well, knowing that to notice was to invite a fight. Even after five years, Niall still rarely left our walls, and could not bear to be alone, the lasting legacy of the ordeal that had cost him his voice. I knew that he could protect himself and his family—he had turned himself into one of the best fighters I'd ever seen, which was the reason none of us wanted to fight him. But not even a good sword and a strong arm could turn back the memories that still haunted him, and I was grateful to Maelan for stepping forward to stand between our youngest brother and those shadows.

Conversations trailed off in different directions, and before long, so did my brothers, each to his respective house and bed. I crossed the urla without really paying attention, my thoughts on my upcoming journey and what I hoped to find at the end of it. So intent was I on my planning that I nearly ran Niall down. He jumped back and laughed, eerily silent, then nodded towards my house and turned to go inside. Intrigued, I followed him.

"What is it?" I asked as he set the long, flat chest he was carrying down on my bed.

He shrugged one shoulder and opened the box, taking from it a bundle that he handed to me. I unwrapped

54

it and found myself holding a sword, beautifully worked and balanced, with an amethyst the size of a raven's egg set into the hilt. I admired it for a moment, then looked at Niall.

"I have a sword, Niall."

He grinned and took out his wax tablet, writing something and handing it to me. I set the sword down and read: *It's a wedding present for Eogan.*

"Oh. Niall, it's a wonderful gift."

He smiled and drew other things out of the box—a pair of finely worked armbands in silver and gold; a pair of matching torcs set with amethysts; an amethyst brooch in silver and gold, with ornate patterns of filigree and granulation; fine bronze and silver fibulae for a woman's gown; delicate gold bracelets and filigree earrings; and matching rings bearing the emblem of a boar—the High King's clan symbol. Niall laid them all out on my bed and stood back, waiting for my reaction. I looked at each piece in turn, then realized what this treasure trove meant and stared at my youngest brother in shock.

"You've accepted the offer?" I asked. "You're going to serve as the High King's smith?"

He grinned and nodded, and I could see the color rising in his face. Then he waved his hand over the treasures spread out on my bed, and I understood the other question he was asking. Was it enough? Was this a fitting tribute for the High King from his sworn man?

"Niall, it's perfect. Eogan chose well. When will you go to court to…" I stopped. The question I wasn't going to ask was just how Niall was going to swear allegiance to the High King? He shrugged and ran his fingers through his hair, then took up his tablet again, writing for a long time before handing the tablet to me.

When Eogan asked, he told me he was willing to take my oath in writing. So I wrote it up and Oscar witnessed for me. He'll be taking it with him to the wedding. And Eogan understands that my forge will be here, and not at Dun-Righ. I know I should go to the wedding. But I'm not ready to deal with that many people staring at me. Will you carry this to Eogan for me?

I smiled and handed the tablet back to Niall. "Brother, I'd be happy to."

* * *

The next day was spent in preparations, making certain that everything was ready, packing clothing and gifts for the High King and his new bride, as well as a selection of pretty baubles that Niall insisted I take with me. For courting gifts, he informed me with a sly grin. I also met with the messenger, a slightly-built young man with gingery curls and a sharp face who reminded me of a young fox, and who introduced himself as Turlach. I had always flown to the High King's baile, so I wanted to know more about what to expect on the road. From Turlach, I learned that we would be on the road for nearly three days. This information fascinated me—in my raven form, I could cover the distance between Dun-Morrigan and Dun-Righ in a day. When I mentioned that to him, he laughed and pointed out that there was no straight road from the one to the other. I had flown over hills that a chariot could not pass through. Our way would take us away from Dun-Righ at first, towards the coast where we would pass our first night. The second day would take us along the coast and then inland through the bogs, camping that night in the shadow of the great forest of Uragh. We would pass through the forest and reach Dun-Righ near sunset on the third day. I found myself eager to leave, curious about this new way of traveling and looking forward to the trip and what I might find waiting at the end for me.

By the end of the first day, I was convinced that I should have flown. Roads are dusty and bumpy, chariots are unstable, and horses are slow. By the time we set our camp that night, I was tired and irritable, feeling as if the rough road had jarred loose every tooth in my mouth and rattled every bone in my body. At least Turlach wasn't laughing at me. Or if he was, he wasn't doing it where I could see him. Once we had made camp, I shifted form and took to the skies, stretching my wings for the first time since we'd left Dun-Morrigan. I didn't go far—I was the guard, after all—but I could see nothing beneath me but sand and rocks, scrubby bushes and stunted trees, and the rolling vastness of the sea. I soared higher and higher, until my breath grew thin and I could go no further, imagining that I could just barely see over the edge of the world. Then I laughed and spiraled slowly back to earth, shifting to human form and landing a few feet from where Turlach was ladling fragrant stew into bowls. He smiled as he handed a bowl to me.

"Feel better?" he asked. "You seemed… uncomfortable the last few miles."

I smiled in return. "Yes, I do. Thank you." We ate in silence, passing a skin of mead back and forth across the fire and watching the stars appear one by one over our heads. Once we were finished, I cleaned the bowls and the pot while Turlach rolled himself in his cloak and went to sleep. When the moon set, I would wake him to guard while I slept, but for now I sat with my back against a large rock, staring up at the skies and thinking.

Night watches are long and boring, and even more so when an aerial inspection has already showed that there are no humans for miles in any direction. I sighed and listened to Turlach snore, letting my thoughts wander. Wondering what it would be like, to mate. I was no stranger to bed-play, but I thought that there must be something different to it when it was with your mate. Something more. I tried to think what it might be, what it possibly could be. Perhaps it was the mead, or the moonlight, or my own fertile imagination, but I found myself growing aroused. I tried to ignore it, tried to turn my thoughts to other, more mundane, things, until at last the torment grew too great for me to bear.

Moving as quietly as I could, I stood and walked a short way down the beach, making certain that I could still see the camp and the fire. I made short work of my clothes, stripping out of my feather cloak, my shirt and trews before lying down on the water-smoothed rocks that were still warm from the sun. Slowly, I ran my fingers over my cock, humming softly under my breath as a shiver of pleasure raced through me. Pausing to spit into my hand, I resumed my play, tightening my fingers around my shaft, running my thumb over the head, pumping slowly at first, letting my mind range and call forth memories of some of the women I'd bedded, thinking especially of one in particular: Nuala.

Our brief tryst was doomed to failure from the start—for some reason she never explained, she disliked children. She could barely tolerate the then five-year-old twins, and she'd left me when Mother had brought two-year-old Cuanu to the baile. Despite that, I still remembered her fondly, and she often featured in my late-night fantasies. She'd been a lively one, willing to do or try anything having to do with sex, and she'd delighted in pinning me to the bed and playing with my cock until I begged for her to mount me. Having a lover who didn't defer to me was a new experience, and having someone who took such immense pleasure in dominating me in bed was intensely arousing.

I remembered her laughing as she sat on my stomach with her back to me, rolling my cock between her warm, greased hands before she started playing. Then it was one hand on my cock, pumping hard, and the other hand playing with my testicles before dipping lower to slide her long, clever fingers into my arse. When I could no longer bear her toying with me, and when she finally deigned to listen to my pleas, she turned to face me and slowly lowered herself down onto my cock, taking me deep inside. Then, unbelievably, she sat there, her arms folded across her chest, her eyes sparkling, daring me to do something. Anything. I closed my eyes, biting down on a moan as I started pumping harder, remembering how I ran my hands up Nuala's sides, pulling her down onto my chest and then rolling onto my side so that we were facing each other, her leg thrown over my hip. Holding her like that, I started to move, slowly at first, watching the high color bloom on her face as she moaned. I cut off her moans with a kiss, and she ran her nails over my ribs and up my back, her leg on my hip tightening as she started moving faster against me, urging me on. That was all the encouragement I needed—I pushed her onto her back and braced myself on my arms so that I could thrust as hard as I knew she liked. At the first stroke, she yowled and locked her legs around my hips, pushing up against me and raking her nails down my chest. Moving as one, neither of us lasted for very long, and fell together to lay in a sated, sweaty tangle in the middle of the ruin that had been my bed.

On the beach, I gasped as I came, biting down on my lip so that my moans would not wake Turlach. My seed splattered all over the cool evening sand, and I lay there on the slowly-chilling rock and once again wondered what had ever become of Nuala. As always, I prayed to my mother that my old lover was well, and praised her memory if she had passed to the lands beyond. Then I rose and picked up my clothes. *Time to get back to my duties*. I took a brief swim in the chilly waters to wash off, then dressed and walked back to the campsite. As I sat down, Turlach propped himself up on his elbow.

"You didn't have to leave," he said in a low voice. "I wouldn't have minded. To tell the truth, I wouldn't have minded watching. Or helping."

I coughed, surprised, then said, "I thought you were asleep."

"I was. Woke up to piss and heard you." I saw the flash of his teeth in the firelight and realized with a start that Turlach was a very handsome man. "I don't suppose you like men?" he asked, sounding hopeful.

"Ah… no. One of my brothers does. I prefer women."

He laughed. "Of course. That's my luck for you. Of all the ravens out there, I would meet the wrong one. Which brother?"

"Petran. I'll introduce you, if you like."

He hummed softly. "I'd like that. What's he like?"

"He's a harper," I started to answer, and was interrupted by Turlach's gasp of pleasure.

"Really? I love harpers. They have the best hands." He laughed again. "I may actually start looking forward to this wedding after all. I'm going to hold you to that offer."

"You do that," I murmured, listening to him shifting around as he lay back down to sleep. The rest of my watch passed quickly, and it seemed that no time at all had passed before I was wrapping myself in my feathers and lying down to sleep next to the fire. As I did, I heard Turlach's husky whisper, "My turn."

* * *

The next day was uneventful, and much more bearable. I spent most of the morning in the air, pacing the chariot and keeping watch that way, until we reached a part of the road overhung with trees. I could no longer see clearly, so I landed and rode with Turlach in the chariot. The previous night seemed to have opened the way for us, and he was much more talkative today, telling me about himself and about the country through which we drove. He was just 20, he told me, younger than I'd originally thought. He was the son of a charioteer, and he himself had been a charioteer since he'd turned 15. My lack of a charioteer of my own fascinated him, until I told him that I didn't even own a horse, and wouldn't know what to do with one if I did.

"You've really never handled a horse?" he asked, amazed.

"What need do I have for a horse?" I asked in response. That drew a laugh out of him, and he offered to teach me to drive.

"Not here, though," he amended. "This road needs watching, and we'll be in the bogs soon. Tomorrow, in the forest. Now, tell me more about this brother of yours?"

61

"You're very single-minded," I accused, laughing. He laughed with me, then graced me with an innocent smile.

"I'm a charioteer. The horses do all the work when we're not in battle. What else is there worth thinking about?"

"Petran is twice your age," I pointed out.

He went from innocent to wanton in a moment, leering at me. "Even better. I like older men. They have more experience, and they know so much more. I can't wait to meet him." He glanced at me. "Why are you going to Dun-Righ so early? If you don't mind my asking, that is."

"I don't mind. I'm hoping to find a wife."

"Ah," he said, nodding sagely. "And you're hoping that one of those high-born fillies at Dun-Righ will suit you?" He shrugged. "I watch them, even though they don't interest me. And you'd be better off looking someplace else. Those girls… all they want are a high-born husband to give them children and status and a baile of their own to rule. There isn't much… substance to them. They're all silk and paint and not a brain in their pretty heads. Do you understand me?"

I nodded, frowning slightly. "I do. I'll have to see for myself."

He glanced at me sidelong, then shrugged. "If you think you must. But I'll warn you. I've seen too many good friends taken to bits by those high-born bawds. Guard your heart and your purse, Diarmuid *Ri na Fiach dubh.*"

His epitaph amused me. It wasn't often that people actually called me what I am—King of the Ravens. In my own home, I was simply the oldest brother. In the village of Scath, I was the overlord and protector. Outside that circle, I didn't know what was said about me and mine.

I'd never thought to ask, never had anyone I could ask who would be able to answer me truthfully.

"Turlach, what do you know about us? About me and my brothers?" I asked, suddenly curious beyond measure.

"Just what they say," he answered, shrugging slightly. "I've heard a lot of things. People tend to talk around us, you understand? This is the most conversation I've had while driving in years." He frowned, obviously thinking. "I've heard that you're all sons of the Battle Queen. I've heard that you're normal men, and that you just claim to be Her sons, and that you make people believe you through trickery. I've heard that you're all great sorcerers, and that you have the High King in your thrall. It's the first that's true, isn't it?"

"Yes."

"I thought so. There's something about you, something… different. You're not like anyone I've ever met before," he smiled and met my eyes. "Let me know if you ever decide to get a chariot. I'd be honored to drive for you."

I smiled back at him. "And does that offer have anything to do with my brother, the harper?"

He managed to look affronted before breaking into laughter. "Perhaps a little. But I like you, too. None of the high-born I've driven have ever been so…" He paused for a moment, then shrugged one shoulder, a most raven-like gesture. "… So friendly. Most of them don't care anything for someone who isn't as high-born as they are."

I nodded. I had the same impression of many of the people I'd met in Eogan's court. "I understand. I like you, too. And I'd be honored to have you drive my chariot. As soon as I get one."

63

He laughed again and drew back on the reins, drawing the horses to a stop. "I'll hold you to that, too. Now, we're about to enter the bogs. I'll need all my attention on the road, and you'll need to keep a watchful eye. There are bog-men in there who prey on travelers, and we're too tempting a target for them to let us pass. I'm going to drive as fast as is safe, but still…"

"Bog-men?" I looked at the road ahead and stared in shock—there was no road! "Turlach…"

"There are markers on the safe passage," he answered my unspoken question. "I know what to look for but I need to pay attention. And yes. Bog-men. There are safe ways to get a small party through the bogs, but no way to safely bring through a large enough attack force to clear out the bog-men." He frowned slightly and looked at me. "I'm going to need to go pretty fast, and it will be a rough trip. Will you be all right?"

I took one of the light spears from a socket built into the side of the chariot and grabbed hold of the chariot rail with my other hand. "I'll be fine. Go."

He grinned, then shouted to the horses; the chariot lurched forward and into the bogs.

* * *

I am never riding in a chariot ever again.

I still planned to get one, and to bring Turlach into Dun-Morrigan as the charioteer, but I swore in my mother's name that never again would I ride in one of these torturous contraptions. That was what I repeated to myself as we bounced and jolted through the bogs, following a road that I couldn't see. I never once saw the markers Turlach mentioned, never knew just how it was that he was navigating without having us end up drowning in the murky waters that I knew lurked under the mossy surface of the bog. I couldn't see how anyone could ever live in this place—either Turlach was telling tales, having fun at my expense, or these bog-men he mentioned were all mad. But I kept my watch, even though there was nothing to see. The land around us was flat, with few, sparse bushes. There was barely anything that could hide a man, let alone a band of bog-men.

Up ahead, I could see a line of trees growing steadily closer, and knew that we'd be out of the bogs soon, and into the great forest where we'd spend our last night on the road. I scanned the area ahead of us, then glanced behind. As I turned, a sudden movement caught my eye—I turned back and saw nothing but more scrubby bushes waving in the breeze.

Just as I realized that the bushes we had already passed hadn't been moving, that there was no breeze, the bog exploded. Men surged out of the water, shedding their camouflage and brandishing spears and swords. I hurled my spear and killed the one closest to us, then had to grab for the rail as Turlach snapped the reins and urged the horses into a gallop.

"They won't follow us into the trees!" he shouted. "We're almost there!"

I nodded, holding on with one hand and taking another spear with the other, watching the way we had come to make sure that there was no one following. I heard Turlach shout, turned, and had just enough time to see the fallen tree that had been hidden from view in a natural dip in the road, and the armed men there. Before I could do anything, Turlach screamed and fell, a spear in his shoulder. I fumbled for the reins and dragged back on them as I'd seen Turlach do, but we were going too fast. There was no way to stop. The horses leapt, clearing the tree easily.

The chariot was not as lucky.

My last memory was of the chariot hitting the tree, and of being thrown through the air. I'd been trying to save Turlach, and hadn't shifted to raven form, so I fell, landing hard on my right shoulder. I remembered hearing something crack, then everything was swallowed by pain and darkness, and I knew nothing more.

* * *

I woke dizzy and nauseous, with my entire right side awash in pain. I started to try and move, to see how badly I was hurt, then heard voices and fell still. *Men, nearby, arguing with each other*. I lay still and pretended to be unconscious, watching them through half-lidded eyes.

They were, I thought, the same ones who attacked us, but I could see now that these were no outlaws, no raiders who lived by their wits. Each of them was dressed well, and when they spoke, it was with the clear and cultured tones of the nobility. That didn't stop them from acting like common thieves, though; they were pawing through the contents of the boxes that had been loaded on the chariot, each claiming their share of our clothes and goods, and of the gifts that had been intended for the wedding. The arguing I'd heard was over the sword that Niall made for the High King, and ended with one of the fake bog-men—a big, ugly man with dirty blond hair— drawing the blade and stabbing the other in the arm. He brandished the bloody sword, laughing until another man, this one thin and dark-haired, came up and slapped him, taking the sword and giving it to the wounded man. He turned on the burly blond, berating him, and I realized that this must be the leader. Then I saw that he wore my torc around his neck, and my feather cloak—my own skin—thrown over his shoulders.

Seething, unable to do anything, I watched silently, seeing what I could of the area. This didn't look like the road, or even the bogs. There were trees here, and the ground, although wet, was solid. I'd been moved, taken to their camp. Turlach was nowhere to be seen. I had no idea if he was even still alive, or if they'd simply dropped his body into the bogs. I shivered in the chilly damp, trying not to think about my fate. I didn't even know why I was even still alive. Surely they weren't going to try and demand ransom for me?

Then another argument broke out, and this one was over me. The burly blond was at the forefront. He wanted me dead, arguing loudly that I was a risk. I had seen them, I could identify them. They'd already killed the one, and they were being paid to kill me, so that was what they should do. I felt a pang of guilt over Turlach's death, mingled with shock over why we'd been attacked. They had been hunting me? By my mother, why?

The dark-haired leader listened to them and shook his head. "You might have been given orders to kill, but I wasn't, and I won't allow you to kill him, either. We'll call down the curse of the Morrigan if we kill her own blood. We don't need to kill him, anyway. All we need is his skin as proof, and we have that." He drew my cloak from his shoulders and tossed it over his arm. "Bind him, take him out into the bogs and leave him there. He'll live or die on his own. Either way, we've clipped this raven's wings."

At his command, they were on me, pulling me to my feet. I tried to fight them and couldn't, hampered by a right arm that refused to move. One of them grabbed my right wrist and dragged it behind me, and I nearly blacked out from the pain. When I could see again, it was too late—my arms were bound behind me. They forced a dirty cloth into my mouth and bound it there, and one of them cinched a rope around my neck, tugging on it like a leash.

"Don't let him see where you take him," I heard the leader call out from somewhere behind me. Another strip of cloth was secured over my eyes, leaving me in darkness. I heard them laughing around me, and then I was prodded to my feet. The leash around my neck tightened, and I had no choice but to follow where they led.

I stumbled and staggered behind them, kept on my feet by the jeering men who surrounded me, who poked at me with sharp fingers and laughed when I tripped and fell into the muck. The ground under my feet grew softer, and I could feel the water seeping into my shoes as we walked. I'd lost all sense of direction almost immediately, as well as all sense of time, so it was a shock when they pulled me to a stop.

"Live or die on his own, he said," one of the men said to me. "Well, this is as good a place as any."

Almost immediately, I was shoved from behind. I stumbled and ended up on my knees, and from there was forced down onto my stomach. My ankles were lashed together, then I heard one of them laugh as my legs were bent and the end of the leash tied off to my ankles. Whoever it was pulled the rope tight enough that my heels were almost touching my arse, and I was nearly strangled by the pressure of the rope across my throat. Someone prodded me with their foot, and I heard their laughter slowly receding as they moved away. Soon, all I could hear was the wind, the distant, mournful call of the birds, and the hammering of my own heartbeat in my ears.

I lay as still as I could, fighting the urge to struggle against the ropes, knowing that if I did, I'd cut off my breath and lose consciousness again. Instead I forced myself to think. Someone was hunting for sons of the Morrigan, someone who knew our secrets, knew what the feather cloak meant. That meant that none of my brothers were safe, nor were Sorcha and the children. But they'd made a mistake in letting me live. Ravens are clever, far more clever than mere mortals. I'd escape them, win back my skin and my pride, and see their heads on the wall at Dun-Morrigan.

Moving my arms was torture, and I couldn't move my right hand at all without sending excruciating pain up and down my side. But my left hand was fine, and I was far more flexible than my captors thought I was. I found a knot in the rope and tugged on it, trying to work it loose with my nails. By the time I'd worried it free, I was growling curses into the gag, trying not to scream from pain. Either I was lucky, or the men who bound me had been careless—the knot that I picked free was the one that bound my ankles. With some careful wiggling, the ropes fell loose, freeing my legs. I took a long breath and got to my knees, turning my attention to the blindfold and somehow removing it. That turned out to be harder than freeing my ankles.

Rubbing my face against my shoulder did nothing except make the pain increase to the point that my teeth ached. Shaking my head made my hair hurt. Finally, I sat down and drew my knees up, rubbing my face against my trews and leaving trails of mud all over my skin as I pushed the cloth up and off. Slowly, I got back to my feet and looked around. There was nothing I could do about the rope around my neck, the gag, or the fact that my hands were bound. I was going to have to find my way out of the bogs, then find a way to free myself. The sky above me was growing darker, and for a moment, I thought it was close to sunset. Then I turned and saw the dark clouds swelling over the horizon; there was a storm coming, and a big one at that. As I watched, the black clouds flickered with lightning, and I heard the distant rumble of thunder. Whatever I was going to do, I needed to do it before that storm hit.

The storm had to have been coming from over the sea, which gave me direction. I turned my back on it and started to walk, picking what looked like a solid path, stopping every few feet to test the ground in front of me. I could swim, but the last thing I wanted to do was find out if I could get myself out of the water with my hands tied behind my back. Behind me, the thunder rumbled again, louder, and I tried to speed my pace. My hands were starting to go numb. I needed to find a way to free myself, and quickly.

When the thunder boomed again, I glanced up and regretted it; the storm was nearly over my head, and a cold wind had picked up, whipping over the bogs and cutting through my wet clothes like a knife. I growled another curse into the gag and stopped to get my bearings and see where my next steps would take me—and heard, echoing from somewhere off to my left, the sounds of men laughing. I couldn't go that way. So I turned right, and started towards a line of trees that looked to be a mile or so away. That had to be Uragh, and there I would find, at the very least, shelter from the storm.

My luck gave out not far from the trees. Eager to find shelter and help, I started rushing, stopped testing the ground in front of me, and I made a mistake. A path that I thought was solid turned out to be a deceptive layer of moss over waist-deep water. I slipped and went under, came up sputtered and coughing, struggling to find footing on the mud and rocks below the surface. I twisted my left knee, fell and went under again, surfaced cursing and discovering even more pain as I tried to put weight on my now-damaged leg. As I foundered, trying to work my way back onto solid ground, the storm broke over me, with driving wind and sheets of icy rain that cut my visibility down to nothing and made my struggles to find dry land even harder than before. At long last, exhausted and shaking, I managed to roll back onto the path and lay there, spent. At that moment, I could no more have gotten to my feet than I could have flown, and in the delirium that comes from unceasing pain, it seemed to me that my best course of action was to lay there in the mud and sleep.

* * *

Truly, I never expected to wake again, but wake I did, into darkness that echoed slightly, and told me without seeing that I was inside. I was warm and dry, covered with a fine, woven blanket, and lying in a wide bed that was piled deep with sheepskins. Someone had stripped away my wet clothes and tended to my wounds while I slept. My aching left knee was wrapped tightly in bandages, as was my left wrist. My right arm was immobile, bound to my chest with long strips of cloth, which helped alleviate the pain somewhat. I searched my memory and could remember nothing after I'd crawled out of the water, except for a dim memory that might very well have been a dream—voices of a man and a woman, both of them singing healing spells over me. I had no idea where I was, or how long I'd been asleep. Or, more importantly, what had become of the brigand who took my cloak, and how to find him.

I heard the footsteps of someone coming closer, and a woman came into the room, carrying a horn lamp. She set it down on a table and came to sit on the edge of the bed.

"How do you feel?" she asked.

I could only stare at her, struck dumb. Up until that moment, I had no idea of what it would be like when I finally found *her*, finally found my mate. Now, at last, I knew, and I understood why Niall had told me that there would be no doubt when I did find her. And I understood just why he'd been in such despair when he thought Sorcha dead. I could barely see her in the dim light, but already I could tell that she was the most beautiful woman I'd ever seen. For a moment, I saw spots before my eyes, then realized it was because I'd forgotten to breathe.

"Are you all right?" she asked, and I could see the worry in her lovely face. "You suddenly had the oddest look."

I smiled. She'd know soon enough what caused that look. "I'm fine," I said, then looked down at myself and grimaced. "Perhaps not fine. But I'm not sick. Thank you. Was it you who saved my life?"

She nodded, then looked at me. "I found you in the storm and brought you back here. What were you doing out there?"

I sighed. "I was on my way to Dun-Righ, and my chariot was attacked. They took me captive and left me out in the bogs to die. I was trying to find my way out."

She frowned and looked away for a moment, then turned back and started to worry the edges of the blanket between her fingers. "You're very lucky," she said softly.

"I'm lucky that you found me," I answered. "Was I dreaming, or were you singing healing chants?"

"You heard me?" she asked, and the bloom of roses in her cheeks made her even more glorious in my eyes. "I…"

"You sing like a lark, my lady. I would be honored to hear you sing again." Sing, speak, breathe, whisper my name in the darkness… I was suddenly glad of the blanket, glad of the weight of it. It hid the fact that my cock was rock-hard for want of her. I wanted so badly just to touch her hand, to convince myself that I wasn't dreaming. She leaned forward and touched my bandaged shoulder; I wasn't expecting it, and gasped at the contact. She jumped back, her eyes large.

"Did that hurt?"

I shook my head quickly. "No. No, my lady. Please, go ahead."

She hesitated for a moment, then nodded and ran her hands over my right shoulder, her fingers probing for I knew not what. Whatever it was that she found seemed to satisfy her, and she took up the lamp and looked me in the face, taking my chin in her hand and staring into my eyes, holding the light close. I could see that her eyes were soft and gray as winter clouds, and again, I forgot to breathe.

"Does your head pain you at all?" she asked. "You had a lump the size of a goose egg."

I forced myself to answer, "No pain in my head. My knee hurts, and my shoulder."

She nodded. "I expected that. Your shoulder is broken. I've set it as best I can, and hopefully you'll still be able to move your arm once it heals, if you're careful and your luck holds out. Your knee is simply twisted. You'll need to stay off your feet for a few days."

"Yes, my lady," I said. "Can a message be sent? I was expected in Dun-Righ…"

She bit her lip and shook her head. "I'm sorry. There's no one to carry a message. I live alone here."

"Alone?" I repeated, confused. If it had been her that had been singing over me, who, then, was the man who had sung with her?

She rose and folded her arms over her chest. "I live alone," she said again, with more than a hint of steel in her words. "I prefer it. Now, I should let you sleep. I'll be in the next room, if you need anything."

I didn't want her to go, but I could think of no way to ask her to stay. So I let her draw the blanket up over my chest and walk away. As she reached the door, I called to her, "I don't know your name, my lady. I am Diarmuid."

She turned to look at me, and a soft smile played over her lips. "My name is Grainne."

* * *

I slept, and when I woke, there was sunlight streaming through the windows, and I could hear Grainne singing in the other room. I shifted under the blanket, and realized that I needed to get up.

"Grainne?" I called, struggling to sit up. I had just swung my legs over the edge of the bed when she came in.

"What are you doing?" she demanded. I looked up at her and saw her in the daylight, and again lost my breath and my wits. She was so beautiful it hurt, and I wanted her more than anything I had ever wanted in this lifetime. Her dark hair was the exact color of my own wings in the sunlight, and cascaded around her shoulders in a glorious fall of silk. Her skin was like new cream, and her eyes were accentuated by the fine gray gown she wore. She frowned at me, and it took me a moment to realize what I'd done to upset her. I shook off the spell her beauty wove about me and grimaced.

"I need to visit the midden."

She looked horrified. "You can't walk that far."

"I can't hit it from here," I insisted. She scowled at me, and I felt the insane urge to kiss her lips and make her smile again. She shook her head and sighed something under her breath, then came towards me.

"You'll have to lean on me. You can't walk that far on that leg."

All at once, I realized that as much as I needed to piss, I needed to stay under the blanket that much more. I felt my face grow warm, and sputtered, "I'll need trews."

"Yours are a ruined mess. I'm trying to clean them," she answered. "If it helps at all, Diarmuid, I'm no modest maiden. I've seen a man naked before. Now, do you still need the midden or should I bring a bucket?"

I sighed and let her help me up. She had to have noticed my erection, but she said nothing. She simply helped me balance as I limped out of the house and out to the midden, and I was surprised by how little my leg hurt. A sign of her skill as a healer, I assumed. I was steady enough that Grainne left me to walk the last few feet to the midden, pointedly looking away while I did what I needed. When I was done, she insisted on helping me back towards the house, and I saw where I was for the first time.

We were in Uragh, far enough into the forest that the little house was mostly hidden by trees and high bushes. If I hadn't known it was there, I would have had a hard time seeing it, the foliage concealed it so well. From my limited viewpoint, I could still see that there were no outbuildings of any kind, nor any kind of cultivated land. I turned my foot on a stone, and paused for a moment as I shifted my arm around Grainne's shoulders. Then I looked at her and blinked. She wasn't tall—the top of her head barely came to my chin—and she could help me walk only with some effort. How had a woman alone managed to get me out of the bogs and to her house, a journey of at least a mile?

"Ready to go inside?" she asked. I nodded and turned to her, only to see her glance around. I felt her shiver slightly, and I knew she was afraid of something.

"Grainne, what's wrong?" I asked, looking around.

"Nothing. We should go in. You shouldn't be on your feet," she urged me into the house with gentle pressure, and through the small outer room. In any other house, this might have served to keep the family livestock safe. Grainne had turned it into a tidy little work-room. I could see bundles of herbs hanging from the rafters, and a table holding tools of the healer's craft was pushed against the wall. There was a cooking pot hanging over the firepit in the middle of the floor, and I saw what looked like blankets rolled up near the outer door. She steered me into the inner room, settled me back onto the bed and covered me with the blanket. As she did, I noticed her eyes lingering, just for a moment, on my now-flaccid cock. She looked away almost immediately and the color rose in her cheeks again.

"I'll fetch you something to eat," she said, and hurried out. I lay back in the bed, thinking.

She had been telling the truth when she told me that she lived alone, of that I had no doubt. There was no sign of anyone else living in this place. No servant, no family. No man at all in her life. Yet she was, by her own admission, not a maid. And she was, I realized suddenly, hiding from something. Or someone. Her behavior outside the house, her nervous survey of the surrounding area, her desire to get out of the open and back into her safe, hidden lair, all spoke of her fear of discovery.

She came back in, carrying a towel-wrapped bowl. "I can help you eat, if you like. I'd rather not have to clean the blanket."

"Grainne, who are you hiding from?" I asked softly. She stopped in her tracks and stared at me.

"How…?" she breathed, and I could see how frightened she was. I wanted to get out of the bed and hold her, protect her from the world. The best I could do was sit up and hold my hand out to her.

"Let me help you, Grainne," I offered. "Let me protect you."

"You can't," she answered, her voice cracking from fear. I felt a wave of anger, and fought it back down, keeping my hand extended.

"Who is he?"

She looked like she wanted to burst into tears, and her hands were shaking so hard I feared for the bowl. "Diarmuid, you can't. No one can…"

"Who is he?" I repeated.

Her eyes met mine, and I saw the tears starting. "My

husband," she whispered, then turned and ran from the room.

* * *

She didn't return for what seemed like hours, and when she did, it was with another bowl. Her eyes were dry, and her face ashen.

"I brought you something to eat," she whispered from the door. I smiled at her and sat up, swinging my legs over the edge of the bed and making room for her to sit on my left. When she sat down, she was close enough that her thigh was pressed against mine, and I was thankful for the fold of blanket I'd kept across my lap. "I'm sorry about… before," she murmured.

"You don't have to be," I answered, keeping my voice low and gentle. "Grainne, I meant what I said. Let me protect you."

She laughed once, bitterly, and turned so that she could run her fingers down my bandaged and immobilized arm. "I don't think you're in any shape to protect anyone, Diarmuid mac Morrigan."

"I still have another arm."

"You don't have a sword. And you can't stand."

"For you, my lady, I'll fight on my knees."

She looked at me, her eyes wide and startled. I smiled at her, and she tentatively smiled back. "I believe you would. Are you hungry?"

"I could eat a bear, fur and all."

"Oh." She looked down at the bowl, then up at me, her lips twitching slightly. "I don't have any bear. Would rabbit do?"

"Any fur?" I teased. "It's the best part."

"I'm sorry, no. I don't care for it," she answered, all seriousness except for the twinkle in her eye. "It gets stuck in my teeth."

I laughed, and she laughed with me, relaxing slightly. I let her feed me, enjoying having her close, watching the fear slowly drain from her until at last she was laughing with me as I jostled her hand and she dribbled broth down my chin and over my chest.

"You did that on purpose," she accused, setting the bowl aside and reaching for a cloth.

"Of course I did. I love having rabbit stew all over my face," I answered lightly. She giggled and started to wipe my chest. I couldn't help it; I closed my eyes and let myself bask in the pleasure of her touch. When I opened my eyes again, she was staring at me.

"Diarmuid…" she said tentatively.

I didn't hesitate. I leaned forward and kissed her gently, tasting her lips for the first time. I wanted so much more, but I refused to push her, refused to frighten her again. So I pulled back and waited, watched her touch her lips with trembling fingers. She smiled and the roses bloomed in her cheeks once more.

"Do that again?" she asked.

I reached for her, pulling her close and kissing her once more, ignoring the pain that the motion sent through my injured shoulder. This time, I kissed her the way I wanted to, harder, more possessive, my tongue brushing against hers to taste her breath and the sweetness of her mouth. She moaned against me, one hand creeping up my neck to tangle in my hair. Then, abruptly, she pulled away.

"I… I can't," she whispered. "You're so wonderful, and… I can't. I'm married."

"I don't care," I said. "Grainne…"

She stood, and I could see her shaking. "No, Diarmuid. I can't. I want… I'm sorry." She hurried from the room, leaving me alone with my desire and my frustration.

* * *

I lay awake late into the night, wishing that she would come back. I stopped myself from calling out to her dozens of times, unwilling to cause her pain by asking her to choose. This was something that I hadn't ever considered, that the one to whom I was fated to be bound for eternity might belong to another. There was no way past this that I could see. She was married, and despite the fact that I knew she wanted me as much as I wanted her, I could not in good conscience ask Grainne to betray her husband, no matter how much I needed her. She was bound to another.

Finally, I could bear the empty bed no longer. I slowly got to my feet, wrapped the blanket around me, and limped to the door. In the dim glow of the coals and the light of the moon through the window, I could see her sleeping, curled in her blankets near the fire. Deliberately, I turned and made my way to the outer door.

The forest outside was painted silver by the moon, with long shadows cast over the path to the midden. I'd noticed a great fallen tree along the path when we'd come this way before, and that was where I stopped, dropping the blanket over the tree trunk and sitting down to stare up at the moon. I ached with desire, unable to do anything about the terrible burning need that threatened to consume me whole. For a moment, I considered trying to find some small relief, but my memories of Nuala were sour to me now, and I knew that they would never again arouse me as they'd done before. What I'd had with Nuala had been a mere shadow of what I might have with Grainne. If she'd only accept me.

The worst part of this whole messy situation was that I was trapped here. I was going to be forced to spend every waking minute for the next several weeks with a woman I wanted and who did not want me, until finally I was healed enough to fly home. And it was with that thought that my world came crashing down around my ears. I wasn't going to be able to fly home. I wasn't going to be able to fly anywhere, ever again. My cloak was gone. By the time I was healed enough to even walk the rest of the way to Dun-Righ, a month or more would have passed. There would be no way to find the man who had taken my cloak—any trail would have long since gone cold. Perhaps it would be for the best if I simply walked off into the forest and disappeared…

"Diarmuid?"

I never heard her approach, didn't hear anything until she called my name. I turned and saw her standing in the moonlight, her blanket wrapped around her like a cloak, so beautiful that she made my heart hurt. I closed my eyes and turned away.

"I'm fine. I needed…" I stopped. I knew what I needed, and I knew that I would never have it.

She broke the silence, "You were right, earlier. I am hiding." She came closer, moving to stand in front of me. "I need for you to understand."

I nodded. "Tell me."

She took a long breath. "I married at 17. A good marriage, better than I thought a fatherless girl like me would ever have, to a man who'd buried three wives before me. He had no children, and he wanted a son. He told me on our wedding night that I was to give him that son. When I didn't… he turned on me. For three years, every month when my courses started, he would beat me for not being pregnant. Every month, until I thought I would die from it. I ran for my life, back to my village. My brother brought me here, and I've been hiding ever since." She looked up, then back down at me. "He's a brutal man, my husband. If he finds me… if he finds me with you…"

Finally, I understood. "Grainne, I'll protect you. Or I'll take you to Dun-Righ and the High King himself will protect you."

"And who's going to protect you?" she asked. She looked at me, and shook her head slowly. "I don't understand. I've known you a day, and I feel…"

"As if you've known me a lifetime? As if there was something you were missing, and you didn't know it until you found me? As if everything you ever wanted and needed in your life was standing right in front of you, waiting for you to take it up?" I finished. She nodded, her eyes wide. I smiled. "Grainne, *acushla*, I know."

"You feel it, too?" she stepped closer, until her blanket brushed against my knees. I fought down the urge to pull her closer, contenting myself with reaching up and toying with a lock of her hair.

"Grainne…" I hesitated, then slowly explained to her the way of my blood. That we mate once, and that once for life. That we never know who, or what, or when, until we find that right person. Then I paused, trying to think of some way to tell her how much I needed her. How nothing was ever going to be right, ever again, unless she was at my side from now until the stars fell from the heavens. I wasn't even certain the words existed. In the end, I met her eyes and whispered, "You are my mate. Seeing you, I know it. I am yours, and I always will be yours, even if you turn away and leave me. Without you, there will never be a moment of happiness for me ever again. I cannot make you love me, cannot make you want me, but please believe me when I say that I love you, and that I will love only you for the rest of my life. I love you, Grainne."

The only sound for a moment was the wind in the trees around us. Grainne's eyes never left my face, and I held myself perfectly still under her gaze, holding her eyes with mine and willing her to see the truth there. Without warning, she leaned forward, catching my face in her hands and kissing me with a passion I wasn't expecting. Her kiss was everything I'd dreamed of and more, even better than the brief kiss that we'd shared before. Dimly, I was aware of her blanket slithering down to puddle around her feet. Awareness sharpened when I realized that she wore nothing underneath. I slid my hand up her thigh and over her hip, pulling her to me, briefly marveling at how well our bodies fit together.

"I couldn't bear it if he hurt you," she murmured against my lips as she pulled back. "If something happened to you…"

I nipped her lower lip, making her gasp and giggle. Then I met her eyes. "You're mine now. You were meant to be mine from the moment you first drew breath. As I was meant to be yours. Nothing can stand between us. And nothing will. If he tries to take you from me, I'll kill him."

She caught her breath. "You would do that?"

"To protect you and keep you by my side, *acushla*? I'd challenge the gods themselves." I tightened my arm around her and kissed her throat. "I want you, Grainne. Let's go back to the house."

She giggled again, running her fingers through my hair. "What's wrong with right here?"

I blinked in surprise, and let her do what she would. She used gentle pressure to push me back so that I was reclining on the fallen tree, holding myself steady with my hand on the stump of a branch over my head. With a wonderfully wicked smile, she straddled me, sitting on my lower belly before lying down over me and resting her chin on folded hands that she propped onto my chest. I could feel the rough tree bark digging into my back through the blanket, and chose to ignore it.

"Comfortable?" she asked, shifting slightly, squirming against me and making me buck upwards slightly. Not as much as I wanted—I had no purchase, no leverage, and I told her so. She laughed and pushed herself up, balancing over me. "If you want to go back, we can. But I don't want to wait."

Who was I to argue with my mate? I grinned and set my grip. "Take your time, *acushla*."

She smiled sweetly, raised herself up just enough, and then slowly lowered herself onto my aching cock, surrounding me with tight, wet heat. I closed my eyes, feeling her tightening around me, feeling her cunt pulsing in time with her heartbeat. Her hair brushed against my stomach as her hand slowly crept up my chest until her fingers found my left nipple. I moaned as she toyed with me, realizing too late the corner that she'd backed me into: I couldn't move with her! The only thing keeping the both of us on the log was me, and the only things keeping *me* on the log were Grainne's weight and my tenuous grip on the branch! If I shifted, tried to thrust upwards, we'd both fall. I was completely at her mercy, and she knew it. And, if I was not mistaken, she was reveling in it.

She was moaning, her head thrown back, her fingers splayed wide on my stomach as she moved over me, taking me deeper and deeper until she finally came to rest against my hips. She stayed still for a moment, then she slowly started to rock, grinding against me. Her hands started moving, trailing over my belly and chest, skimming over bandages, tickling me gently and making me fight to stay still and not tip the both of us onto the ground. It was enough to drive a man mad! My moans quickly turned to gasps of pleasure as Grainne started moving faster, driving herself down onto me, making short, guttural sounds in her throat that quickly elevated to moans, and from there to keening. Her movements became sharper, shorter, more abrupt, her hands fell still, and I could feel her orgasm building around me, spurring my own arousal to greater heights. I heard someone shouting, and realized that it was my own voice calling her name, begging her to come, to let me come. She started thrusting harder, so tight around me that every movement was tortuous pleasure. Then, without warning, she leaned down, licked my nipple, then bit me, just hard enough that I knew I'd been bitten. I howled and came, dimly aware of Grainne's voice joining mine in spiraling up to serenade the moon. She fell limp over me, and I marveled again at how well we fit together, how comfortable she felt lying on me. Until the tree bark digging through the blanket got to be too much.

"Grainne?" I murmured softly, afraid that she'd fallen asleep.

"Hmm?"

"We need to move."

She moaned softly and buried her face in my neck. "Oh, but you feel so good."

"I'll feel better in bed." I nuzzled her hair and breathed a sigh of contentment. This would be the last thing I saw before I slept and the first thing I saw when I woke for the rest of my life. It was something to which I was very much looking forward to becoming accustomed. " *Acushla*, this tree is digging into my back."

"Oh," she gasped and pushed herself up, sliding off me and helping me to stand up. I leaned against the tree and pulled her to me, reaching up and pulling her face to mine for a long, deep kiss that left her moaning against my mouth and clinging to me. I pulled back slightly and whispered against her lips, "Bed?"

"Oh, yes."

Together, we gathered up the stray blankets and walked hand-in-hand back down the path to her house. Every so often, I had to stop and kiss her, just because I could. She giggled and cuddled against me, and then would whisper, "Bed," and lead me on. Truly, if she hadn't been guiding me, I probably would have walked into a tree within ten paces. For me, on that night, there was nothing else in the world, in all of existence, except for Grainne. My mate.

If it had been a perfect world, I would have picked Grainne up and carried her into the house, laying her in the bed so that I could stand over her and admire her beauty. In reality, I limped through the door behind her, following her into the bedchamber and sitting down on the bed when she bid me to do so. She looked down at the blankets in her arms and frowned.

"I need to shake these out, or we won't be able to sleep with them. Lie down and I'll be right back."

I remember her leaving, remember lying down and thinking how frustrating it was that lying on my left side so that I could see her come in meant that I didn't have a hand free to hold her. I remember hearing her moving around, and the snap of the blankets as she shook them out. And I remember thinking that closing my eyes while I waited was a wonderful idea. I'd just rest for a moment…

* * *

Maelan grinned at Niall. "It's just a market, Niall. No one is going to attack us here. Relax."

Niall scowled at his older brother and shifted slightly, keeping one hand on the hilt of his sword. The look he gave Maelan spoke volumes: How did I let you talk me into this?

"You wanted something pretty for your wife, remember? She's giving you another nestling? Who is currently making her sick to her stomach all day, every day?" Maelan reminded Niall, who sighed and nodded. It hadn't taken much for Maelan to talk Niall into coming with him to the village market, but then, Niall had been distracted. The past few days had been dreary in Dun-Morrigan—Sorcha had been ill from dawn to dusk, and Niall had been fretting and irritable. Finally, Maelan had gone and brought the midwife up from Scath, who assured both Sorcha and her mate that this kind of sickness was normal for some pregnancies, and the fact that Sorcha had never been taken with pregnancy sickness before meant nothing. The midwife left after giving Sorcha some potions and a list of foods to avoid,

and after telling Niall not to worry so much. Silently, Maelan wondered if Niall had listened to her at all.

"Look there, Niall. Silks. That green would look nice on Sorcha." Maelan pointed at a display. Niall shrugged one shoulder, looked at the table, then looked again, a frown on his face. Without warning, he stalked away. "Niall!" Maelan called as he hurried after his brother.

Niall waved one hand at him, stopping at another table and pointing. The man behind the table frowned, then picked something up and handed it to him. "This, my lord? Very pretty piece."

Maelan caught up with Niall and peered over his shoulder to see the brooch in Niall's hand. It was a pretty thing, silver and gold, set with a large, clear amethyst. Niall ran his fingers over the surface, then did something that Maelan had seen him do a thousand times—turn the piece over. To check the workmanship, he'd explained once, back when he'd still had his voice. As Maelan watched, Niall's eyes widened. He took a long breath, then launched himself over the table, catching the merchant by the front of his shirt and pinning him against the wall, a bared dagger across the man's throat. It happened so fast Maelan barely had time to react.

"Niall!"

Niall shook his head, then nodded towards the brooch, which had rolled to a stop in the dirt next to Maelan's foot. Maelan frowned and picked it up, studying it for a moment. The piece looked oddly familiar…

"Niall, this is your work!"

Niall nodded once, and the trapped merchant moaned softly. Without turning, Niall started to whistle. It took a moment before Maelan recognized the tune— Conchobar's Wedding.

"This is one of the wedding presents that you sent with Diarmuid?" Maelan asked, suddenly cold. Niall nodded once and Maelan drew his sword.

"I've got him, Niall. Go get the others. Oscar will have a great deal of fun finding out what this piece of shit did to our brother."

* * *

I woke first, well after dawn, and spent an endless age just lying there. I couldn't remember Grainne coming to bed but she was there when I woke, sound asleep next to me, her cheek pillowed on her arm and an amused smile on her sleeping face. I could guess what amused her so. Part of me wanted to wake her, hold her, burrow under the blankets with her and never, ever come out. Instead, I decided to let her sleep. Slowly, I climbed out of the bed and went into the other room. There, the cold hearth welcomed me and helped me to make my mind up as to what I was going to do. I'd light the fire and make the porridge. If it wasn't ready when she woke, at least it would be started, and if it was ready, then I could serve it to her in bed before crawling back in with her.

Lighting a fire one-handed turned out to be more difficult than I thought, but I managed without waking Grainnc. Once I had a good blaze going, I filled the pot from the water barrel in the corner and tried to discover just where Grainne kept her food stores. There were no bags of meal hanging from the rafters, only herbs. The shelves were full of crockery and not much else. The only place left was a solid looking chest that stood under the window. I opened it and stared for a moment in shock. There, half-covered by one of Grainne's gowns, was my cloak!

I took it out of the chest and buried my face in my feathers, feeling a suddenly, heady wash of relief. Ever since I'd first awakened, there had been a tiny trickle of fear in my mind that the man who'd taken my cloak would destroy it and, in doing so, destroy me. But now, now I was whole.

"Diarmuid?" I jumped and turned to see Grainne standing in the doorway to the bedchamber, wrapped in a blanket and looking deliciously rumpled. Her eyes widened when she saw what was in my hand. "You went through my things?"

I shrugged, my mind reeling, suddenly remembering now how she'd called me by my full name when I'd annoyed her the day before. She'd known the entire time who I was, had hidden my cloak away. To protect it? Or to keep me prisoner? Something inside me fractured, and I said the only thing I could think of. "I was going to make something for us to eat. I couldn't find the porridge meal. Grainne, how…?" I stepped towards her, and stopped when a man's voice snapped, "Don't move!" I turned towards the door and froze, seeing the arrow first. Then I recognized the man who was aiming it at me—the dark-haired man who'd attacked us on the road, and who had stolen my torc and cloak.

"Donal!" Grainne went to his side, taking his arm. He shrugged her off and pushed her behind him. "Donal, stop!"

"You… know him?" I asked, suddenly tired. I slung my cloak over my wounded shoulder. "Is this the husband you were so worried about?"

Donal went white with fury and spit onto the ground. "Don't insult me!"

"Diarmuid, this is my brother. Who is going to put the bow down!" Grainne stepped out from behind him and came across towards me, ignoring Donal's warning hiss. "Diarmuid, I was going to give it back to you. I swear to you, by all the gods, I was! Once you healed enough to wear it again. I was afraid you'd push yourself, and that you wouldn't heal properly."

I looked into her tear-filled eyes and believed her, so I reached out my hand and cupped her cheek. "Thank you, Grainne." She smiled and moved into my embrace, resting her cheek against my chest.

In the doorway, Donal had lowered his bow and was leaning against the doorpost. He looked at us, then sighed. "So, Diarmuid *Ri na Fiach dubh,* I suppose you'd like an explanation?"

"It would be a start," I answered curtly. "You killed my charioteer and left me to die."

Grainne went stiff and turned to glare at Donal. "You said no one would be killed!"

"And no one was!" Donal answered sharply.

I stared at him. "Turlach—"

"Is alive," Donal answered. "In truth, he's right now at my house in the village, and not happy about it. But he understands that the others will kill him if they find him." He sighed and set the bow aside before speaking again. "I ordered the others not to attack, but… Grainne, it was Ruaidri. He tried to kill the charioteer, would have killed both of them if I hadn't stopped him." He met my eyes. "I swear to you, Diarmuid, my plans were to stop you at the fallen tree and take you captive. I didn't want to kill anyone. Everything went wrong when Ruaidri threw that damned spear. I did the best I could to keep you alive. I was even going to come back and let you go once I'd hidden Turlach away, but you got loose on your own. It took me hours to find you in that storm."

"I lied to you, a little," Grainne said softly. "It wasn't me that found you in the bogs, Diarmuid. Donal did. He carried you here and asked me to care for you."

I nodded. That, at least, answered one of my questions. "I remember someone saying that they had orders to kill me," I said to Donal. "A big man. He said something about being paid to kill me. Why?"

"That was Ruaidri. And I don't know. My orders were to bring you to the bitch who holds my leash. I found out that he'd been given different orders when you did. I'm starting to think she doesn't trust me anymore," Donal answered with a bitter laugh. "Not that it matters. They were my men. I'm responsible. I will pay whatever forfeit you ask. Just…" He paused and looked at Grainne, then looked back at me. "If you ask my life, then I ask that you protect my sister."

"I would do that even if you didn't ask it," I answered. "I will decide on your forfeit later. For now, how do I know I can trust you?"

"You can," Grainne answered, tightening her arm around me. I smiled and hugged her, kissing the top of her head. As I did so, Donal coughed and straightened.

"Grainne, is that the way it is?"

Grainne looked over her shoulder. "It is."

He nodded, running his fingers through unruly dark hair, then shrugged. "So be it. I suppose I can put up with a pretty featherhead. Anyone is better than Guaire, after all. Now, how badly is he hurt, Grainne? How soon can we move? I can have Turlach here in an hour."

"Not that soon, brother. Diarmuid won't be flying for weeks. Perhaps months," she answered, touching my bandaged shoulder. "He can't walk far, either. Not on that knee. A week, perhaps two, before he'll be able to leave."

He grimaced. "You're not going to be safe here that long. Ruaidri is due back in the village tomorrow, and she's coming with him. If she finds Turlach, she'll know I'm plotting. And if she finds out that the cloak I gave her is fake…"

"What?" I interrupted. Grainne sighed softly, her breath warm on my chest.

"We have a lot of explaining to do, Diarmuid. It will go better over something to eat, I think."

"And it will be less distracting for me if you put some trews on him, woman," Donal added. He shook his head and grinned at me, then laughed as Grainne stepped in front of me and snapped, "Mine!"

Donal grinned. "But he's pretty, Grainne!" he said plaintively. "Can I at least admire the view?"

Grainne made an indignant squeak and grabbed my arm, dragging me out of the room so quickly that I almost fell. She stopped in the doorway and steadied me, glaring over my shoulder at Donal, who I could hear laughing. Once we were inside the room, Grainne turned to me, her expression serious. "I'm sorry. He's not usually so… vulgar."

"It's fine, Grainne," I answered, and her face was so serious that I couldn't help but tease her. I smiled. "I am amused that you and your brother seem to have similar taste in men. Do I even have trews, or do I have to keep on distracting your brother?"

She scowled at me, seating me on the edge of the bed before she left the room, and coming back a few minutes later with my own trews, now battered and stained. She had to help me dress, which took longer than it should have, simply because neither of us could stop touching each other for very long. I found that I needed to touch her, and that there was an almost desperate need to pull her back into bed with me. I knew that she felt the same way; there was a heat in her eyes, an urgency in her touch, that told me clearer than words that she wanted a repeat of the night before as much as I did. When she kissed me, I almost gave in to my desires, almost let her push me backwards onto the bed. Then I heard Donal cough in the other room, and realized that there was one thing I needed now more than her. I needed to understand what had happened to me, who was hunting me, and why. It was harder than I thought it would be to push Grainne aside and stand up, but she understood, rising on tip-toe to kiss my cheek before taking up her own gown and starting to dress. I left her there and limped out into the other room, finding Donal there, stirring the pot.

"You couldn't find the meal because I was late," he said, making what I assumed was an apology. "I bring supplies every third day. That would have been yesterday, but with the ambush… What has she told you?"

"That you're hiding her from her husband," I answered. Donal nodded and pushed a bench towards the table.

"Sit. She'll pull my hair out by the roots if I keep you standing on that leg. The porridge will be ready by the time we finish talking, and then we can eat and plan. We were born here, you know. This cottage, it was our mother's," he looked up at the rafters. "She died when I was 12 and Grainne was five. No one wanted us, so I took care of Grainne as best I could."

I looked at him curiously. "No one?"

"Our mother was the village whore. I think they were afraid of bad blood or something," Donal shrugged and came over to sit across from me, folding his left hand

94

over his right in an odd gesture. "Like I said, I did the best I could. I apprenticed myself to the village healer, moved the both of us in with her in the village. When Grainne was old enough, old Imag started teaching her about healing, too. Said that maybe Grainne would make the village a fine healer in time. But… Grainne got older, got prettier, and people started thinking that Grainne was just like our mother. The boys started coming around looking for things Grainne didn't want to give, and I had to knock some sense into their heads. The village elders started making noise about driving the whore and the troublemaker away. That was about the same time Guaire passed through the village.

"He saw Grainne, and he came to me and proposed marriage that same morning. Proper bride-price and everything, just like she was a high-born girl. I told Grainne we'd be idiots not to take the offer." Donal took a long breath. "She left with him that day, and the next time I saw my sister, it was three years later, and I almost didn't recognize her for the bruises. So I brought her back here, nursed her, kept her hidden. She's been hidden here now almost two years, and we've been lucky. Guaire came back here looking for her, more than once. I knew our luck wouldn't last. So… I swore in blood to a high-born witch, swore that I'd serve her if she helped keep Grainne safe." He spread his hands, and I saw finally what he was hiding—his right hand was missing the smallest finger. He saw my gaze and held his hand up. "As I said, I swore in blood. She took this as a token, to seal the bargain and to keep me in line. A small price to pay, to keep Grainne safe. But now… she's the one who ordered me to take you. She wants your head on a platter, Diarmuid, and she wants to do it herself."

"Why?" I asked. "Donal, who is she?"

"Her name is Aine, and that's all I really know. She lives out in the bogs, keeps her baile hidden with strong magic and trickery. You can only find her if she wants to be found. When she calls me, I go. I don't have a choice." He raised his mutilated hand, then looked past me; I turned to see Grainne standing in the door, wearing a green gown that made her look as though she'd walked out of a story. Something about Fand, the beautiful wife of the sea god Manannan mac Lir. I'm sorry, Uncle, but my wife is much more beautiful than yours.

"He doesn't know how long he's been here, Donal."

I frowned. "Of course I do. You found me in the storm two nights ago."

Donal's lips twitched. "That storm was nearly six days ago. How's your leg?"

I couldn't find words for a moment, then stammered, "Why?"

"We kept you asleep so that we could work strong healing magic on you, Diarmuid," Grainne answered, coming over to sit next to me on the bench. "And so that we could make a false cloak."

"I am not going to have the Battle Raven rise against me and mine because I took the life of her son," Donal said firmly. "But I had to give Aine something. She has a fake cloak, and thinks that you fell into the bogs and drowned. I'd hoped that your leg would be better healed than it is, so that you could take the road to Dun-Righ. Now… I'll have to bring Turlach out here to keep him out of Ruaidri's way. And then see if I can get a horse."

"How long will that take?" Grainne asked.

"Too damn long. A day, maybe two," Donal answered, standing up so that he could ladle porridge into bowls. He served Grainne and me, then sat back down across from us. "Grainne, I want you out of here. When Diarmuid and Turlach leave, you're going with them."

Grainne sat up straight. "And since when do you give me orders, Donal?"

I stopped with my spoon halfway to my mouth and stared at her. "Does he have to? Was there ever any question of you leaving with me?"

She softened and rested her hand on my thigh. "No. I just have had enough of being ordered about."

"I'll remember that," I said, leaning over and kissing her cheek. Across from us, Donal coughed, dragging our attention back to him. He pointed at his sister.

"Grainne, if the witch has decided I'm not to be trusted, then she might decide that whatever she could do to me wouldn't be enough to punish me. She might decide to take it out on you. I want you someplace safe, someplace Guaire mac Bressail can't reach you."

My spoon fell from my hand, bounced off the table and clattered onto the floor. I ignored it, staring at Donal. "Guaire mac Bressail? About my age, thinning hair? Always looked like he'd swallowed a toad and wasn't enjoying the experience?"

Donal's jaw dropped. "Yes. You know him?"

"A long time ago. I met him at Dun-Righ." I frowned, thinking back. "Ten years? More? It was before Eochaid died. I remember the man being a turd. He insulted Eogan and was banned from the High King's court. I think Eogan maintained the ban because I've never seen him at court again."

Grainne was nodding when I looked at her. "That is him. He used to rail about it at night when he was in his cups."

I looked from her to Donal and back. " *Acushla*, I don't understand why you're still in hiding. Guaire isn't hunting you anymore. He's been dead almost a year."

Her face went white and she jerked as if she'd been slapped. "He's dead?"

"He died in a cattle raid. Fell from his chariot and broke his neck," I answered. I turned to see Donal's wide eyes. "You didn't know?"

He shook his head, then stood up and walked away, his shoulders slumped. I watched him pace across the room until he turned to face us again. In a strangled voice he said, "I swore to that witch half a year ago. She told me then that Guaire was still hunting, that he was getting closer, and that she'd use her magic to keep him at bay if I served her."

"She manipulated you," I said.

He nodded. "She knew I'd do anything to protect Grainne. I practically told her that myself! So she kept me jumping at shadows so I'd follow and obey."

"Donal, what will happen to you when she learns you've turned on her?" Grainne asked. I looked at her and saw in her eyes that she already knew the answer. Donal shrugged and turned away.

"Something messy, I expect. Don't you worry about it. You and Diarmuid just… get to Dun-Righ. You'll be safe there, and you finally found someone who loves you and who'll treat you the way you should be treated. That's enough for me. For what it's worth, you have my blessing."

Grainne rose from her seat, tears welling in her eyes. She stood still for a moment, then she whirled and ran from the room. I stood up slowly, but I didn't follow Grainne. Instead, I crossed the room to face Donal, offering him my hand. He looked at me, a puzzled expression on his face, then took my hand.

"Thank you," I said. "For your blessing. It means a great deal to me."

He smiled. "It means more to me to see her happy and loved. What that bastard did to her…" He stopped and looked down. Then he met my eyes. "You take care of her, Diarmuid."

"I intend to. And you, if I can."

He frowned. "What?"

"My brother is a sorcerer. If anyone can free you from the hold that Aine has over you, Oscar can. Come with us."

I saw the flare of hope in his storm-gray eyes. He nodded once, quickly, then let my hand go. "I need to get back. Turlach doesn't have any sense, and he might come out looking for me if I'm gone too long."

I grinned. "Tell him he doesn't get out of teaching me about chariots that easily."

Donal smiled weakly in return. "Look for us before dawn tomorrow. And be ready to leave. I'll bring a horse if I have to steal one." I nodded, and he hurried out of the house and down the path. I watched until I could no longer see him, then limped into the other room to see to Grainne. She was lying on the bed, her face buried in the blankets; she didn't move when I came in and sat down next to her, laying my cloak on the foot of the bed. Feeling awkward, I started to rub her back. Almost immediately, she rolled over and looked up at me, her face streaked with tears.

"He's gone?" she asked. I nodded, and she hiccupped. "I didn't get a chance to say goodbye."

"He'll be back tomorrow morning with Turlach. And he's coming with us."

Her eyes got very round. "He is?"

"I insisted. Once we get to Dun-Morrigan, my brother Oscar should be able to free him from any compulsions that witch might have put on him," I answered, with more confidence than I truly felt, shoving aside thoughts of the one spell I knew Oscar had never been able to break, the one that had cost Niall his voice.

Grainne wiped one hand over her face and sat up. "He can do that?"

"He's one of the strongest sorcerers in Eire."

Her smile was breathtaking, her joy infectious as she threw her arms 'round me and kissed me. I laughed as I hugged her back, enjoying having her close, having her happy. I turned so that she was sitting in my lap and held her close against my chest. She giggled and rested her cheek on my shoulder.

"Donal says he'll be back before dawn, and that we should be ready to go."

She nodded. "There isn't much I want to take. Some clothes and food is all. I should work on your leg some more, see if I can strengthen it. Donal is better at this type of healing than I am. I seem to be better with illnesses than injuries."

"I'm sure my brother's wife will appreciate that," I said. When she looked up at me, I explained, "My youngest brother and his wife have two children, and they're expecting a third. You know how children get sick. Sorcha will love having a healer in the family."

Grainne smiled and then tipped her head back so that she could look at me. "Children?" I waited for the rest of the question, and she bit her lip before asking, "Do you want children?"

I kissed the tip of her nose. "If you want to give them to me."

100

She blushed. "I might not be able to have children. Guaire blamed me…"

"Guaire was an arse," I said firmly, cutting her off. "He had three wives before you, and none of them bore him a child. That speaks to the problem being him, not them, and not you." I kissed her again, lightly, on the lips. " *Acushla*, we will try. And if you bear me a child, I will rejoice. If you do not, I still have you, *a rún mo chroí*."

Her blush deepened, and she met my eyes. "Should we start now?" She didn't give me a chance to answer, catching the back of my neck in her hand and pulling me down for a deep kiss, her tongue gently caressing mine. I felt her other hand reaching between us, fumbling at my trews. I twisted, laying her down on her back and wishing once more than I had the use of my right arm. My left was trapped under her, so all I could do was let her touch me, her nimble fingers loosening my trews. Her hand slipped between skin and cloth, and I gasped as she grabbed my half-hard cock.

"I want your children, Diarmuid," she whispered. "I want to be your wife. I love you."

"I love you, too," I whispered back. Then I screwed up my brow and looked down at the two of us. "Unfortunately, I can't do anything about how much I want you while we're in this position."

Grainne had the most wonderful giggle. She shifted and rolled onto her side, pressing up against me and kissing my throat before gently pushing me onto my back. She tugged my trews down over my hips, freeing my cock, then straddled me, her skirts pooled around us like the leaves of a water lily. Lying down on top of me, her left hand resting just under the line of bandages, she skimmed the fingers of her other hand over my cheek, and her face grew solemn.

"Diarmuid, we'll get through the forest safely?" she asked.

I sighed and shrugged my shoulder. " *Acushla*, I don't know. I hope so." I frowned. I didn't even have a sword anymore. "Grainne, what do you have for weapons?"

She bit her lip and shook her head. "Cooking knives. A spit. That's all."

"It will have to do. Perhaps Donal will think to bring something." I looked up at her and slid my hand under her gown, running my fingers up her thigh. "Now, I thought we had other plans here?"

Grainne smiled at me and pushed herself upright, running her hands over my chest, my belly, and ribs with long, sweeping motions that left me humming with pleasure.

"Not even getting undressed?" I murmured, stroking her underneath her gown, running my fingers through the damp tangle of hair between her thighs. "Such a wanton."

She pinched me. "Bad blood," she said. "I heard Donal tell you. My mother was a whore. So am I."

"I never said that!" I protested, pushing myself up on my elbow and almost unseating her in the process. "I'd never call you a whore, Grainne."

"You might be the only one. The entire village certainly thought I was."

"They're idiots, all of them," I said. "I know exactly what you are, *acushla*, and it's not a whore."

She looked at me quizzically. "Then what would that be? What am I, Diarmuid?"

I smiled and sat up so I could face her, holding her so that our noses were almost touching. "The Raven Queen," I told her. "My queen." Her eyes widened, and she repeated the words softly. I pulled her body to mine and kissed her lips gently. "Once we're safe in Dun-Righ, we'll seal this between us. You'll be my mate for always." I was going to tell her about the cloak, about her becoming immortal and gaining her own cloak, but she decided that I'd spoken enough, and kissed me, pushing me back down on the bed.

Our lovemaking the night before had been wild. We ignited like dry tinder, our passion burning just as hot, and burning out just as quickly. Last night was the first spark of discovery, the uncontrolled flame of lust. I knew this would be different, this would be more akin to Niall's forge flame than the conflagration of a forest fire. Now, we burned as one, controlled power and sustained heat, a flame that would last, and that could be used to create something wonderful. If the rest of my nights turned out to be like this one day, then I would someday die a very happy man indeed.

She began by touching me, firm caresses that left me gasping and squirming under her, whispering pleas and trying to coax her into something more direct. She ignored me, following the path of her hands with her mouth, until I was certain that there wasn't a square inch of bare flesh on my chest that she hadn't explored with lips and tongue. When I reached for her, Grainne pushed my hand back down and laughed, sliding down my legs, out of my reach. I knew what she was going to do before she stopped moving, and as her lips closed over my cock, I almost came right then and there. She giggled again, and that delightful sound became even more as it vibrated through me, traveling up my spine and into my brain; I bucked under her, gently, and she responded by putting one arm across my lower belly and pressing down. I understood her message instantly— *Don't move!* So I tried my best to obey, which was harder than I thought. To just lie there and let her lavish such fond attentions on my cock and not be able to do anything to reciprocate was near impossible. I was just about to reach for her again when Grainne discovered something that distracted me completely.

She bit me.

It was a little thing, gentle, just hard enough that I knew what she was doing. But it was shocking, something that no one had ever done to me before. She started at the very tip of my cock and then oh-so-slowly nibbled her way down the length, leaving me fighting to keep still and yowling like a cat in heat. Then she licked me, long slow strokes of her tongue to bring her back up so that she could swallow me again, taking me deep into her throat. I was close to the brink and I knew it, and I couldn't seem to find anything even vaguely approaching a word to tell her. Not that she seemed to care—when I came, howling like a *bean-sídhe*, into her mouth, she laughed delightedly and licked me clean. Then she crawled up my body and kissed me, deeply and passionately, until my head spun of it.

"I've been wanting to do that since I first saw you without your trews," she whispered against my lips. "You taste as good as I thought you would."

I groaned softly and held her tightly. "I want to taste you."

She giggled and blushed, then shook her head. "No. You'll hurt yourself. That will have to wait until you're healed."

I grumbled at her, told her she was a horrible tease, to treat me thus and not let me do the same for her. She laughed and pounced on me again, like a kitten with a piece of string, starting once more to torment me with teeth and lips and tongue until amazingly, she again coaxed me to rise. She knelt above me like a goddess, teasing me with the slow stripping off of her gown until she at last revealed herself in all her beauty, in all her glory. With slow, aching tenderness she lowered herself onto my cock, moaning as she enveloped me, sliding softly around me until our hips met and we were joined as one. I slid my hand up her thigh, over her belly to her breast, finding the erect nipple with my fingertips. She moaned again and leaned forward to grant me better access.

"Lean down, *acushla*," I murmured. "Let me taste you."

She leaned forward, bracing herself on her hands; I cupped her breast and brought her nipple to my lips, suckling gently and delighting in the taste of her skin, then moving to sample the other. She moaned and giggled, and I could feel her arousal, feel her growing wetter around me, tightening around my cock until I could bear it no longer and thrust upwards. She gasped and laughed, pushing herself up out of reach and starting to rock.

"Don't you move!" she gasped, breathless. "You'll hurt yourself!" Grinning, I thrust up into her again, and she moaned softly before she mock-scowled at me and muttered, "Don't make me tie you to the bed!'

"Promises…" I mumbled. Any other teasing I might have made was lost as she rolled her hips and sent my wits wandering. I rested my hand on her hip and closed my eyes, feeling her orgasm building around me, feeling my own soaring to meet hers. My cries mingled with hers as we peaked; she collapsed over me as we soared and floated back to earth, and I wrapped my arm around her and held her tightly as her breath warmed my throat. Eventually, she shifted slightly, and we lay together, the sweat on our bodies slowly drying, my trews hopelessly tangled around my legs. Grainne had rested her head on my good shoulder and was running her nails over my chest. I cuddled her close and buried my face in her hair.

"When will we be married, Diarmuid?" she asked me.

"Soon. When we reach Dun-Righ," I answered. "Oh, a day or so after, actually. I want my brothers around me when I marry. I think you'll like the way ravens marry, Grainne."

"I will?"

"Have you ever wanted to fly, *acushla*?" I asked. She looked up at me through her hair, and I smiled. "The only magic I have is the magic to grant you your own wings. You'll be able to fly with me, Grainne."

Her eyes lit up, and she grinned like a little girl. "Oh, I can't wait!"

I laughed, then said, "Do you want to know what I can't wait for?"

"What?"

"I can't wait for this arm to heal enough that you can unwrap me," I looked down at the bandages crossing my chest.

"So you can fly again," she said. I shook my head.

"I want both arms to hold you, Grainne," I answered. "And, eventually, I want to be on top."

She laughed and threw her leg over mine. "Who says I'm going to let you?"

I roared with laughter until tears blurred my vision,

hearing her laughter in harmony with mine. She managed to stop first, crawling over me to get off the bed and picking up her discarded gown. She put it back on and leaned over me, kissing me deeply before standing back up and helping me to pull my trews back into some semblance of presentability. Then she folded her arms over her chest and looked down at me.

"I should work on your leg. The healing will take less time if you sleep."

I nodded and settled myself more comfortably on the bed, watching as she moved around, picking up small things and putting them down.

"We can come back later, Grainne."

She looked over her shoulder and smiled at me. "Will you always know what I'm thinking?"

"I don't know. Ask me again in twenty years."

"Just see if I don't!" she said, laughing. She came back and sat down on the edge of the bed, resting her hand on my knee. My last memory as I fell into sleep was of her voice, singing the healing chants over me.

* * *

I woke when Grainne screamed, bolting out of the bed before I was even fully awake. I heard the sound of a slap, followed by a sound I never wanted to hear again—Grainne crying. Rage swallowed me whole, and I grabbed the only weapon I could find before rushing into the other room.

Dusk had come while I slept, and the outer room was almost dark. There was still enough light that I could clearly see the big man who had invaded our hiding place. He had Grainne bent face-down over the table, her arms twisted up behind her back, her gown pulled up to bare her from the waist down. He was fumbling for his trews, and didn't see me, didn't notice me at all until I brought the heavy pottery wash-basin crashing down on his head. He roared in fury and staggered back, releasing Grainne and turning to see me. I recognized him then as one of the men who'd attacked the chariot. His eyes went wide when he saw me, and I knew in that moment that if he got his hands on me, I was a dead man.

"You!" he roared.

"Diarmuid!" Grainne called, and I saw something flash in the half-light. On instinct, I reached out and grabbed it out of the air, discovering that what she'd tossed to me was the spit—a metal rod as long as my arm. I held it as if it was a sword and advanced. The attacker looked at my pitiful excuse for a weapon and drew his own blade; as he did, I saw the flash of amethyst and realized that he was carrying the sword that Niall had made for the High King. I tried not to react, but I knew the spit was not going to be able to stop a weapon of my brother's forging.

It didn't. He charged, the sword raised. I blocked with the spit, and the metal held just for a moment before shearing neatly in two, the cut-off end clattering to the floor. I stepped back, the short end of the spit still in my hand, casting around for another weapon. There was nothing, and my attacker was advancing, the sword held ready and a cruel smile on his face.

"You should have stayed in the bogs, bird," he said. "Would have been better than throwing your life away for a worthless little whore."

I snarled at him, "Grainne is my wife."

He just laughed. "Oh, fine. So I'll let you live long

enough to see her taken by a real man." He stepped closer, and I backed up and hit the wall. With nowhere else to go, I tightened my grip on the spit and prepared myself, planning to dive at the man and do what I could to stop him. I had no idea what that would be, but I wasn't going to let him hurt Grainne.

He leered at me, then froze and shouted. He spun, and I saw the hilt of a knife sticking out of his back. In his pain, he seemed to forget all about me; he let out a roar of anger and attacked Grainne. I could tell the knife wound wasn't going to be enough to kill him, and dove forward to stop him before he grabbed Grainne, who scrambled out of his way and grabbed up another knife. I was on him before he'd gone two steps, knocking him to the ground and using what remained of the spit as a cudgel, beating him over the head and shoulders until he stopped moving. Grainne stared at me with wide, frightened eyes and whispered, "Is he dead?"

I got off his back and felt his throat, finding a strong pulse. Shaking my head, I stood up, wincing at the new, sharp pain in my leg. "He's alive," I told her. "Give me your knife."

Without a word, she did so, coming just close enough to hand it to me before dancing back and away from the man who lay prone on the floor but had started to groan and stir. I didn't even hesitate, shoving him over onto his back and slitting his throat. Then I picked up the sword and looked at Grainne. "Do you know him, Grainne?"

She nodded, one hand cupping her cheek. I could see a bruise starting there. "His name is… was Tadc. He's the miller's oldest son. He lives in the village, and he's one of the ones who caused the trouble that Donal told you about."

"Is that so?" I leaned back against the wall and took a long breath, not liking what this meant. There was nothing to be done for it—we had to run. "Grainne, help me get dressed. Then pack some food. We're leaving, before someone else comes looking for us."

"But Donal…"

"He'll have to catch up with us," I interrupted her. "Grainne, we have no time. I recognize him from the attack. He had to have been given this," I held the sword up. "by Ruaidri. They know, *acushla*."

She nodded, her face drawn and pale. "He knew. He knew I was here."

"Then others probably know, too. Hurry, Grainne!"

* * *

We left the house as the sun set, with Grainne carrying a small bundle and trying to steady me. I was limping badly, worse than I had before, and every step sent pain shooting up my leg, despite the fact that Grainne had insisted on splinting the leg as if it were broken. I ignored the pain, focusing on getting us away from the house before we were found. I kept the sword I'd taken from Ruaidri at my belt, and my suspicions to myself. I assured Grainne that Donal would catch up with us, but privately, I doubted that her brother still lived. I'd find out later— for the moment, my priority was to get Grainne to safety.

"It will be dark soon," she said softly.

I nodded. "We keep going. We have no choice. There's some light, at least. We'll keep moving until moonset. I want as much ground between us and that house as we can manage before we stop."

"Diarmuid, your leg…"

"When we stop, *acushla*. I'll manage."

It was hard going. Grainne helped me as much as she could, her arm a comforting presence around my waist, under my cloak. I kept my arm over her shoulder and concentrated on putting one foot in front of the other, trying my hardest not to see the pinched look on my beloved's face, the ugly bruise on her cheek, or the despair in her eyes. She insisted on stopping to rest after an hour of walking, more for my benefit than hers, I thought. It was then that we heard the hounds.

She heard them first, almost dropping the waterskin that she was about to hand to me. "Diarmuid?" she whispered. "Did you hear? Were those wolves?"

I listened, and heard the baying on the wind. "No. Hounds. They're after us."

She wilted. "There's no place to hide."

"There's no point. They have our scent," I said, closing my eyes. I was exhausted from the pain, and couldn't think. If only we could fly…

I caught my breath and opened my eyes. "Grainne, come here! Come here and kiss me, *acushla*," I demanded.

She stared at me as if I'd gone mad. "What?"

"Do you remember what I told you? That when you became my wife, you'd have wings of your own?"

She saw what I meant immediately and backed away, shaking her head. "No! I won't leave you to them!"

"We have no choice!" I insisted. "You'll be safe in the trees, and in the morning, you can go to Dun-Morrigan and find my brothers. Bring them after me."

"But they'll kill you!" Grainne shrilled.

"Not immediately," I said softly. "Donal says she wants my head."

"But…"

"I'll try and stay alive long enough for you to bring my brothers back for me," I interrupted. She scowled at me, and I sighed and took a different approach. "Grainne, if we did make a child between us…"

Her jaw snapped shut. I saw the tears in her eyes and knew that I'd won. She'd go, for the sake of our hope for a child. Silently, I prayed to my mother that we had, just in case I was wrong and they killed me outright. *Give her that much, Mother, in case I die tonight.*

"What do I have to do?" Grainne asked softly. I didn't answer at first, listening to the hounds. They were closer now. Much closer.

"Come here and kiss me, *acushla*," I held my arm out to her, and she came to me and tipped her head back.

"I love you, Diarmuid."

"I love you, too." I whispered, pulling her close and kissing her deeply.

Of all my brothers, I've always been closest to our mother. It comes from being first-born, I suppose. I am the only one who can hear her, albeit very distantly. This time was no different; I called to her silently: *Mother, hear me! She is the one, my mate, my heart. Give her wings!* In the distant corners of my mind, I heard the sounds of a raven calling, and Mother's bright laughter. Then the magic flowed through me and into Grainne. By the time I ended our kiss and straightened, my Grainne wore her own cloak of blue-black feathers. She looked down at them in wonder, then jumped at the sound of the hounds.

"Now that you have your own cloak, you know how to change, and you know how to fly. My mother gave you all that you need to know," I said, speaking quickly. "Get away from here. Get up into the trees and stay there until dawn, then fly straight over the hills, towards the sun. Dun-Morrigan is on the highest peak. You'll be safe there."

She looked up at me and nodded, then stood on tiptoe and kissed me quickly. "I'll be back," she told me. "I'll bring them. Don't you dare die!"

"I'll do my best not to," I promised. I stepped back and watched as she took her raven form for the first time, flying off into the night. I hoped that Grainne would leave the area, start moving towards the east, towards Dun-Morrigan. I didn't want her to see them kill me. Once she was gone, I put my back against a stout tree and waited, my sword in my hand.

The dogs, thankfully, were leashed, dragging the hunters along behind them as they bayed and barked and threw themselves against their collars in their eagerness to reach me. That alone gave me hope—it meant that they didn't want me dead immediately. If they had, they would have let the dogs tear me to pieces. I stood my ground and watched as the hunters surrounded me, their torches creating a ring of flames around me. Then Ruaidri walked into the circle, his own torch held high. He stood before me, just out of my reach.

"Where's the whore?" he asked, raising his voice to be heard over the barking of the dogs.

I met his eyes, not bothering to hide my contempt. "I assume you'll be taking me to see her. And where is your leader?"

He spat at me, the glob landing just short of my foot. "My lady is dealing with the traitor. Where's the woman, bird?"

I smiled slowly. "Gone. Out of your reach."

Ruaidri snarled and gave orders without turning. "Five of you, keep searching. She can't have gone far. Find her and kill her. Someone bring the cart. The Lady wants him safe behind her walls before dawn."

I heard the cart approaching, but I couldn't see past the torches. It wasn't until the men drawing the cart pulled it into the circle of hunters that I saw the cage. For a moment, I thought perhaps there was another dog inside the cage, it was so small. Then I realized they meant the cage for me, and I lost my head entirely.

I have always had an unreasoning fear of cages, something I could never explain. It was also something that I'd never been able to rid myself of, no matter how I tried. The idea of being caged was simply too much for me to bear. So, in a mindless state of near-panic, I attacked Ruaidri. He wasn't expecting such a rash move from me, and didn't have a chance to draw his sword before I was on him. I could have killed him, if it hadn't been for the man standing behind Ruaidri, who unleashed his hound. The beast attacked me, knocking me off Ruaidri and going for my throat; I went from trying to kill to struggling to stay alive in a heartbeat, and I could barely hear Ruaidri curse and shout orders over the barking, slavering dog. Then the dog was pulled away, and two men grabbed me and pulled me to my feet, holding me in place as Ruaidri stalked forward and slapped me across the face. I shook my head, feeling blood running freely from my nose, and saw the knife in Ruaidri's hand. For a moment, I thought he was going to kill me, and I was shocked when he slipped the blade under the bandages that held my right arm still and cut them free. Once my arm was free, he leaned down and cut the bandages holding the splints on my leg. Then he rose and smiled at me as he took my cloak from my shoulders.

"Get him into the cage and secure him," he ordered as he walked away. The two men holding me started to push me towards the cart, heedless of my struggling. The cage itself was small; small enough that once I had been forced inside, my shoulders were pressed against the bars and my back was against the top, leaving me folded in on myself, my chest against my thighs. My knee ached, and my arm was practically on fire from the pain; I would have kept my arm clasped to my chest to protect it, but my captors had different ideas. They reached into the cage and grabbed my arms, pulling them out to the upper corners of the cage, ignoring my screams of pain as they lashed my wrists to the bars. This was repeated with my legs—they were dragged apart and my knees and ankles were bound to the bars, leaving me immobilized and helpless. Then a blanket was thrown over the cage, cutting of my sight, and the cart started to move.

* * *

Maelan leaned against the doorpost of the feast-hall, trying not to fret and failing, knowing that the others were feeling the same way. The merchant had died too quickly, telling them nothing, and leaving Oscar beside himself with anger at his failure to see the spells that had killed the man. The next morning, Niall had done the unthinkable, taking the twins and flying to Dun-Righ, only to return the next night with nothing. Diarmuid had never reached the king's halls, and there was no sign of him. They had each taken turns overflying the route that the chariot had taken, which had done nothing—the trail was a week old, and any signs of an attack or an ambush had been washed away by the heavy storms that had rolled over the land a few days after Diarmuid had gone.

As Maelan watched, Niall stood abruptly and stalked across the hall towards him. He stopped an arm's length from Maelan and glared at him, then walked out into the fading sunlight. Maelan shrugged as he passed, then smiled at Sorcha, who followed on Niall's heels.

"Maelan..." she started. Maelan shook his head.

"It's all right, Sorcha. I know. This is worse for him than for the rest of us combined, I imagine."

She sighed, relaxing slightly. "I was hoping you understood. He knows Diarmuid did everything to find him, and he's trying to figure out what else he can do."

Maelan snorted. "Oscar's scrying failed, searching the road failed, Eogan's hunters failed. I can't think what else we can do!"

Before Sorcha could answer, a piercing whistle interrupted her. Maelan spun and ran out of the feast-hall, hearing the others behind him. Outside, Niall stood on the urla, his eyes on the sky. Maelan looked, squinting slightly, and saw it: a raven, plainly exhausted, flying towards Dun-Morrigan.

There was a flicker of movement in the corner of his eye, and Maelan turned to see that Niall had taken flight. Following him into the air was Petran, the two of them streaking like black bolts through the darkening air towards the small raven.

"That's not Diarmuid," Ronan muttered. "And it's not a natural bird, either. Who is it?"

"From the looks of it, Diarmuid found what he was looking for," Cathal answered. "Maybe she knows what happened."

"She'd better," Oscar said darkly.

Maelen said nothing, watching as Niall and Petran flew to meet the other raven and wheeled to escort her back to Dun-Morrigan. Niall landed first, and was able to catch the pretty, dark-haired young woman as she fell out of her raven-form and dropped the last few feet to the ground. She clung to him for a moment, shaking, then looked up and saw the others.

"You... you're Diarmuid's brothers?" she gasped.

Sorcha brushed past Maelan, carrying a blanket; she knelt and wrapped it around the woman's shoulders. "You're safe now, sister. What's your name?" she asked.

"Grainne. I... Diarmuid..." She looked distraught, and without warning, started to weep. Niall looked over her head at Sorcha, who shook her head and gathered the weeping woman into her arms.

"It's all right, Grainne. You're safe now."

"Where is Diarmuid?" Oscar croaked. *Grainne sniffled and scrubbed her face with her hand.*

"In the bogs, I think. I don't know. He sent me away, to find you," she answered. *"They put him in a cage and took him away."*

"Why didn't he fly away with you?" Maelan asked.

"His shoulder is broken," Grainne said. *"He's hurt, and they're taking him to the witch who lives in the bogs. She wants him dead."*

Oscar scowled. "A witch in the bogs? Impossible. I'd know of it."

Grainne looked up at him, and Maelan could see the ugly bruise on her face and the dark rings of exhaustion under her eyes. "You're Oscar? The sorcerer?"

"I am."

She sighed softly. "Diarmuid said you would be able

117

to help us. Help my brother. The witch has a hold over him. She took his finger…"

Oscar snarled. "A blood witch. What's she called, this bog witch of yours?"

"Aine. My brother says her name is Aine."

Oscar sniffed. "Not a name I know. Whoever she is, she didn't come through the college of sorcerers."

"Or she was there before you were, Oscar," Ronan offered. "Nothing says she's a young one, especially if she's hunting for Diarmuid. Can you find her, Oscar?"

"Given time…" Oscar started to say, and was cut off by Niall's whistle. He held up his wax tablet; Oscar took it and read aloud:

Diarmuid doesn't have that kind of time. We must be on the wing at dawn.

Oscar snapped the tablet closed. "And just how do you propose that we find him, little brother? I've already scryed for him and found nothing."

Niall pointed at Grainne, who flinched away from his finger and whispered, "Me? What can I do?"

Niall smiled and reached out, tapping Grainne's chest. Then he looked at Sorcha and gestured, pointing first at his wife, then at himself. Sorcha looked thoughtful, then laughed.

"Oh, of course! She's Diarmuid's mate!"

Niall grinned and reached out to tap his wife on the nose. Then he looked up at Oscar and arched his eyebrow, a look that Maelan could read clearly: Figured it out yet, sorcerer?

Apparently, Oscar had. He narrowed his eyes and studied Grainne for a moment, then looked at Niall. "You're proposing taking a woman who is clearly not a warrior into battle? Diarmuid won't thank you for getting his mate killed, Niall."

118

Niall rolled his eyes and shook his head, gesturing for his tablet and catching it when Oscar tossed it back to him. He scrawled for a moment, then handed the tablet to Sorcha, who read what Niall had written:

We don't have to take her into battle. We just have to take her far enough to find Diarmuid. Then someone can take her on to Dun-Righ. With Diarmuid hurt, that will be the best place to take him once he's safe.

"I can take her," Cuanu offered. "I'm not the best in a fight, in any case."

"And Fergus can stay here with Sorcha and the little ones," Petran added, looking back over his shoulder at the big man, who nodded and smiled at the sound of his name.

"I stay and look after the nestlings," he agreed. "Cormac is teaching me hurling."

Maelan heard Sorcha groan softly, and fought back the urge to grin. As he turned, he saw Grainne stand up slowly. "What do we have to do?" she asked, the blanket clasped tightly around her.

"First? We need to find something for you to eat," Sorcha answered, rising and putting her arm around Grainne's shoulders. "No one is going anywhere before dawn. You'll eat and rest, and then we'll plan." She led the shivering Grainne into the feast-hall. The others followed, until at last only Oscar, Maelan, and Niall were left standing in the rapidly growing darkness.

"A blood witch named Aine," Maelan muttered. "What would she want with Diarmuid? Why want him dead?"

Niall shrugged one shoulder and pointed at each of them in turn. Oscar frowned, but it was Maelan who voiced the thought.

119

"You don't think it's just Diarmuid she's after?"

Niall shook his head, then frowned and slowly touched his throat, then touched the bracer on his left wrist. Under that bracer, Maelan knew, were a series of pale white scars. Maelan flinched at the memory of how those scars had come to be.

Oscar made the connection as well. "Arlaith. She was a blood witch, too. No, brother. That would be too much of a coincidence. The woman is dead, and the brother was a magicless barbarian who is worse than dead. This is something else. Something new."

Maelan frowned, looking off into the distance, studying the stars as they slowly bejeweled the night sky. "Oscar? Did you ever find out who trained Arlaith? You've never said."

Oscar glared at him for a moment, then stalked away into the darkness. Niall wrapped his arms around himself and shook his head.

"We'll find him, Niall," Maelan murmured.

Niall nodded, then turned and walked towards the feast-hall. Alone, Maelan stared back up at the sky, looking for answers until it seemed the stars were laughing at him. Finally, he went back into the feast-hall to help make plans for the dawn.

* * *

In the last few years, watching Niall struggle to put the pieces of his life back together, I'd spent some nights thinking on how I would face my end. How, I wondered, would I have survived what he went through? Would I break? Or would I stay defiant, as he had? I knew the answer now. All it had taken to break me was deprivation and pain. I had no idea how long I had been in the cage. Long enough that the air under the blanket had grown thick and stale. I had been given neither food nor water for the entire journey, nor had they allowed me any freedom to move or to relieve myself. It had been impossible to rest or sleep because of the position in which I was bound and the pain I was suffering. So when the cover was whisked away and I was left blinking in the sudden bright light, I was faint with hunger and thirst, my clothes were fouled and filthy, my voice was gone from screaming, and I was nearly out of my mind with pain. I no longer cared where I was or who was waiting for me. I just wanted it to end.

"So, this is the proud Raven King?" a woman taunted. I didn't bother to raise my head. I heard someone walking around the cage, saw the hem of a gown as she stopped in front of me. "And this is the real cloak?"

"It is, my lady," I heard Ruaidri answer.

"Good. Put it on my bed, Ruaidri. I'll enjoy sleeping on the pelt of the man who murdered my children."

That made me raise my head, for what little good it did—I could see no higher than the woman's knees. "Children?" I croaked. "I murdered no children…"

She knelt, and I saw her for the first time. She was older than I'd thought, older than I by 10 years or more, and strangely familiar, though I was certain that I had not met her before. Her nut-brown hair was heavily streaked with gray, and her face, lined though it was, would have been handsome if it had been less cruel. There was a light in her green-flecked eyes that said that she would enjoy flaying my human skin from my back and sleeping on that as well. This, then, was Aine.

"Have you forgotten my children, oh Raven King?"

she asked. When she smiled, I realized why she was so familiar.

"Arlaith…" I murmured. She nodded.

"My daughter. My son. Both my children lost to your hands, Raven King. Now I take my revenge on you and your brothers."

I scowled, anger burning clear the fog that clouded my mind. "Your daughter was going to murder my brother."

"And yet your brother lives," Aine said coldly. "My daughter is five years dust. My son is not even that, condemned to spend the rest of eternity as a *deamhan aeir*."

I coughed, shocked. Oscar never would tell me what he had done to Ailill, so I'd always assumed that he'd simply killed the man. Never would I have dreamed that Oscar had been so vengeful as to curse any man, even one who'd threatened our youngest brother, to a horrific living death.

"Interesting," Aine murmured. "You didn't know."

"I didn't," I admitted. "I would never have allowed it, if I'd known."

She frowned. "How strange. I believe you." She rose, moving away from the cage. "No matter. My children cry out for vengeance. I will see them at rest."

"And what will that do, Aine?" I called out. "Will it bring your children back?"

"It doesn't have to," she answered. "I will have nine feathered pelts on my walls to pay for my children's lives. And my son, at least, will be free."

"Impossible!" I gasped. "You can't make a man from a *deamhan aeir*! The spell can't be unworked."

She laughed at me. "Oh, you know so little. Come. I'll show you." She gestured, and the cage shuddered and rose from the ground. I held my breath as it moved forward, seeing my surroundings for the first time. I was in the middle of a large courtyard, under a westering sun, and the cage was slowly floating towards a large hall. Aine and Ruaidri preceded me through the door, and then stood as I moved past them and towards the center of the room.

The first thing I saw there was a large, badly burnt piece of wood that had been cut roughly to stand about knee-high. It wasn't native to this hall, and stood simply in the center of the space, as out of place as I was. Nearby, I saw two more cages. The occupant of one cage cried out when he saw me, "Diarmuid!"

"Be still!" Aine snapped, pointing at the cage. Turlach yelped and fell silent, and the cage that I was in floated to the ground next to the wooden stump. This close, I could see the scorch marks were mingled with strange, brown mottled patches that didn't look like they were caused by any fire.

"Do you know where this came from, Diarmuid?" Aine asked, walking around to the other side of the wood and facing me.

"Should I?"

"My daughter's hall. This was once one of the roof supports in the feast-hall. The very one, I think, to which your brother was chained."

I frowned, looking at the wood. "Eogan ordered the place burned."

"Just so," Aine agreed. "I salvaged this from the ruins. You see, your brother imprisoned my son within the pillar. He is here now, waiting to be freed." She ran her fingers over the top of the wood. "My darling son."

In response, the wood shrieked, a sound that made

my blood run cold, and a voice that I barely recognized screamed, "Give him to me!"

"Soon, my darling boy," Aine crooned. "Soon. The spells will be that much more potent when the sun goes down." She looked at me, and her eyes glittered with madness. "Now you see your fate, Raven King? Your blood will be spilled on my son's prison, and that will be the final part to the spells that will at last free him. Then we will take our revenge on the rest of the ravens, and then on the little upstart who sits in Dun-Righ. When this is all over, my son will have his father's throne." She turned away and gestured to Ruaidri to follow her, leaving me to face a now-silent Ailill. I looked at it for a moment and shook my head, dismissing as my imagination the waves of malevolence and hunger that I thought I could feel rolling off the thing. Delusions caused by hunger and pain, I decided, and tried to force myself to think of a way to escape.

"Diarmuid!" I heard Turlach calling from behind me and to my left. "Diarmuid, are you all right?"

I bit down on a hysterical laugh and made myself answer, "No. No, I am not all right. You?"

He laughed, once. "Not really."

"And Donal? Turlach, where is Donal?"

There was a long silence, then Turlach answered, "He's here. In the other cage. Diarmuid, I think he's dying. What she did to him... I'm surprised he isn't dead already."

So was I. I closed my eyes, thinking hard. I was thinking clearly now, the haze of pain and exhaustion burned away by complete, abject fear. I tugged ineffectually at the bonds on my left wrist, then sighed and called out, "How long since they took you, Turlach?"

"Two days. They took me when Donal left to bring supplies to his sister, and they took him when he got back to the house," Turlach answered.

Two days? That meant that Grainne should have reached Dun-Morrigan last night. If they were coming… *Please, Mother, let them come soon!*

There was nothing else to be said, and we waited in silence as the shadows grew longer and the darkness grew deeper. To my growing horror, I realized that Ailill's wooden prison glowed slightly in the gloom, a dirty reddish-brown that was the color of dried blood. What I'd thought I was imagining before I could feel clearly now— the predator trapped within the wood knew I was here, knew I was trapped and helpless, and it wanted my blood. Preferably by sipping it from my still-beating heart. I fought back a wave of panic; I knew that Aine would never be able to control Ailill once she freed him. Nor was I certain that anyone could destroy him. My own mother was said to have battled against an army of *deamhan aeir*, but that was so far back in time that the story was a bare memory of a myth. I certainly didn't know how to fight a *deamhan aeir*, or what weapon would kill one. I hoped that Oscar knew. Damn the sorcerer!

"Diarmuid?" It wasn't Turlach that called my name. I barely recognized the slurring, pain-filled voice as Donal's.

"I hear you, Donal."

"Grainne?"

"She's safe," I called. "I sent her to my brothers."

"How?"

There were some secrets I wasn't willing to shout out into an empty room, no matter who wanted to know.

"Trust me. She's safe," I answered. He didn't answer me, and I sighed, letting my head fall, ignoring the pain that shot down my side as I did. That was when I realized something that made me catch my breath and curse softly: Aine had called my cloak my "pelt!" She *knew*! Suddenly, her desire to take my cloak as a trophy made sense, as did Donal's making the fake cloak to give to her. But for the life of me I couldn't imagine how she had learned our secret! Arlaith hadn't known, had thought the cloak simply a talisman from which she could siphon power.

My thoughts were interrupted by the sounds of shouting from outside the hall. I tried to turn to see but could not. "Turlach, can you see?"

"No... Yes! Fighting! I see... I see Eogan's men!" Turlach sounded jubilant, and I couldn't blame him. After Ailill feasted on my blood, no doubt he'd sample from the other two cages provided for him. I heard a cage rattling, and Turlach shouted aloud, "Here! We're in here!"

As if summoned by Turlach's shouting, Aine and Ruaidri came hurrying back into the hall.

"Ruaidri, bring him out and prepare him. We have no time!" Aine ordered before she left through another door. Ruaidri ran straight towards my cage, his knife bared. Before he reached me, I saw a darker shadow streaking through the gloom near the floor. In the instant before Ruaidri saw it, the shadow became Niall, rising with a bared sword that he sheathed underneath Ruaidri's breastbone before dancing out of the way. The big man kept moving, carried on by his momentum several steps before collapsing to the floor in a boneless heap. Niall shoved Ruaidri's corpse over, spit on him once, then roughly pulled his sword free. He wiped it on Ruaidri's shirt, sheathing it as he came towards me and knelt next to the cage. He looked at me, shook his head, and drew his knife, sawing at the leather thongs binding my right wrist. As he started working, Ronan appeared on my left, starting to work on the bindings there.

"Eogan's men are taking care of the guards. Once I've done this, I'll see to the other two, get them out to the healers," he said quickly, talking over my head to Niall. "That was a nice dive, Niall. Teach me to do that, will you?"

Niall grinned and reached through the bars, taking my wrist in his hand and lowering my arm slowly, all the time watching me closely. Grainne must have told them about my shoulder, something for which I was grateful.

"I'm fine, Niall. Hurry. The witch is still somewhere around here." I felt the bindings on my left arm fall loose, and then the ones on my left leg. Ronan rapped his knuckles on the top of the cage and hurried away, and Niall leaned down to start cutting the last two bindings holding me prisoner.

It was at that moment that Aine appeared out of the darkness. I pulled back, hitting my head on the top of the cage as I shouted the alarm. Niall turned in shock and start to rise. Which was exactly the wrong thing to do—her thrown spell hit him full in the chest, knocking him onto the floor. I heard him breathing, and I could see the cords standing out in his neck as he fought to move.

"So, this is the little one who caused all the trouble?" Aine asked, walking over to stand between me and Niall. She looked down at him and shook her head, then bent and picked up the dagger that Niall had dropped. "It must be. Her spells are all over him. Why this one, I don't know. She never did have any taste, that daughter of mine. But I suppose he is pretty, in a rough sort of way. And he'll do. Won't he, my dear?" She gestured, and Niall got to his feet, his movements jerky and abrupt. He staggered forward drunkenly, his eyes wide as he fought the spell drawing him forward. It forced him to his knees before the wooden monstrosity, then leaned him over the thing so that his cheek was pressed against the charred surface. I could see the panic in his eyes, and wondered where Ronan had vanished to. The wood was rocking now, and I could hear a high-pitched keening that seemed to come from somewhere deep inside it. Niall could hear it, too, and from the look on his face, I knew that if he'd been able to, he would be screaming.

"Aine, leave him alone!" I shouted. "I'll be your sacrifice, willingly! Let him live!"

"You have no say in the matter," Aine answered, walking around my cage, her eyes on Niall.

"Aine, please." I looked at Niall, and threw whatever dignity I had left to the winds. "Please. Let him live. He has children, Aine."

She stopped and looked at me. "Children?"

I nodded slowly, wrapping my hand around the bars. "Two. A boy and a girl. And another on the way. Please, Aine?"

Aine studied me for a moment, then looked down at Niall, who had his eyes squeezed shut. With the hilt of the dagger, she tapped his cheek until he opened his eyes.

"You have children?"

To my surprise, Niall mouthed the word, "Yes."

"Pretty little things, I imagine?" Aine asked with a smile. She looked over her shoulder at me, then back down at Niall. "My children were pretty little things, too." She raised the knife, and I lunged towards the front of the

128

cage, knowing that I wouldn't be able to reach, that I wouldn't be able to stop her.

I didn't have to. Ronan shifted in mid-air and caught Aine in the side, grappling with her before knocking her to the ground and sending the dagger flying. She collapsed, and as her concentration shattered, so too did the spell holding Niall. He shoved himself away from the wooden altar, stumbling back until he tripped and sprawled full-length on the ground, breathing heavily and shaking.

"Niall?" Ronan called. "She didn't hurt you, did she?"

Niall shook his head and slowly got to his feet, drawing his sword as he did. He slowly walked around behind my cage, and I heard the sound of metal against metal as he smashed the lock and swung open the door. Gratefully, I crawled out; he tried to help me to my feet, but my legs wouldn't hold me and I almost pulled him back onto the floor.

"Let him sit, Niall," Ronan called, sounding amused. "Go find Oscar and have him come take care of this foul thing." He waved his hand and only then noticed the blood running down his fingers. He looked down at his bleeding hand in surprise, then shook it, spraying blood across the floor. "I didn't realize she scratched me," he said, laughing.

I don't know what happened. Perhaps some of Ronan's blood landed on the wood. Or perhaps Aine did something. But I will always remember the image of Ronan standing there, laughing and wiping his bloody hand on his shirt, just before the red mist rose behind him and swallowed him whole. He shrieked, once, in mortal terror and mortal agony, a sound I will never be able to forget. Then he was gone, and Ailill stood in his place, a naked monster that once was a man.

I vaguely remembered Ailill as being a big man with a scarred face. This… thing resembled that memory only in the scar. His skin was deathly pale, almost blue in color, and when he smiled, his teeth were small and pointed, like a beast's. And his eyes, when he turned them on me and Niall, were glowing red.

"Ailill!" Aine's voice rang out joyfully. "It worked!"

He turned and smiled, a look that made me want to scream and run. Aine seemed oblivious to the malice in her son's eyes, going to him and throwing her arms around him. He laughed then, and took his mother's shoulders between his hands, holding her at arm's length. Once his attentions were turned from me, I felt someone tugging at my arm and looked up to see Niall trying to drag me to my feet. I got up slowly, feeling the blood coming painfully back to my legs, limping along with him as he pulled me towards the door. His face, I noticed, was wet with tears. That was when I noticed that I was sobbing as well.

"You freed me, Mother," Ailill said quietly, in a voice that somehow filled the hall, and would have turned blood to ice.

"Yes. Now you can fulfill your destiny, my son," Aine sounded jubilant, almost euphoric. Ailill merely nodded.

"Of course, my destiny," he repeated. "To be a puppet king. To sit on a throne that was never meant to be mine and let you rule through me."

Aine gasped, and I wasn't certain if it shock, or because he saw through her so quickly. "No! No, my darling…"

130

"I have a new destiny now, mother," Ailill interrupted, and Aine whimpered and tried to pull away. Even from where I stood, I could see blood running down her arms from where Ailill's nails had pierced her flesh. Niall started forward, stopping when I grabbed his arm.

"No!" I whispered. "We don't know how to fight him!"

He hissed softly and stepped back, then jerked his head over his shoulder, towards the door. I nodded my agreement, let him lead me.

"Where do you think you're going?" Ailill called. I took another step, and bumped into something solid. When I turned, I could see the barrier between us and the door, glowing softly in the darkness. Niall grimaced and shifted his grip on his sword, stepping in front of me. Ailill laughed and turned his attention back to the struggling, crying woman in his hands. "Mother," he crooned. "You've done so much for me. Now you can do one thing more."

"Ailill, please…"

I looked away, up at the roof, and noticed that the glowing barrier that kept us from escaping only covered the walls. The smoke hole was clear. I took Niall's arm and whispered into his ear, "You can get out. Find Oscar. He's the only one who can fight this thing."

Niall looked at me and shook his head. I shook him gently and pointed towards the ceiling. He sighed and nodded, so I released his arm and let him fly. As he vanished through the smoke hole, Aine screamed once, a sound that was almost immediately cut off. When I looked, I saw why, and fought to keep my gorge from rising.

Ailill had ripped her throat out.

131

He let the body fall and turned towards me, licking Aine's blood from his lips as he approached. He paused for a moment and looked around, then shrugged. "He flew away. Silly bird. He should have known how futile it is to run from me. I'll find him. I'll find all of them and I'll devour them all." He looked at me and smiled, his teeth stained gruesomely carmine. "You're first. Did you know, Raven, that divine blood tastes glorious?"

I was backed up against the barrier, with no escape, no weapon, and no hope. I could barely stand on my own feet, and my head was starting to spin. So, naturally, I answered him, "It does?"

"Oh, yes. This isn't the first time my mother has attempted to free me. I've drunk deep of mortal blood since your brother imprisoned me in the wood. Just the few drops of your brother's blood was far, far better than anything I've ever tasted," he said. He licked his lips again, and I took an involuntary step back, pressing hard up against the barrier. "Perhaps Mother had the right idea," he continued. "Perhaps I'll keep you in cages, you and the rest of your brothers. I can drink you slowly, savor every drop." He reached out and ran his hand up my chest, catching me around the throat and squeezing, his claws digging painfully into my skin. "Perhaps not you, though. I am hungry, Raven. I'll eat your heart, drink your blood while it's still hot." He leaned in close, his body cold against mine. His breath in my face smelled like carrion. "I'll keep your eyes, I think. I'll put them in mead to save them. They'll give the brew a special flavor and it will make me think of you…" He licked my cheek and I shuddered, trying to push him away, feeling as if I were pushing against a tree. He laughed, and I closed my eyes.

I felt more than heard a series of pops, and the barrier

that I was pressed against disappeared; I fell backwards with Ailill on top of me, landing hard, then having the wind knocked out of me by his dead-weight on my chest. He scrambled up, leaving me lying there, and I heard him shouting in rage. Then someone had my arm and was pulling me, coaxing me to my feet. I opened my eyes and saw Grainne.

"What… what are you doing here?" I gasped.

"I came with the healers. Get up!" She helped me to my feet and pulled me towards the door, past Oscar, past Niall and Petran and Maelan, stopping near the wall when I could go no further. I leaned against the wall with Grainne keeping me on my feet, and I watched as my brothers walked further into the hall. Ailill laughed when he saw Oscar, throwing his arms open wide and calling out, "Father!"

Oscar stopped, looking stunned. "What? How dare you call me that?"

"You made me this way. Who better should I call father?" Ailill asked. "You can't stop me, you know."

"I can. You haven't fed. You're weak. Holding that barrier against me took all of your energy, didn't it?" Oscar raised one hand; I saw a flash of light, and Ailill fell back, hissing.

"I won't let you stop me. Not when I've barely begun," Ailill snapped. He rose into the air, fading away into a red mist. Just before he vanished completely, he laughed and called, "Never another night's quiet sleep, ravens! Never another moment's peace! I will have you all!"

Oscar cursed and sent a bolt of pure power flying, but it passed harmlessly through the mist and blasted a hole in the roof of the hall. Ailill was gone.

"Diarmuid?" I looked up to see Petran standing at my side, his face pale. "Diarmuid, where is Ronan? Niall... he won't write it. Where is my twin?"

I swallowed hard and tried to clear my head. "He's... Ailill took him. He's gone."

Petran moaned softly and turned, walking away. I stood up and tried to follow him, but my head spun violently and my legs turned to porridge. I heard someone shout, "Catch him!" just before the darkness swallowed me whole.

* * *

I awoke comfortable, in a room I didn't know. Sunlight was streaming through the windows, casting golden stripes over the bed and over my cloak, which lay at the foot of the bed. My arm was again bandaged and immobile, and I could feel weight and stiffness on my leg that spoke of splints. And Grainne was there next to me on the bed, curled up under her own cloak, fast asleep with her cheek pillowed on her hand. I reached out and brushed her cheek with my knuckles, and she blinked and smiled at me.

"You're awake?" she whispered.

"I think so. If not, I'm enjoying this dream."

She smiled sleepily and reached up to brush the hair out of her eyes. "How do you feel?"

I started to answer, then stopped and considered the question. There was still a little pain, but nowhere near as much as there had been. I was hungry, but not as much as I remembered being before. And there was a raw, aching wound in my heart that I knew would only be filled when I saw the bastard who murdered my brother dead at my feet. I nodded. "Better."

134

"Good. The healers here are very good." Grainne sat up and took my hand. "Are you hungry?"

"Starving. Got any bear?" I asked.

She laughed. "With or without the hair?"

"Without, please. Where are we?" I looked around again. The room was very nice, but the wood furnishings smelled too new to be someplace I'd been before.

"Dun-Righ," Grainne answered, surprising me. "This is one of the guest halls that they built for the wedding." She leaned down and kissed me, then got off the bed and went around to the door. She opened it and looked out, calling, "He's awake."

Before she was away from the door, it swung open further and Oscar walked in. Behind him came Cuanu, Cathal, and Petran.

"Maelan and Niall went back to Dun-Morrigan," Oscar said when he saw me looking. "They worried for the children."

I nodded. "You should all go back, as soon as possible. Oscar…"

"You don't have to say it, brother. I'm aware that I made a…" Oscar stopped and grimaced. "A very grave error in judgment. I should have just killed him."

"Yes. You should have," Petran growled. I looked at him, and had to look away. The pain in every line of him was too much for me to bear. I wondered how he wasn't screaming, until I realized that he was. Silently. And would be for the rest of his life. We'd lost a brother. Petran had lost the other half of himself.

"We have worse problems, Oscar. He knows about the cloaks. He knows what they are," I said. I tried to push myself up, and found myself weak as a kitten; Grainne had to help me, then prop cushions around my back so that I didn't fall backwards.

135

"A lucky guess," Oscar scoffed.

"No. He knows," I insisted. "Aine knew. I don't know how, but they knew."

"I might be able to answer that," a new voice said, and my brothers stepped away and made room for him to enter. Eogan was as tall as I, and younger by 10 years. His auburn hair was braided with golden beads, his beard neatly trimmed. He looked every inch a king, and yet I still remembered him as a babe, toddling around behind me the years I'd spent fostering in his father's hall. "Diarmuid, I'm glad to see you awake at last," he said as he closed the door behind him.

"At last?" I repeated. "How long was I asleep?"

"Three days," Grainne answered. "You don't remember?"

I shook my head slowly. "No. Should I?"

"Consider it a blessing that you don't," Cuanu said quietly. "You spent most of it screaming."

I looked at Grainne, who nodded and murmured, "Nightmares."

Eogan cleared his throat. "I think I know how Aine knew, Diarmuid. It's because of Eochaid. He never could keep a secret when he was in his cups."

I frowned. "Your father? How did he know of it?"

Eogan nodded slowly and looked down, then looked back at me. "Our father, Diarmuid. He told me, on his death-bed, that you were his son. That he lay with the Morrigan in the sacred marriage, and that you were his first-born. He always wanted to acknowledge you, but he swore to the Goddess that he wouldn't. That you would be hers alone. But he knew about your powers. About your cloak. And… I think he might have been the one to tell Aine."

I couldn't think of a single word to say in response. I'd always been fond of Eochaid, had mourned his death bitterly. I'd never known, never suspected, that he'd been anything more than a foster-father to me. And Eogan...

"I always did think of you as a little brother," I whispered. He laughed and nodded.

"I know. So, that, I think, answers your mystery," he said. He grew somber and folded his arms over his chest. "Now, I've heard from your brothers and from my charioteer about this thing that now haunts Eire. A *deamhan aeir* is loose in my kingdom. Already there are reports of animals slaughtered, and children missing. Tell me what you intend to do about it."

I blinked, taken aback by Eogan's sudden vehemence and was saved from answering by Petran. "We're going to find it, and we're going to kill it."

Eogan nodded. "Good. How?"

Oscar frowned slightly. "That, my king, remains to be seen."

Part Three
The Raven and the Fox

In an instant, your entire world can change. I know this for a fact.

Last year, when summer dawned on the land, one could take wing and fly from one shore of Eire to the other and see people at their labors, farmers and herdsmen and the like. You would see children at play, with their mothers standing by, and if you were taken with the notion to land, you would be welcomed as a traveler and offered a bite and a bed, and all the gossip you could stand. Last year, all was well with the world.

No longer. Now, when one of the sons of the Morrigan must leave Dun-Morrigan, we dare not go alone. In twos and threes we travel, and when we do go, we see men watching suspiciously, armed to protect what is theirs. We see no women, no children, for they are hidden away for their own safety. Though how one can protect themselves from the likes of a *deamhan aeir* is not a question that anyone has been able to answer. The people are afraid, and they look to the High King to keep them from their fear. The High King, in turn, looks to us for answers. Answers that we have not yet been able to provide him.

In truth, the sons of the Morrigan are as frightened as the people in the villages. Last year, we never thought of our own mortality. We never thought we could be defeated. Hampered, yes. We'd had that proven to us. But defeated? Of course not. Killed? Out of the question.

How painful that lesson was to learn, and how well we learned it. We took it to heart, and it changed us all. I suppose that it was because of that lesson in mortality that there was a rush of marriages in Dun-Morrigan. Maelan was first, making his marriage with the falling of the leaves. He brought saucy, golden-haired Caitilin, the tavern-keeper's daughter, into his house, revealing to all of us that the reason he'd spent so much time at the tavern was that he'd been waiting for his mate to notice him. Cathal was next, wedding his Alis with the first snows of the year, and for the first time in months, we again heard our merry brother laughing, a welcome sound in our too-quiet halls. And as the snows faded and spring again started to green the hills, Oscar—Oscar, of all people—brought shy, quiet Muirenn into his house as his bride and his apprentice.

This rash of marriages made sense, I suppose. A form of defiance, laughing at fate and creating life in the face of certain death. If we survive until next summer, we will more than likely be awash in babies. Yes, it makes sense, and somehow, I cannot understand why. We all heard Ailill's promise—nay, his curse—as he escaped: *Never another night's quiet sleep, ravens! Never another moment's peace!* He will hunt us, and he will destroy us, as easily as he destroyed my twin. How then can any of us justify taking a wife, or bringing a child into the world? How can we put beloved innocents into such mortal danger?

And yet… There was Turlach, the delightfully foxlike charioteer who was given into Diarmuid's service as a favor from the High King. Diarmuid would be a long time healing from his injuries, the king's healers said, and would likely favor that arm all of his days. He certainly wouldn't be flying until midwinter at the very least. Hence, the need for a charioteer. I had not seen Turlach before, being absent from Dun-Morrigan on the day when he arrived to take Diarmuid on his ill-fated trip to Dun-Righ. I met Turlach for the first time on the day that we'd saved his life. Met him, and recognized him. I knew very well who he was. More important, I knew *what* he was. He was mine. My mate.

Somehow, he knew as well. I remembered wondering at the stunned look on his face when I introduced myself to him the first time. At first, I was bitter. It seemed at the time to be unjust, somehow, that on the very day I lost the better part of myself, I should have found the missing piece of my heart. Unfair that I should not be able to share the joy of discovering my mate with the one with whom I shared a life. Unfair again that I couldn't be free to accept him into my life. I made up my mind that I could not, would not take him as my mate until that thing was dead. I had already lost too much to this monster. I refused to give it another life.

Unfortunately, I could not get Turlach to see it that way…

* * *

After rescuing Diarmuid and Turlach, we brought them back to Dun-Righ, along with the body of Grainne's brother. Once we reached Dun-Righ, Turlach vanished.

Occasionally, I would see him at a distance, but for some reason, he refused to come near me. At first, I thought he was frightened, or that he associated me with the trauma he'd just been delivered from. Perhaps he found me unattractive, or far too old for him. Diarmuid soon put me to rights; it turned out that Turlach recognized the bond between us for what it was, and he welcomed it. He was avoiding me out of respect for my loss, Diarmuid told me, although from what I learned later, I'd say rather it was from concern for his own self-control. Whatever the reason, Turlach stayed out of my sight until the day I left Dun-Righ. That morning, he cornered me in the guest-hall where I'd been sleeping.

"Petran?"

I turned from my last-minute packing and found him standing in my door. The look on his face should have warned me that he was up to something. He was looking at me like a starving man might look at a feast.

"What is it, Turlach?" I asked as I turned back to my work, settling my harp into its padded traveling case.

"I came to see how you were," he answered, and I heard the door close. I shrugged one shoulder and didn't turn around.

"Tired," I answered. "I'll be glad to be back in Dun-Morrigan. Perhaps I'll be able to sleep again."

I heard him coming closer, and looked over my shoulder to see him standing there, concern plain on his face. "You haven't been sleeping?" he asked.

I shook my head, running my fingers over the wood frame of my harp. "No. Too many ill dreams. Too many memories."

"I'm sorry, Petran." He was quiet for a moment, then touched my shoulder. "I haven't heard you play yet."

141

In truth, I was supposed to have played for the High King's wedding. But I'd made some excuse I could no longer remember, and I'd avoided the feast entirely. The words had turned to ashes in my mouth, and I found that there was no joy in my harp these days. I closed the lid of the harp case and turned towards Turlach. "Perhaps you will."

He smiled, and it lit up his face. "I'd like that. Perhaps over the winter…"

I stopped him. "I don't see myself coming to Dun-Righ this winter."

"I'll be at Dun-Morrigan," he said, and told me of the plans for him to serve Diarmuid. When he was done, he smiled slightly and met my eyes. His eyes, I noticed, were green and gorgeous. "I'll enjoy Dun-Morrigan, I think. And… I'd like to get to know you better, Petran."

The husky hopefulness in his voice was just enough to start my cock to rising. I wanted to get to know him better, too, inside and out. I turned away, and in a voice that I barely recognized as mine, I said, "Over the winter. Perhaps."

"Petran?"

I turned towards him and was taken completely by surprise when he kissed me, taking my face between his big hands, then wrapping his arms around my neck when I didn't pull away. I meant to push him back, push him away, but for some reason, my arms went around his waist instead, pulling him closer to me. He laughed against my lips and pushed me backwards until my back was against the wall, his body pressed against mine, his hands gliding down my chest. He found the hems of my shirt and slid his hands underneath, his warm fingers grazing over my ribs. This seemed like the most sensible

142

thing to do, so I followed suit, tugging his shirt up and running my hands over his skin, as warm and soft as the finest sueded leather over wonderfully solid muscle. He groaned his pleasure and released my mouth to start nibbling his way over my jaw and down my neck, while his clever hands started working at the ties on my trews.

Somewhere in there, my mind started working again, and I realized what I was doing, and with whom, and I remembered what I'd promised myself. Silently, I cursed myself and slowly drew my hands back. "Turlach," I said, my voice harsh to my ears. "Turlach, stop. We can't."

He chuckled and licked the hollow of my throat. "Why not?" Before I could answer he pressed his hips to mine, and I could feel his hard cock burning like a brand through both his trews and mine, brushing up against my own erection and making me want to forget my vow. I moaned in frustration and need, and he took that as a sign to continue, slipping one hand into my trews. I grabbed his shoulders and pushed him back, holding him at arm's length. He stared at me, confused.

"What... Petran, what's wrong?" he asked. "You've gone white as milk!"

I shook my head slowly and let Turlach go, putting my trews to rights and stepped away from him before my resolve crumbled. Another two steps between us, and I shook my head again. "No. No, Turlach. Not now. Not... not yet."

His eyes widened. He took a long breath, and it was as if I'd broken the fragile pottery of his dreams. He crumpled, and I saw the guilt rising in his eyes.

"I... I shouldn't have pushed..." he stammered. "I... I just wanted... I wanted you. I've been wanting you, since even before I met you. I feel... I feel like I've been looking for you my entire life. Now that I've found you, I couldn't... I couldn't wait any longer." He flushed red and looked down, looking for all the world like a child caught doing something he ought not be doing. "I didn't mean to hurt you, Petran."

I wanted to tell him that he hadn't hurt me, that it wasn't his fault. I wanted to tell him that I wanted him, too, and the real reason I'd pushed him away. But I looked at him and knew that if I went to him, tried to comfort him, that I'd never have the strength to push him away again. So I ran, like the coward I am, bolting from the room and taking wing as soon as I reached sunlight, flying away with only my cowardice to accompany me.

I had, in the haze of lust and guilt and fear, completely forgotten what Turlach had just finished telling me. Which meant that I was completely unprepared when, a month after I returned to the house that was now mine alone, Turlach arrived with the falling of the leaves, bringing Diarmuid and Grainne home. I was in my house when I heard my brothers calling welcome and the sound of the chariot wheels and harness. When I went out onto the urla to greet Diarmuid, Turlach was waiting for me, holding something wrapped in a cloth in his arms. When he saw me, he paled slightly, then came towards me and cleared his throat.

"Petran?" he said softly. "You left this. I didn't want it to get damaged in the cart, so I carried it here for you." He held out the bundle with both hands, waiting for me to take it. He never once met my eyes, and once I had the bundle, he fled. When I unwrapped it later, I found my harp-case, and inside, nestled next to my harp, a single perfect rose. A peace offering? An apology? I had no way of knowing, but I carefully put the flower away

That meeting set the tone for the next several months—one of us would see the other, perhaps there would be a cordial greeting shared, and perhaps a brief conversation of inanities. Then the one who had spoken first would turn tail and run as if the entire force of the Fianna were pursuing him. I imagine that our antics amused my brothers and their new brides greatly throughout the oddly quiet winter months. In spite of me, I would often catch myself spending hours during the day hidden away on some perch so that I could watch Turlach. He had made a comfortable home at Dun-Morrigan, very quickly becoming a favorite playmate of Niall's children, who tagged along behind Turlach like a pair of puppies. Endlessly patient, Turlach was always ready to play catch-me-if-you-can with Niamh, and he was more than willing to teach Cormac everything that he knew about horses. I think that Turlach endeared himself forever to Cormac by taking the boy to the village and coming back with Cormac astride a shaggy pony that the boy proclaimed was his very own horse. And it was Turlach who went out on horseback to fetch the midwife on the night when Sorcha went into labor, when a snowstorm raged over Dun-Morrigan and none of us could see to fly to the village. After the birth of infant Ronan, I know that there was a long private conversation between Turlach and Niall, and I later saw Turlach proudly wearing an armband of finely decorated gold.

It was late in the winter when I started to find reasons to make late-night errands that would take me past the guest-hall that had been given to Turlach as his own. It was on one such night that I heard someone calling my name. There was no one in sight, and when it was repeated, I realized that it was Turlach calling to me.

145

I didn't see him anywhere, so I guessed that he was calling from inside his house and walked up to the door to see why… and was treated to the sight of Turlach, his beautiful body illuminated by firelight. He was lying on his bed completely naked save for his armband, his eyes closed, one hand wrapped around his cock, the fingers of his other hand in his mouth. He moaned around his fingers, writhing in pleasure, and then arched backwards so that he could slide his saliva-slicked fingers into his arse. His breathing grew ragged, and he moaned and called my name over and over until he came, his seed splattering over the bed and onto the floor. He went limp, and I fled, shifting and flying away into the darkness, not wanting him to see me. I came close to crashing into a wall that I could not see, but I made it back to my own house and lay awake most of that night with an achingly hard cock and the glorious memory of my Turlach, wrapped in pleasure, calling my name as he spent. For days after, even the sight of him was enough to set my blood aflame, and it fired my determination to defeat Ailill so that I could bring Turlach into my bed. However, there was nothing for me to fight that season save for my own desire.

After the winter snows set in, and messengers could no longer reach us, Oscar had set up some complicated system powered by sorcery that allowed him to speak with the druids and sorcerers at Dun-Righ. To our surprise, it was quiet for months, as if Ailill was only a nightmare shared among us all as a jest. And yet, as winter turned to spring, the monster resurfaced, and we quickly learned the tales of villages razed, entire herds of cattle vanished as if they'd never been, and the rising count of the dead. There seemed to be no pattern to the attacks, no way to predict where Ailill would strike next. No way to defend against him.

One damp spring morning, after one such report, we all sat around the large table in the feast-hall. We no longer ate at this table—it was the only one large enough in Dun-Morrigan to keep a map of the attacks, marked out with scarlet-painted beads nailed into the wood. Oscar added the newest site, then sighed and shook his head.

"He's building his strength," he said. "Taunting us. The man was smarter than he looked."

Niall reached out and touched the beads, then dipped his finger in a cup of water and traced a large circle around them all. He frowned and touched the center of the circle, then shook his head.

"No, I don't think so, Niall," Maelan said. "He can't be flying that far that fast."

"Who says? How fast does a *deamhan aeir* fly?" Diarmuid asked. "Does it fly? That last… he just seemed to disappear. Can he do that? Disappear and then reappear someplace else? Oscar?"

Oscar frowned. "We know next to nothing about the powers of a *deamhan aeir.* Have you asked Mother?"

Diarmuid grimaced. "She hasn't answered me."

Cuanu spoke next, "I've found nothing in the histories. Nothing at all. It's as if the historians have never heard of these monsters."

I drummed my fingers on the table. "I've found nothing in the ballads either. Nothing save the story of Lir's children, and that just tells that Aoife was made into one for her crimes. It seems that no one makes songs about their encounters with a *deamhan aeir.*"

"Probably because no one survives long enough to write one," Cathal muttered. I glared at him, but privately,

I agreed. It would be hard to sing of an encounter with a monster when one was the main course for the monster in question.

"So how do we *fight* it?" Diarmuid snapped, standing up and stalking around the table.

"You'll find a way." We all looked up then to see Grainne coming into the feast-hall. She went to Diarmuid's side and rested her hand on his still-weak right arm. "Any pain this morning?"

"No, *acushla*. Thank you," he answered, leaning down and kissing her. Then he looked at the table. "Perhaps new eyes? Grainne, do you see any pattern here?"

Grainne frowned and walked over to the table, slowly circling it so that she could see it from all angles. She cocked her head to one side. "Where is Dun-Righ?"

"Here," Oscar tapped the spot.

She nodded. "And Dun-Morrigan?"

Oscar touched that point, then frowned and dug through his bag of beads, coming up with two blue ones. He placed those in the appropriate spots, then looked thoughtful. "Where's Turlach?"

"Playing hurley with Fergus and Cormac. They're all covered in mud," Grainne answered, Next to me, Niall rested his face in his hands and groaned silently, prompting a forced laugh around the table.

"Why do you need him?" Diarmuid asked.

"I think we need his eyes. The eyes of someone who doesn't yet fly." I flinched at his words, and almost missed what he said next. "We aren't looking at this the right way."

"I'll get him." Grainne stood on tiptoe to kiss Diarmuid's cheek, then quickly walked out of the hall.

She returned shortly with Turlach behind her, red-faced and breathing hard, his clothing mud-splattered and filthy. He was laughing, but sobered quickly when he saw us sitting there. He bowed deeply and asked, "You sent for me, *A Ri*?"

"Turlach, come and look at this. See if you can make any sense of it." Diarmuid gestured to the table. "The red beads mark the sites of Ailill's attacks."

Turlach's eyes went wide as he saw the number of beads. "So many?"

"We can make no pattern of this. We were hoping you might be able to see something we do not," Oscar explained. "The blue beads are…"

"Dun-Righ and Dun-Morrigan. I can see that," Turlach interrupted, already studying the tabletop. He moved around to look at it, then looked up. "Do you have chalk? Paint? Something I can mark this with?"

A pot of paint was found quickly, and we all stood and let Turlach work, watching as he drew random lines that connected the red beads, and that ran past the blue ones. He frowned as he worked, then reached over and picked up another blue bead, setting it on a clear part of the table, near one of the painted lines. Finally, he looked up. "I'm done."

"And what is it that you've done?" Cuanu asked.

"The roads. You were missing the roads." Turlach set the paint aside and studied the map. "That makes sense. Why would you know the roads? You fly over them. You probably never even see them."

"It's true. Now, do you see a pattern here?" Oscar wanted to know.

"I… think I do," Turlach said slowly. "Look, see these here?" He pointed to a grouping of beads that before

149

had not seemed to have any significance. Now, I could see that they were all connected by a single line of paint. "This road is a major one for traders, one of the major sea-roads. This village here?" He tapped another red bead, one on the coast. "It's a good-sized fishing village. They salt fish there and the traders carry it inland."

"It was," Diarmuid murmured. "It's gone now."

Turlach's eyes went wide. "Gone?"

"Wiped out entirely."

Turlach shuddered, his face going pale, and it was all I could do to keep from taking him in my arms. He looked at the map again and caught his breath. "All villages. These were… all villages. None of these are… were bailes. He's hunting the defenseless."

Diarmuid nodded once. "We know. Turlach, is there any pattern here?"

"I think so," Turlach repeated. "The attacks, did they start here?" He pointed to the bead that marked the sea-coast village, and then traced a line along the painted road. "And they moved this way?"

"Yes. With one or two exceptions," Oscar answered.

"Then he's traveling as a trader," Turlach said firmly. "No one looks closely at a trader. He's probably stolen the goods from one of the first people he killed, and is somewhere on the road." Turlach paused and then tapped the map. "About here, I'd say."

"Why there?" I asked, moving to stand behind him so that I could see if perhaps I might be able to understand how he was figuring this out. I tried to ignore his shivering as I leaned close and touched his shoulder, or the fact that it took him a moment to gather his thoughts and answer.

"Because a horse can only travel so far. If he's

traveling as a trader, then he has a horse and a cart for camouflage. And… When was this last village attacked?"

"Two days ago," Oscar answered.

"Then he's around here somewhere," Turlach said, tapping the map solidly.

"Fine. Wonderful. We know where he is. How do we *kill* him?" Maelan asked.

"I have a better question," Turlach said. "You don't see this pattern because you don't know the roads. Why haven't the people who do know the roads seen this? Have the High King's men seen what I've seen?"

"Yes."

We all jumped at the sound of Muirenn's voice, and Oscar rushed to the door to meet his new bride, who was standing in the doorway, visibly shaking. She looked up at Oscar, and I could see even from where I sat just how close she was to bursting into tears.

"What is it?" Oscar asked, in a gentle voice I'd never heard him use before.

"A report from Dun-Righ," she whispered in a voice that somehow seemed to carry to the far reaches of the hall. "I didn't mean to touch the spell-workings, Oscar. I was looking for the scrolls you asked for. I jostled the crystal and triggered the spell, and… they found him. Ailill. It was just as Turlach said. He was posing as a trader, traveling. They found him just outside a village he'd… ." She stopped and her breath caught, shuddering like a bird in a trap. She blinked and looked down, taking Oscar's hand and holding on tightly. "He killed them."

"Another village…" Diarmuid murmured. Muirenn's head shot up.

"No," she blurted out. "Not just the village. The war-band that found him. They're all gone. That… *thing* destroyed one of the High King's war bands. Destroyed them completely, down to the horses and the charioteers."

"Mother of us all," I heard Maelan say. "How can we hope to defeat something like that?"

Before anyone could say anything in response, a strangled voice asked, "Which war band?" I turned and saw that the question had come from Turlach, who was holding onto the table's edge as if he were afraid the table would fly away and take him with it. "Which war band?" he repeated, his voice harsh.

Muirenn stared at him for a moment, then shook her head. "I… I don't know. It didn't tell me."

"Turlach?" Diarmuid said gently, walking around the table.

Turlach looked up at him and choked out, "My father… he's a charioteer in Cerball's band."

"I'll find out, Turlach," Oscar said immediately

Diarmuid sighed and looked at me, gesturing for me to stand up. "Petran, take Turlach to your house. He shouldn't be alone."

I was about to protest, but as I opened my mouth, someone slapped me across the back of the head, hard. I whirled and glared, but both Maelan and Niall were behind me, and neither gave any sign of having done it. Instead, they were both glaring daggers at me. I turned back and realized the room was deathly quiet, and all of the rest of my brothers were all staring at me. Then Diarmuid came over to stand in front of me, and in a low, dangerous voice, he said, "See to your mate, Petran."

I opened my mouth to protest, to say that Turlach wasn't my mate, but was silenced by the clatter of Niall's wax tablet landing on the table in front of me. I looked over my shoulder to see him standing over my shoulder, his arms folded over his chest, and his eyes as hard as I've ever seen them. So I turned back and picked it up, opening it to see the words: *Do not deny him, Petran. You will not get another chance.*

I looked back at Niall, who nodded once and took the tablet back. Without a word, I stood and went to Turlach's side, putting my arm around his shoulders and drawing him out of the hall. I tried to ignore how good his body felt against mine, how right it felt to have him in my arms, steering him gently towards the guest-hall that had been given to him as his own. I didn't trust myself to bring him into my own home, no matter what my brothers said. If I brought him into my home, it would be only a few short steps to my bed. So I brought him to his own house, his own bed, and I intended to leave him there. But he grabbed my arm and wouldn't let me go.

"Petran, don't leave!" he pleaded. I could feel his hands shaking, and realized with a start just how young he was. I mean, I knew he was young, younger than Niall by a few years. But he'd never struck me as being young. Not until now. I nodded and sat down on the bench that ran under his window. He perched on the edge of the bed, rubbing his hands together as if they were cold, and studying the floor for a long time before murmuring, "Petran?"

"Yes?"

"Why don't you want me?" He looked up at me and I was shocked at the hollow look in his eyes, the despair I found there.

"I… I never said…"

"You pushed me away. You won't come near me. You won't…" He stopped and looked down. "I don't understand. Diarmuid says that this…" He gestured

153

between the two of us "… this… bond, that it's forever. That once you find your mate, you're mated for life. He never said it could be wrong."

I swallowed hard. "Because it can't. Our mother set it up so that we bond with the right person. She's… protective, that way."

He sniffed. "She might start being protective other ways. It would be helpful."

I couldn't help it. I grinned. "I know. I think she might be busy. There must be some fighting in some other kingdom." I sighed and shook my head. "Why are we talking about this now, Turlach?"

"Because if I have to think about that… thing doing to my father what he did to your brother, I'll either scream or go mad," he answered solemnly. "And since you've driven me halfway mad already, I figured that was the shorter road. So why don't you want me?"

"I never said I don't," I answered.

"You never said you do, either."

"Turlach, I… I just… No. We can't!" I insisted.

"Why not?" he asked, getting to his feet and coming to stand in front of me. "I swear to you, Petran, by sacred Epona herself, I love you. I want you. I want only you."

I looked up at him and met his eyes. "I know. Turlach, I feel the same."

He closed his eyes and turned away. "You don't. You can't. Not if you can turn away from me so easily. Petran, did you know that I was already half in lust with you before I even met you? Diarmuid told me about you, when we were on our way to Dun-Righ. He told me, and I knew I wanted to meet you, maybe have a good time with you. Then I saw you, and I knew that you were what I was looking for my entire life. I've always liked men.

154

I've always liked older men, and I have always adored musicians. Turns out that I was just waiting for one in particular. Because when I saw you, I realized that everything I have ever wanted, everything I was waiting for, was you." He took a long breath and continued in a softer voice, "I'm going to ask Diarmuid to release me from service. I'm going back to Dun-Righ."

"What?" I blurted out, jumping to my feet. All I could think of was that if he left, he'd end up in some war-band somewhere, facing Ailill. "You can't!"

"You're very fond of that word, Petran. Why can't I?" He turned on me, anger and hurt clear on his face. "I can't stay here and live like this. I'm going mad for the want of you, and you don't see it. It's like a hunger I can't fill…"

"I know."

"Every day it gets worse, seeing you and not being able to do anything about it!"

"I know!"

"I am never going to feel about anyone the way I feel for you! And losing you is going to be like losing part of myself…"

"I KNOW!" I raised my voice to a shout, startling him into silence; Turlach stared at me in shock, then his jaw dropped.

"That's it, isn't it?" he whispered. "That's the reason." Miserable, I nodded, putting up no resistance as he took my hand and pulled me over to sit on the bed. He sat down next to me, keeping my hand in his. "Now tell me," he ordered.

I took a deep breath and tried to order my thoughts. "I… Has anyone told you yet why Niall doesn't speak?"

Turlach looked confused. "No. I assumed he was born that way. Like Fergus, except not simple."

"Don't let Niall hear you say that," I warned, and Turlach smiled slightly. I'd seen him spar with Niall, and I knew that he understood. "No, Niall wasn't born like that. He was bespelled, by Ailill's sister."

"Oh!" Turlach gasped. "Now it makes sense! I heard some things last year while I was a captive. Things that I just didn't understand. That's the bit I was missing. All right. What does that have to do with us?"

"Because when Niall was taken by Arlaith and Ailill, he found Sorcha there." Quickly, I explained about Niall and Sorcha, about how Niall had trained with Sorcha's father. "Ailill and Arlaith killed Sorcha's father and took Sorcha as a slave. We all thought her dead, and we thought we were going to lose Niall, too."

Turlach frowned. "Lose him how?" I stayed silent, and Turlach gasped, "Wait, you mean… you thought he was going to kill himself?"

"We were afraid he would," I said, starting to rub my thumb over Turlach's knuckles. "Losing his mate, especially as young as he was…"

"How young?" Turlach interrupted.

"He was 17 when we found the forge burned," I answered.

Turlach nodded, then frowned. "I'm still not seeing the connection."

I turned to face him. "I'm not as strong as Niall. Losing Ronan almost killed me. I couldn't…" I stopped, not even wanting to say the words. I didn't have to. Turlach nodded and tightened his grip on my hand.

"I understand now. Except for where I don't." He looked at me quizzically. "Petran, we're bonded already. Even if you decide to never seal the bond between us, it's too late. We're mated. I know it. You know it. How does denying it protect you at all? If something happens to me, the bond is still going to be severed." My jaw dropped, and I realized just how right he was, and just how stupid I had been. Turlach laughed at the look on my face, then leaned over and kissed me gently before saying, "Petran-my-love, you're an idiot."

I stared at him in shock, and his lips twitched. A moment later, we were roaring with laughter, great whooping gales of mirth that cut off abruptly when Turlach kissed me, pushing me backwards onto the bed. He straddled me, catching my wrists in his hands and forcing them over my head, pinning me to the bed. I didn't struggle, even though I could have overpowered Turlach easily. Instead I let him take control, losing myself in his touch and in the taste of his mouth, as sweet and as tart as good cider. His tongue caressed mine and I moaned against his mouth.

"Turlach?" I heard Diarmuid's voice and felt Turlach stiffen in surprise. He rolled off of me and sat up, letting me rise so that I could see my brother in the doorway, his eyes wide.

" *A Ri*?" Turlach said slowly, his face crimson. He glanced sidelong at me and tried not to smile.

"I… ah…" Diarmuid started, then shook his head and grinned. "I came to tell you that we heard from Dun-Righ. Your father is fine. He sends his regards."

Turlach let out a long breath and slumped slightly; I reached out and squeezed his shoulder. He smiled his thanks at me and then turned to Diarmuid. "Thank you, *A Ri*."

"You'd best start calling me by my name, I think," Diarmuid answered. He gestured at the two of us. "I'm glad to see that you two have… settled your differences,"

157

he said, smiling. He left, and I leaned back on my elbows and laughed. Turlach lay down next to me, pressing up against my side and draping one arm over my midsection.

"I'm glad, too," he said. "Shall we continue to settle our differences?"

"Not here," I answered, rolling towards him and kissing him quickly. "My house."

"Why there?" Turlach asked, getting up and helping me to my feet.

I slung my arm over his shoulders and steered his towards the door. "Because my bed is bigger," I answered. "And because my harp is there."

"Your harp?" Turlach stopped and looked up at me. "You're going to play for me?"

"If you'd like that," I said, tugging him along with me. "You get to decide if you want it first or after."

"Oh, such decisions!" Turlach laughed as we walked. Inside my house, I let Turlach make himself comfortable while I took my cloak off and laid it aside, then took my harp from its box. As I lifted the harp, the dried flower fell out onto the floor; Turlach stooped and picked it up and handed it back to me.

"Is that the rose I put in there?" he asked, sounding surprised. I smiled and nodded, sitting down with my harp in my lap. It had been a long time since I'd played, and it took me longer than I'd thought to tune it to my satisfaction. When I looked up, I was surprised to see Turlach stretched out on my bed, completely naked. He smiled and stretched like a cat, posing for me.

"What's this, then?" I asked, leering at him.

"I thought it would save time," he answered, visibly preening under my gaze.

"It's distracting."

"I could put my trews back on," he offered.

"No. It's also inspiring." I ran my fingers over the harp-strings, just barely touching them with my nails, thinking about Turlach, about what I felt for him, what we could have together. The words rose up within me, struggling to be free. I smiled and started to play:

Oh, love of my love, do not hate me,
For love, I am aching for thee;
And my love for my love I'll forsake not,
O love, till I fade like a tree.
Since I gave thee my love I am failing,
My love, wilt thou aid me to flee?
And my love, O my love, if thou take not—
No love for my dear love from me.
O dear love, take my love,
Love of my heart, thy love,
Love without fear or failing;
Love that knows not death,
Love that grows with breath,
Love that must shortly slay me;
Love that heeds not wealth,
Love that breeds in stealth,
Love that leaves me sorrowing daily;
Love from my heart is thine, and such a love is mine
Is found not twice—but found, is unfailing.

I finished, rested my hand over the harp-strings to dampen the sound, and looked up to see Turlach staring at me, slack-jawed. I blinked in surprise and set my harp aside. "Turlach?"

"That… that was beautiful," he whispered. "All for me?"

I stood up and crossed to the bed, sitting down and pulling him to me, whispering into his ear, "All for you. Always for you. I'm sorry, *a shiorghra.*"

The endearment made him smile. "Forever? I like the sound of that."

I nodded. "It will be forever. When you become my mate, you take on my immortality."

His eyes widened. "Immortal. But…?"

"We can be killed, but we stop aging at some point. I think at about 40 or so. Diarmuid hasn't really changed much in the past few years," I answered. "Now, is forever acceptable to you? You won't get tired of being married to an old harper?"

Turlach sputtered amusingly for a moment, then stopped and pointed at me. "You… you're teasing me!"

"Yes. Yes, I am," I answered, grinning.

He laughed and started tugging on the lacing of my jerkin. "You're wearing too many clothes."

"Really?" I murmured, enjoying myself, letting Turlach tug at my clothes and toss them to the floor, watching him and his obvious arousal. His cock arched up proudly, almost touching his belly, and I hungered for a taste of him.

"Far too many," he agreed, pushing my shirt up over my head. He ran his hands down my chest and sighed, "I've been dreaming about this."

"I know," I admitted quietly. "I… I saw you."

He stopped and looked at me. "You saw me?"

"You… you called my name," I answered. "I heard you, so I came to see and…"

He smiled sweetly. "Did you enjoy watching me, Petran?"

"You have no idea. I could think of nothing else for

days," I told him, leaning down and kissing him before I stood up and stripped off my trews. "I don't think I was ever so hard as I was the night I watched you pleasuring yourself."

His smile grew broader and, somehow, more brazen. "Oh, I think I can put that to the test. Come here, my love." He opened his arms, and I went to him, letting him pull me down onto the bed, his body warm and solid against me, mouth welcome and soft on mine.

To my great surprise, the bold, impetuous Turlach who had pursued me so ardently on that last day at Dun-Righ vanished almost immediately, and was replaced with a sweet, almost submissive lover, with an eagerness to please that was completely charming. He let me push him down onto his back, then smiled up at me and asked, "Tell me what you like, Petran?"

I propped myself up on my elbow and grinned down at him. "I like you."

"That's not what I meant. What can I do to please you?"

I pretended to think about it, then leaned down and kissed him again. "Breathe. Anything else is extra."

"Petran!" He sounded like he was torn between indignation and laughter, and the laughter was winning. I shook my head to cut off any argument and ran my hand down his chest.

"Hush, love. Let me love you. That's all I want." I let my hand trail down over his belly and from there to his hip. He was so beautiful, and so innocent…

"Turlach, how many lovers have you had?" I asked, suddenly curious.

He was quiet for a moment, then shrugged. "Two. Not for very long, either. They weren't what I wanted, and I think they knew it." He looked a little sad. "I started playing at being a flirt, because it tended to drive people off. I really didn't want anyone else who was just going to be disappointed and leave me. I knew that when I found what I was looking for, then I could stop and be… myself."

I nodded and ran my fingers up his inner thigh, making him gasp. "I like you when you're yourself. Of course, I like the flirt, too. I like it when you tease me." He let my fingers trail up and down his leg, until he was almost purring, his eyes half-lidded with pleasure. "Turlach, when was the last time?"

His eyes opened, and he frowned as he thought about it. "Over a year, I think. Yes, that's right."

I nodded. "I'll be careful, then," I said, turning and reaching into a basket that rested on the floor next to my bed, pulling out a flask and setting it on the bed. Then I turned back to Turlach, to find him looking up at me.

"You haven't answered me," he said. "What do you want me to do?"

I smiled down at him. "Let me play. Let me love you." I leaned down and kissed him, slow and deep, tasting his mouth again before slowly tracing the line of his jaw with my tongue. He whimpered and slid his hand up my side, his fingers digging into my back as I worked my way down his neck and over his chest. I paid especially close attention to his nipples; he arched his back and cried out, and I laughed low in my throat, delighted by his reaction. If he was enjoying himself this much before I got below his waist, then he was going to love what came next. I delved into his navel with my tongue, making him gasp and squirm and call my name.

"Ticklish?" I asked before returning to my oral

162

exploration of his body. His only answer was a low moan, one that spiraled up into an impossibly higher range when my mouth closed over his cock. He tasted magnificent, the tiny dribbles that trailed down over his skin salty and tart all at once, and I moaned as I took him deep into my mouth, trailing my tongue over the heavy vein that ran along the underside. I wanted more, wanting every drop that he could give to me, and I could feel his orgasm building, hear it in his increasingly urgent cries of pleasure. He started to thrash, forcing me to pin him down to the bed or else be thrown clear. That seemed to be an extra goad to his pleasure—he shrieked and my mouth filled with a river of thick, salt-and-tart cream. I drank it down greedily, then licked him clean and let him go, dropping a kiss onto his hip before crawling up to rest my head on his stomach. A moment later I felt his fingers in my hair; I closed my eyes and sighed happily.

"… Been wanting that…" he murmured.

"You can put two words together? I'm shocked." I looked up to see him grinning at me.

"Three words, even," he said and laughed. "What about you?"

"I thought I'd let you get your breath back," I said as I rolled onto my back and stretched, picking up the flask as I did, then rolling onto my side and getting up onto my knees. Turlach smiled up at me and started to roll over.

"No, stay like that," I said, stopping him. "I want to see you."

His eyes went wide and he nodded. "Petran, I haven't done it like that before."

"I'll be careful," I repeated. "If you don't like it, I'll stop and we'll try something else." I opened the flask and poured a measure of oil into my hand. "Spread your legs, *a shiorghra.*" As he did, I ran my oiled fingers up his thigh and then down, finding his passage and gently easing one finger inside. He was tighter than I expected, and for a moment I wasn't sure he would be able to take me. Then I heard him take a long breath and felt him relax around me, enough that after a short span of toying with him, I was able to slip another finger in, then a third. He whimpered softly as I stroked him internally, watching him, waiting. Finally, I was sure he was ready, and I slipped my fingers free and took his legs in my hands, pushing his knees to his chest. Leaning on him for a moment, I poured more oil and liberally anointed my cock, then smiled down at his eager, expectant face. "Remember, if you don't like it, tell me."

He nodded, gripping his legs behind the knees. I nodded and shifted slightly, my own cock in my hand, moving into position. He moaned softly when I lay the head of my cock against his arse. "Petran, please… ."

"Coming, my love," I answered as I started to move, pressing into him, gasping as I was surrounded by the most delicious tightness. I had the sudden overwhelming urge to ignore caution and plunge balls-deep into him, and I paused for a moment to fight it, closing my eyes as I felt Turlach grow even tighter around me. So good… I ran my hands up his legs, pulling them to me so that his knees were resting on my shoulders. He yelped, scrabbling at the blankets and catching them in his fists.

"Turlach?" I whispered. "Are you…?" Are you all right? Are you unhurt? Are you mine? I didn't know quite what the end of the question was supposed to be. Somehow, Turlach did.

He moaned and gasped out, "Petran! Please… please… more!"

That was all I needed to hear. I grabbed on to his legs and started to move against him, slowly at first, then faster as he urged me on with moans and pleas for *more, faster, harder, please!* When I looked down at him, it was to see one of his own hands busy on his cock, which had risen again to its former glory. Without warning, he clamped down around me as he came again, and as pleasure took me over, I was suddenly aware that someone was keening, loud, off-tune, and very nearby. As I collapsed over Turlach, I realized that it had been me.

Some infinite time later, when I was certain I could move and breathe again without help, I tugged the blankets up against the chill in the air, settled down on my side and pulled Turlach into my arms, his back resting against my chest, my soft cock nestled against his arse. He sighed happily and turned to look at me over his shoulder, and I took advantage of the position to kiss him. He smiled and lay back down, relaxing with his head pillowed on my arm, and I buried my nose into his hair and breathed in the scent of him, feeling more at peace with myself than I had in a long time. I would have been happy to stay like that for the rest of the night, and perhaps for most of tomorrow, but a high-pitched voice rang out from just under the window.

"Uncle Petran? Is Turlach in there?"

Turlach snorted with laughter and murmured, "I wondered how long it was going to take him to figure out I wasn't coming back."

Before I could ask if Turlach had latched the door, it bounced open and Cormac bounded in. He stopped just inside, looked at us curiously and asked, "Why are you in bed?"

"Napping," Turlach answered immediately. Which was good, because I had no idea what to say.

"Mama says that I can help you move, if you said yes. I wanted to know if you'd say yes."

"Move?" Now Turlach was confused. Good. I needed company.

"She said you'd finally be moving in with Uncle Petran," Cormac answered. "And she said that it was about time, and that Uncle Fergus would have seen it faster and done something about it sooner. I don't know what she meant, though."

"Cormac!" Turlach started to scold. I reached around and pressed my hand over his mouth, amused. Sorcha's sharp tongue was almost as cutting as Ronan's had been, but it took far more to make her unleash it. I hadn't realized just how much I'd annoyed her.

"What else did she say, boyo?" I asked, now curious.

"She said it about time that you woke up to what was in front of you, and that it would be good to see Turlach wearing a cloak of his own. Does that mean you'll be able to fly with me, Turlach?"

"Yes," I answered, and heard Turlach's muffled laugh. "And you'd best start calling him Uncle Turlach now. Now be off and tell your mother what you've been up to, Cormac."

"We'll move tomorrow," Turlach added as he shook off my hand. Cormac crowed delightedly and ran back out the door, pulling it closed behind him. As the door slammed shut, I fell back on the bed and laughed until tears came to my eyes. When I opened my eyes again, Turlach was leaning over me, his hair hanging into his eyes.

"What is so funny?" he asked.

"Me," I answered, reaching up and brushing his hair back. "You're right, my love. I am an idiot. I wasted so much time…"

"No regrets, Petran," Turlach said softly. "We have the rest of forever."

I rolled the phrase over on my tongue and found myself smiling. "The rest of forever? I like that."

He smiled and leaned down, kissing me slowly; I pulled him closer and held him tightly. The rest of forever could mean endless days and nights of pleasure, or it could mean a very short time indeed. It all depended on the whims of the monster at loose in the world, who could destroy us all as easily as I might swat a fly.

"You're thinking too much," Turlach whispered into my ear. "I can change that."

"You can, hmm?" I focused all my attention on him, and immediately had an idea. "Shall we not think for a while, then?" He grinned and reached for me, then stared at me in confusion when I grabbed his wrist and stopped him. "Not that way," I said. "I have a better idea."

"Better than sex? What?"

"Want to go flying?"

He stopped and looked at me for a moment, then he realized what I meant and his eyes went wide. Without a word, he nodded.

"You'll have to let me up. I need my cloak," I said, and as I hoped, he got up and went to fetch it for me. I took advantage of the moment to slip my trews back on and to put a small flask of oil into my pouch. When Turlach handed me my cloak, I put it on and then rested my hands on his shoulders.

"Turlach, I want to be certain that you understand what I'm asking. Once you have a cloak, you'll be one of us."

"I'll be yours," he said in response. "That's nothing new."

I nodded, conceding the point. "You'll have to be careful. Never let anyone take the cloak from you. Without it, you cannot make the change. And if something should happen to the cloak, if it were destroyed, you would die."

He looked shocked. "I would?"

"It will become part of you, your other skin. Be careful with it, Turlach," I said solemnly.

He nodded, just as solemn. "I will. I swear it."

There was no answer I could make at that point, nothing I could do but pull him to me and kiss him, silently invoking the magic and letting it flow. I felt him stiffen in my arms, and then he started to laugh, the feel of it bubbling against my lips as I felt his cloak flowing over my hands and down his back. When I pulled back, he had the oddest expression on his face.

"What's so funny?" I asked.

"It tickled!" he exclaimed, then turned and look over his shoulder. Silently, he pulled the edge of the cloak around and draped it across his arm, running his other hand over the glossy black feathers. "It's real. It's really real."

"Ready to go flying?" I asked. He looked panicked for a moment, then startled. "You know how," I explained before he could ask. "The knowledge comes with the cloak. Ready?"

"Where are we going?" he asked.

"You'll see," I answered as I opened the door; I changed and flew out and up, conscious of my mate following behind me, laughing as he spread his new wings and soared after me.

I flew up the side of the mountain, and alighted on a wide ledge of rock. As I landed, I changed back, and shifted over so that Turlach could do the same. He landed well and changed, grabbing onto my arms in his glee.

"That was amazing!" he blurted, as giddy as I'd ever seen him. He pulled the cloak around himself and turned to look down. "Oh. We're... we're very high."

"This is my perch," I said, sliding my arm around him. "Our perch, now. Do you like it?"

"I... I think I'll need to get used to it," he whispered, pushing back against me, away from the edge. "I've never been so high before."

"I'd be surprised if you had," I answered, reaching around and unfastening his cloak, taking it from his shoulders. "Don't look down. Look out. If the air is clear, you can see Dun-Righ from here."

"You can?" He looked in the direction I pointed, then gingerly made his way closer to the edge and squinted. "I... think I see it. This is wonderful, Petran. But it's cold up here. I should have put on my clothes. Can we go back down?" I smiled slowly, loosened my trews and removed them, then set his cloak down behind me and sat with my back against it. He looked at me for a moment, then he realized what I'd done. "Petran!"

"I'll give it back. When we're done. You looked good in your cloak and nothing else." Truth be told, he had looked amazing, his pale skin luminous against the darkness of his feathers. All at once, I couldn't wait another moment. "Come here, *a shiorghra.*"

He crept closer, one arm crossing his chest in a defensive pose. "Petran, what are you doing?"

"Do you want me to stop? We could go back down. Or we could stay here and not think." I took the flask of oil from my pouch and poured some into my hand. With slow, deliberate movements, I anointed my cock, very

169

much aware of how closely Turlach was watching me. When I was done, I looked at him, and was amused to see the glazed look in his eyes. "Do you want to go back?" I asked again. He hesitated, then flushed scarlet and shook his head. I grinned and held my hand out. "Come here."

"Now... now what?" he asked. I waved him closer and took his hand in mine. With gentle words and firm hands, I guided Turlach until he was sitting in my lap, his back to me, my slick cock resting once more against his arse. I wrapped my arms around him and rubbed my cheek against his bare shoulder.

"Now, don't look down," I repeated. "Look out. Look at how beautiful everything is in the setting sun, all gold and glowing. Look at the sky, and think about flying up there with me and touching the scarlet clouds." I felt him starting to relax, felt his head tipping back against my shoulder, and I knew he was ready. He moaned and shuddered all over as I took his cock in my oiled hand and started to squeeze and pull. He started to twist, to try and raise his arms, and gasped in surprise as I tightened my arms around him, holding him fast.

"No. Not going anywhere," I murmured against his shoulder. "I've got you."

"Petran!" He turned his head, and I kissed his cheek, then I started to nibble on his ear, which prompted another moan.

Turlach was every bit as responsive as I'd hoped, and my slow massage of his cock did exactly what I'd thought it would—turned him into a writhing, incoherent bundle of need and desire trapped in the circle of my arms. But while this was a wonderful position to tease and torment him into an orgasm, it wasn't quite right for me; his struggles ground his arse into my cock and while the pressure was wonderful, it wasn't enough, and it threatened to drive me insane with hunger. So, I drew him down so that we were lying on our sides, him still clasped in my arms, struggling and moaning, and me still frigging his cock as hard as I dared. Now, though, I could thrust against him, shifting slightly so that my cock was no longer pressed into the crack of his arse. Instead, I was caught between his thighs, and I could feel the head of my cock brushing against his balls with every stroke. Turlach noticed and responded, clenching his thighs together tightly, arching back in my arms and making such incredible noises that I felt the need to harmonize with him. I could feel his cock starting to pulse in my hand; he yowled as he came, shooting his seed over the edge and down onto the mountain. I followed him over the edge, shouting my own pleasure before I folded over him, pushing him down onto the rocks. He whimpered slightly as I loosed my hold on his arms, and reached back to stroke my hip.

"… Think… think I might… might like heights…" he mumbled. I laughed and reached back to pull both of our cloaks over us for warmth. We lay like that, curled around each other under our cloaks, watching the sun slowly slide down from its heights. Eventually, I sighed and rubbed my cheek on Turlach's head.

"We should go back down," I murmured into his hair.

"Cold?" he asked.

"And hungry." I untangled myself and rose, pulling my trews on and slinging my cloak over my shoulders, watching as Turlach put his own cloak back on. Naked, wearing only his feathers, he was glorious, and I couldn't help myself—I had to pull him back into my arms and kiss him once more.

171

"I thought you were hungry?" he asked, laughing, when I let him breathe again.

"I am. And I want to eat, too. Ready?"

In answer, he shifted and dove off the ledge, his laughter echoing back to me as he spiraled down towards the baile. I shook my head and followed him, racing him back to my house.

We washed and dressed, fetching fresh clothing for Turlach from the guest hall that would soon be a guest hall again. And as we walked towards the feast-hall, I mentally ran through all the possible reactions that my finally taking Turlach as my mate could possibly evoke from my brothers and their wives, preparing myself for as many as possible. I apparently missed one, and when Turlach and I walked into the feast-hall, the sound of riotous applause brought me to a stunned stop. They were standing there, my brothers and their wives, along with two laughing children, all of them clapping as Diarmuid broke free from the flock and came towards us.

"It's about damn time, Petran," he said, hugging me hard. He grinned at Turlach, who blushed and laughed. I slid my arm around Turlach's shoulders and sighed dramatically, prompting more laughter.

"Fine. I was wrong. You were all right," I declared. Then I pulled Turlach closer and kissed him thoroughly, hearing Maelan crow his approval amidst more laughter. When I let Turlach go, he staggered and grabbed on to me for support, giggling like a loon. Laughing with him, I turned to face my family and shouted, "Can we eat now?"

Diarmuid waved us on, and I escorted Turlach to the table where I usually sat, noticing that not everyone was here. Oscar and Muirenn were nowhere to be seen. Sitting on the table there was a flat, square casket, the lid decorated with the images of stylized ravens and foxes. I looked around and saw Niall watching me; when I met his eyes, he nodded towards Turlach and smiled. That told me what was in the box, and I picked it up and handed it to Turlach. "This is for you," I said.

He looked at me, confused, then took the box and opened it. I couldn't see into the box, but I saw the stunned look on Turlach's face and knew that Niall had surpassed himself. Turlach stepped away and set the box down on the table, and took from the padded interior a gold torc similar to the ones that my brothers and I wore, the finials finely worked raven's heads with garnets for eyes. I took the torc from Turlach's shaking hands and helped him to put it on, settling the raven's heads at the hollow of his throat.

"It looks good on you," I whispered, and was rewarded by a truly transcendent smile as Turlach reached up and touched the torc gently.

"Oh, I have to thank…" He turned and almost bumped into Niall, who had come up to us all unnoticed. Niall cocked his head to one side, studied Turlach for a moment, then nodded, a satisfied look on his face. Then he reached out and pulled Turlach into a hard and fast embrace, ruffling Turlach's hair as he let him go. Turlach laughed and mock-punched Niall in the arm.

"All right. Time to eat," Grainne announced, shooing us all to our places. Diarmuid came up behind her and whispered in her ear. She smiled and shook her head. "Not tonight, love." He nodded and took her hand, leading her to the larger table at the head of the hall. I took Turlach by the arm and brought him back to the table where Maelan and Caitilin were already sitting. Maelan smiled up at us as we both sat down.

"Welcome to the family, Turlach," he said, then looked at Caitilin and smiled, reaching out to touch her rounded belly. She dimpled as she smiled back and covered her hand with his.

"How are you feeling today, Cait?" Turlach asked.

"Oh, the little one is doing flips tonight," she answered, laughing. "Sorcha says that's how it is. The little one starts keeping you awake before he's even born."

"I think we'll be hearing an announcement from Cathal before too long," Maelan said as he picked up his cup. "Alis has been looking a little green the past few mornings, poor thing."

"You do well with children," I commented, touching Turlach's hand. He grinned.

"I have three sisters, and nine nieces and nephews at last count." He paused and looked thoughtful. "Although… Aislinn is in Connacht now, and I don't hear from her very often. There might be more."

"Connacht is only a few days flight from here. You can go visit and find out," Maelan pointed out. Turlach's eyebrows rose, and he looked at me. I nodded.

"We'll go, once this is all over." That seemed to be the wrong thing to say. Conversation at our table stopped, and the others started poking at their meals. I sighed and took a long drink of mead, looking across the hall. "Where's Oscar?" I asked.

Maelan shook his head. "Haven't seen him for hours. He…" He stopped, looking past me, and I turned to see Oscar rushing into the hall.

"Diarmuid, I have something important!" he called out, more excited than I'd seen him in a long while.

Diarmuid was still in a merry mood, and he grinned and called back, "What, is Muirenn pregnant?"

Oscar frowned slightly. "Yes. But that's beside the point. Ailill has struck again. And left a survivor. Someone attacked him and drove him off."

Suddenly, it was as if everyone was shouting at once, and I could hear nothing clearly; not until Niall's whistle pierced the din, making everyone fall silent. Then we heard what Niall had, what had made him whistle— the distant sound of a gong.

"Scath!" Diarmuid ran out of the hall, with the rest of us boiling out after him. Out on the urla, I could smell smoke in the air, and hear the gong more clearly. Abruptly, it stopped ringing, leaving the air oddly still. Diarmuid took to the air, circling over our heads for a moment, then gliding back down and shifting back to his human form, his face grim. "Arm yourselves, brothers. Scath is under attack."

* * *

"What do you mean I'm not coming with you?" Turlach demanded, following me into my house. I threw open the chest at the foot of my bed and started pulling out my weapons and my leather jerkin.

"I mean, I need for you to stay here. The women and children need someone to stay with them. Someone who isn't Fergus, who Fergus will take orders from. He trusts you. So do we all." I pulled off my cloak and picked up my jerkin, shrugging it on quickly. "My bracers are in there, too, love. Will you grab them for me?"

He silently went to the chest and picked up the heavy leather bracers, handing them to me one at a time, then helping me to tighten them down. He picked my sword-belt up off the bed and held my sword tightly in his hands. "Petran, I don't want you to coddle me. I can fight."

I sighed and crossed my arms over my chest, meeting his eyes. "I know you can, *a shiorghra*. Which is why we need you here. Fergus can fight, but he's not... He's a child, Turlach. A big child. We can't ask him to guard the baile, or properly protect anyone. He'll listen to you. The children will listen to you. We need you here."

He looked stricken, then nodded and looked away. "Fine. I'll stay." He handed my sword to me and walked away, leaving the house and leaving me behind. I started to call him back and swallowed my words, strapping on my sword and heading out to the urla to meet my brothers. I had no time to assuage my mate's hurt feelings. The village was under attack, and they needed us. It was only as I took to the skies that I realized that my mate had been the only one not to come and wish us well, bid us return safely, or offer a kiss for luck.

* * *

This wasn't the first time that someone was stupid enough to attempt to raid Scath. Far from it. Every few years there was some young idiot with a war-band who thought that peaceful, prosperous Scath was ripe for the picking. Usually, the way this song went was that they'd attack, someone would sound the alarm, and we'd wade in, knock a few heads, take the ring-leader hostage, and let whatever was left of the war-band run away crying and pissing themselves. We never really ever had to kill anyone, and ransoming the idiot who'd thought that taking something of ours was a good thing back to his father was usually more fun than should be allowed in public.

This time, it was different. For one thing, the time

was off. Raids usually came before dawn, not in the late afternoon. And I noticed as we flew over the village that none of the raiders seemed to be taking anything. Food and valuables were being smashed and ground into the dirt, and animals that got in the way were being cut down indiscriminately. I saw one raider grab a girl, slit her throat and throw her body away as if it were so much trash. I made that one my first target, landing behind him and running him through without hesitation.

Things got very busy from that point on. The raiders all seemed to have been waiting for us to land. As we did, they attacked, turning on us with a ferocity that was surprising. I spent an endless time fighting, until my arms ached and my chest burned from breathing so hard. Every so often, I'd see one of my brothers nearby, or one of the villagers, engaged with one or more of the raiders, gore-splattered and grim as they fought to survive. Finally, I turned and realized there was no one left to fight. It was over. I leaned against a still mostly-upright fence and wiped my forehead with the back of my wrist, so tired that when a young girl came timidly towards me and offered me some water, it took me several moments to recognize her as Caitilin's younger sister.

"Orla," I said when I realized who she was. "Where's your father? Is he all right?"

She nodded towards a milling group of people near the tavern. "Over there. He's fine. Trying to help calm people down. Maelan is with him."

"Good." I handed the cup back to her and straightened up, heading towards the group. As I got closer, I saw several of my brothers among the men, and Diarmuid at the heart of the group.

"… Came out of nowhere," I heard someone say as

I got closer. "They didn't want anything. They just wanted to fight."

"Do we have any idea who they were?" I asked.

"Not yet. We've started moving them off to burn the bodies, and so far, no one recognizes them, and they wear no clan-symbols," Caitilin's father Becc answered. "The only strange thing the men have noticed is that every single one of the bodies is missing the smallest finger on their right hands."

From where I was standing, I could see Diarmuid go very still, the color draining from his face. "What?" he said softly.

Becc repeated himself and shrugged. "It's the oddest thing I've ever seen. Never seen the like before."

Diarmuid swallowed. "I have. Aine's men were marked that way," he said, his voice shaking slightly. He turned, and I heard him whisper his wife's name softly. I spun and saw the flames leaping to reach the sky. Dun-Morrigan was burning.

"A diversion. This was a diversion!" Maelan gasped. "Cait!" He was in the air before he'd half-finished shouting. I was about to follow him when we heard the sound of echoing thunder. The ground under our feet shook, and I turned in shock to look at the others, some of whom had been knocked off their feet by the shaking.

"What was that?" someone shouted. I didn't see who, because my eyes were on Oscar. His face had gone stark white, and he was staring up at Dun-Morrigan.

"Muirenn?" he whispered. His face went through an interesting range of expressions, more in one moment than I could remember seeing on him in a day. Confusion. Frustration. Anger. Cold fury. And then… it was as if he crumpled, and a wave of unbelievable grief flowed over his face and didn't go away. "No," he said simply. Flatly, as if denying whatever it was could have unmade it. Then… "No! Muirenn!" The agonized scream sounded as if it had been ripped from his throat with a scythe, and he took two running steps and was aloft, overtaking Maelan and outpacing him in a heartbeat. This time, I followed, terrified beyond measure, uncertain of what we would find when we reached our home.

* * *

Whatever it was that had happened at Dun-Morrigan was long finished by the time we reached the baile, and all that was left for us to find was the aftermath. The fires that we had seen from the village were from Niall's forge and three of our houses—mine, Maelan's, and Cuanu's. There wasn't a living soul to be seen anywhere, save for Oscar, who was kneeling in the center of what had once been the urla, but was now a scorched and blackened circle of ground. I couldn't imagine what had caused that destruction, nor did I care at that moment. I had no idea where Turlach was, and I was mortally afraid that he had been in the house when the blaze had started. I started forward, and stopped when an eerie cry pierced the air. The hair on the back of my neck stood on end as I realized that it was coming from Oscar, who was cradling something in his arms, rocking slowly as this horrible sound was ripped from his chest.

"Oh, Mother," I heard Diarmuid whisper. "Muirenn."

Muirenn? That… thing in Oscar's arms was Muirenn? I stepped back, feeling my gorge rising, remembering Oscar's words hours before when Diarmuid had asked if Muirenn was pregnant, *Yes. But that's beside the point.*

"Diarmuid?" I jumped at the sound of Grainne's voice, turning to see her standing in the doorway of the stone building that housed Niall's storehouse. Her gown was torn and dirty, and she had a bloody sword in one hand. Her other hand held tightly onto Niamh, who was clinging to her side and crying. I heard a step behind me, then I was almost knocked off my feet as Niall ran past me, scooping his daughter up into his arms and holding on to her. Grainne touched his arm gently and guided him out of the doorway, letting Caitilin and Alis out into the air. Alis, I saw, was holding baby Ronan.

I ignored Maelan and Cathal's reunions with their wives. Where was Turlach? For that matter, where was Fergus? Silently, I looked around the ruins of our home, counting faces, seeing who was missing and not liking what I saw. Besides Turlach and Fergus, Sorcha and Cormac were nowhere to be seen. My mind started constructing reasons for those five to be missing. Fergus had gotten hurt. That had to be it. Turlach and Sorcha could always get him to listen and do what they needed him to do, so they must be with him. Cormac… Well, there had to be some reason that he was there with them. He was probably helping his mother. Never mind the fact that whenever Fergus got anything more serious than a splinter, he cried, and the sound of Fergus bawling could be heard in every corner of the baile. Or the fact that Grainne, our only healer, was here and not with Fergus. I could hear her voice behind me, softly talking to someone. Diarmuid, I assumed. Then I heard two words that shattered completely all my carefully built delusions. The words were "Turlach" and "taken."

I spun, almost tripping over my own feet. "What did you just say?" I demanded. "Taken? Taken where?" I felt someone at my elbow, turned and saw Niall, still holding his daughter, his eyes on Grainne.

She looked back at us, and I saw how tired she was, and how distraught. Her voice was surprisingly even when she spoke, "We didn't have a chance of defending ourselves. There were so many men. Too many for Fergus and Turlach to fight. Turlach took a wound in his leg and went down. Fergus they just overpowered, there were so many. Once they had the baile, they separated us, and by the time Ailill arrived, all of the fighting was already over. We," she gestured, indicating the other women, Niamh, and the baby. "Were put into the storehouse. They took Sorcha away, and then Cormac. Ailill ordered his men to take them and Turlach and Fergus. I don't know where. Then…" She faltered, and somehow I knew this was something that she had not yet told Diarmuid.

"Then?" Diarmuid asked.

She didn't meet his eyes. "Then he told the men he was leaving here to wait for your return that they could do what they wanted with us. One of them tried to take Niamh…" She looked down at the weapon that she still carried. "I killed him. Muirenn said that she could stop them, said something about Oscar teaching her how. She told us to bar the door after her, and not to come out until she called for us. Then… she left and we barricaded the door as best we could. The next thing we heard was her screaming, and then… it was like being inside thunder. Everything shook… and when I looked, I saw…" She looked past me and tears started to flow. She turned and buried her face in Diarmuid's chest, crying bitterly.

I turned and saw what… who they were talking about, and the last vestiges of my composure blew away like feathers in a strong wind. Oscar, the Ice Raven himself, crying like a lost child over the body of his mate and their unborn child.

It was Cuanu who went to Oscar first, kneeling down next to him. He pulled the unresisting sorcerer into his arms and held him while he cried. Cuanu was followed by Maelan and Cathal, who had somewhere found a blanket that they spread over the poor little corpse. Together, the three of them managed to get Oscar to his feet and started to steer him towards Cathal's house.

Diarmuid cleared his throat. "The feast-hall, brothers. We have plans to make."

* * *

Everything in the feast-hall had been smashed, all except for our map table. Grainne said something about it amused Ailill, and that he'd wanted to keep it, but I admit that I really wasn't listening at that point. All I could see was the image of Oscar, crying. There was a twisting in my guts, a fear like none I'd ever felt before. That could be me. Turlach might be dead. I jumped when I heard Maelan's voice, and saw that he had come into the hall and sat down at the map table.

"Oscar is resting. Cathal is with him. They will join us when he is able," he said. "Diarmuid, what do we do?"

"I think we need to know more. We need to know what Oscar wrought when he cast this spell," Diarmuid answered. "So we'll need to wait for him."

"Ah… no, you won't," Cuanu said softly from the door.

Diarmuid looked surprised, then nodded. "Of course. You were there. You can tell us the spell?"

Cuanu nodded. "As much as I'd have liked to forget, I can't. It was… something I wish I'd never seen. I'd never really understood Oscar's power before that. He… he took what he needed to know from Ailill's mind. And then… he said it would be best for all of us if Ailill had never been born. He…" Cuanu stopped, frowning, then his voice took on the slight sing-song that he affected when he was reciting something he had learned. " *My curse on you, root and branch. My curse on you, beginning to end. My curse on you, from this day until the gods are no more. Bound unto the wood, body and blood. Bound unto the wood, flesh and bone. Bound unto the wood, from this day until the gods are no more.*" He finished and grimaced, as if he had a foul taste in his mouth. I looked around and found a cup and, amazingly, an unbroken flask of mead. I poured out a measure and handed it to him. He drained it in a swallow.

"I don't understand how Aine broke that spell," Diarmuid said. "Granted, I don't know much about spell-work, but it doesn't sound like there was any way to subvert that curse. Petran, you know more about verse than any of us. Did you hear anything?"

Silently, I ran through the words of the curse, and frowned. Then my jaw dropped. It couldn't be that simple! "Until the day the gods are no more!" I repeated. "That was why she wanted us. She tried blood and body, flesh and bone and it didn't work. She needed us."

"Petran, you're not making sense," Maelan interrupted. Next to him, Niall looked at me, then slapped his forehead with his hand, making his daughter giggle. I nodded.

183

"Niall has it. Don't you see? The prison stood until the gods were no more. And we're each of us part god!"

Diarmuid nodded slowly, pulling Grainne tightly to his side. "So Ailill could also unmake the curse on him by killing one of us?"

"Possibly," I agreed. "But I don't think he wants that. No…" I froze, the words resonating in my head. "Oh, no…"

"What? Petran, what?" Maelan asked.

"Oscar cursed him, root and branch. Root and branch! His children will be monsters, too!"

Niall went white, set Niamh onto her feet and pulled out his tablet. He scrawled quickly and passed it to Maelan, who cursed softly as he read, then read it aloud: *Arlaith promised Sorcha to her brother, if he helped her win the throne. He thinks of her as his property. He took her to get children on her.*

"That doesn't answer why he took Cormac, though. Or Turlach and Fergus."

I could see Diarmuid shiver from across the room. "He took Turlach and Fergus because he likes the taste of our blood," he said. "He told me that he was going to keep all of you in cages and feed from you slowly."

The idea of Turlach being bled to death to feed that thing's hunger was enough to make me want to take to the skies, screaming his name until I either found him or fell to my doom. I reached out and grabbed onto one of the roof supports and held on tightly, more to keep myself in one place than for any other reason. "How do we find him?" I asked. "How do we *kill* it?"

"Wood." I turned to see Oscar in the doorway, looking haggard and ancient, his eyes red-rimmed and swollen. Cathal stood right behind him, his hand on

Oscar's shoulder. "It is wood that is his vulnerability. That was what I was going to tell you. Ailill left a survivor when he last attacked a village. A woman, who turned on him and attacked him with a ladle."

"A ladle?" Cuanu repeated. "She hit him… with a spoon?"

"A wooden one. And she told the High King's guard that Ailill screamed in pain and ran from her, and that he bled as if she'd hit him with a knife and not a spoon," Oscar said. "It seems that when I trapped him in the wood, I created a weapon we can use against him."

Grainne spoke up. "If that's the case, then I think I might know why Cormac was taken. They didn't want him at first. They were going to put him in the storeroom with us. But he got away from the guards and attacked Ailill with his hurley stick. He was trying to protect his mother and brother." Niall nodded, an oddly proud smile on his face. He gestured for Grainne to continue, and she shook her head. "I don't know what happened. We heard a shout, and then nothing until Ailill ordered the men to put Cormac with the others."

"Cormac hurt him," Maelan said, clapping Niall on the shoulder. "Good boy."

"That… doesn't make sense. Why didn't Ailill just kill him?" Cuanu asked. Niall growled at him, and he went pale and held both hands up.

"Calm down, Niall. It's a good question," Diarmuid frowned and looked at Oscar. "Thoughts?"

"Perhaps…" Oscar murmured, starting to pace. "Perhaps he's too damaged? He's been hurt twice in only a few days."

"In that case, we need to find where this thing has gone to ground," I said, standing up. Niall whistled and tapped the blue bead that Turlach had placed on the map only that morning. Diarmuid arched an eyebrow and nodded.

"You think he's gone back there?" he asked.

"He must have. He has no place else to go," Oscar answered. "It's too late to fly there tonight. Diarmuid, you and the others should prepare and rest. Niall, I'll need you and Petran."

"Me?" I asked. "Why do you need me?"

Oscar looked at me, his eyes as cold and hard as granite. "You'll see."

* * *

Confused, I followed behind Oscar as he led Niall and me out of the hall, heading towards his house. I looked at Niall and he shrugged—he didn't know what was going on any more than I did.

"Oscar, what are you doing?" I asked.

"We need a weapon," he answered without stopping. Niall snorted, and Oscar stopped and turned around. "You have something to say, little brother?"

Niall scrawled something and handed it to me. I read aloud: *I have no forge. How do you expect me to make a weapon for you?*

"Did I say we'd need a forge?" Oscar asked. "Come with me." He led us past his house and into the smaller house that lay behind it, where he did his spellwork. As we crossed the threshold, Oscar gestured and I felt as if something pushed through my chest and out my back. I looked at Niall, saw his wide eyes and knew that he'd felt the same thing.

"What was that?"

186

"A barrier. To keep the magic in and to keep anyone else out," Oscar answered. He turned and folded his arms over his chest. "We need a weapon. I need help from both of you to make one. I admit freely that I know nothing of sword-making. Niall, that is why I need you." Niall scowled, took the tablet from me, and handed it to Oscar, who brushed it aside. "I'm not speaking of a bronze sword, or an iron one. We need a wooden sword."

"It will break," I said immediately.

"Not when we're done with it. Niall, I will need your help to form the sword, and perhaps some way to strengthen it," Oscar said. Niall looked thoughtful and nodded, but tapped the tablet and arched an eyebrow. Oscar nodded again and said, "We will work here."

"What do you need me for?" I asked.

"The forge songs," Oscar told me. "Sorcha sings them to release Niall's magic. We need you to sing them now. And we're also going to need you to sing the chants to kindle a need-fire."

"Oh." I closed my eyes and thought, running through the words of the chant that we would need to light the sacred fire. Usually, the need-fire was only sung twice a year, in the spring to invoke fertility and then at the end of the year, when we asked the protection of the gods for the coming year. I'd been taught that it could also be kindled in extreme emergencies, but I'd never done it, never even seen it done. This *did* count as an extreme emergency.

"Shall we get to work?" Oscar asked. He moved to kneel on one side of a wide cauldron that stood in the middle of the room, and gestured for Niall to kneel on his left. I took my position on his right, and saw the bow, the spindle and the stone waiting for me, as well as wood and kindling waiting in the cauldron. How many times had I done this? How many times had I called fire from the wood and called on the gods to protect the village of Scath? Would I ever do it again? I shook the thoughts away and swallowed hard, looking over at Oscar. When he nodded, I set the spindle amidst the kindling and picked up the bow, making certain the cord was wrapped well around the shaft of the spindle. I could smell pitch, and knew that Oscar must have dipped the end of the spindle in the stuff to help the fire catch. Good. I rested the hollow of the curved stone atop the spindle and looked across at Niall, who took the other end of the bow. Together, we started to draw the bow, back and forth, turning the spindle faster and faster. As I pulled, I felt myself relaxing, falling into the rhythms of the ritual, and I started to chant, calling on the spirits of the fire that lived in the wood:

> *I will kindle the sacred fire*
> *In presence of the High Gods*
> *I will raise the sacred fire*
> *As would the goddess Bride.*
> *The encirclement of Bride and of Danu*
> *On the fire, and on the floor,*
> *And on the household all.*
> *I will light the sacred fire*
> *Without malice, without jealousy, without envy,*
> *Without fear, without terror of any one under the*
sun.

As I sang, the fear that had been in me for months slowly started to drain away, leaving behind a chasm that I had no idea how to fill, until Oscar started to chant. I couldn't really hear his words over my own, couldn't follow the thread of melody without losing track of my own chanting. But as he started to sing his spells, I felt the emptiness within me start to fill, the power growing and spreading until it felt as if the excess would simply fountain up from the top of my head. For the first time in six years, I heard Niall's voice, echoing in my head, and I started to sing the forge-songs he needed. I could see his hands moving, and felt as if they were my own, felt as if he, Oscar, and I were sharing one breath, one heartbeat, one purpose.

I had no idea how long we worked together, how long the spell took. I was only aware of Oscar's voice ringing in my ears, calling out "Done!" There was an abrupt shock, and I was alone in my head, feeling lost inside my own skin, and wondering what had happened to the rest of my arms. Across from me, Niall was lying on the ground, looking as if he was ready to sleep for a week. He blinked and looked up at me, then wrinkled his nose at me, which told me that I didn't look much better than he did.

"We did it," Oscar whispered, his voice nearly gone. I turned, slowly, feeling as if I'd had too much to drink, and stared at him. He sat cross-legged on the floor, and across his knees rested a polished wooden sword that fairly glowed in the dim light. Oscar ran his hand over the wood, then held it out to Niall.

"You're the warrior. This is yours to do," he said.

Niall sat up, looked at the sword, then looked at me. I nodded my agreement. "You're the best fighter," I said, suddenly aware just how sore my own throat was. Niall smiled and took the sword.

"Now, we rest. We'll fly at dawn," Oscar said. He

clapped his hands and I felt something pop. "You can go or stay. I'm sleeping here." True to his word, Oscar stretched out right there on the ground and was asleep in an instant. I looked across at Niall, shrugged, and lay down. The floor had never been so comfortable.

* * *

At dawn, we took to the skies, two groups flying in two different directions. Cuanu and Maelan were to escort the women to Dun-Righ, rally the High-King's war-bands, and then meet us at the baile in the bog where we hoped to find Ailill and our loved ones. The rest of us winged out way towards the bogs.

As we'd waited on the scorched urla for everyone to be ready, I'd been pacing, anxious, ready to fly. And Oscar had stopped me.

"He's alive," he said quietly. I stared at him.

"How do you know?" I demanded.

He looked at me, an infinite sadness in his eyes, and reached out and tapped my chest. "You know. You know here. He's alive. Trust me. If he was dead, you'd know." Then he walked away. Those were the last words he spoke to anyone before we shifted and flew off, and they repeated, over and over in my ears. I had to fight to stay with the others—part of me wanted to press on as fast as my wings could carry me. We landed once in the hills, to rest and eat. I ate without noticing, drank what was handed to me without tasting, and was on the wing again almost before the others were ready. Turlach was alive, somewhere up ahead. I needed to find him, save him, before it was too late.

We reached the baile in the late afternoon. Instead

of landing, we circled, looking for any signs of life. It was Diarmuid who called first, seeing the men milling around outside the hall where we had found him and Turlach imprisoned the last time we were here. I saw at least 10 men before Diarmuid called us off, and we wheeled off to find a place to land so that we could plan our next move.

"Where did he find so many men who would follow him?" Cathal asked as we took on our human forms.

"Aine took tokens from the men who served her, so that she could compel them if necessary," Diarmuid answered. "Ailill must have kept the tokens so he could have an attack force. The men he had attack the village were all missing the same finger. Grainne's brother had the same mark." He looked around at each of us. "How many did you all count?" he asked.

"Ten, more or less," I volunteered. "I think I might have counted one twice."

"I saw 10," Cathal agreed. Niall nodded and held up both hands.

"So, 10 men." Diarmuid frowned. "We should wait…"

"No!" I shouted. "We can't wait. He knows we're going to be hunting him. Whatever he's going to do, he's going to do it soon."

"Ten men, Petran," Diarmuid said. "And only five of us. If we attack, Ailill will know we're here. There has to be another way." He looked over at Oscar. "Ideas?"

Oscar shrugged, and I swear he looked bored when he asked, "How long do you want them to sleep?"

"Until dawn."

"Done." Oscar stood and stretched. "Now, the spell will only work within a certain range. Anyone outside that range will not be affected. You'll probably have three or four to worry about."

Diarmuid's eyebrows shot up. "And where will you be?"

"Inside. With Niall. Killing this thing," Oscar answered. He looked at me and nodded. "And Petran will be with us."

"Leaving two of us to deal with the guards," Cathal said, crossing his arms over his chest. "Oscar…"

"If I increase the range on the spell, Ailill will sense it. We have to get inside quickly or he will kill everyone in there," Oscar said, his voice flat. "We have no more time. If we don't get inside now, we will have to wait for dawn."

Diarmuid looked at Cathal, who scowled for a moment, then sighed and nodded.

The spell worked incredibly well; as we flew over the urla and into the roof thatch, I counted eight sleeping men on the ground. Oscar, I noticed, looked very smug, at least until we heard the unmistakable sound of Fergus crying. As quickly as we could, we started making our way through the loose, rotting thatch, making as little noise as we could until we finally made it all the way through and hid in the shadows.

Down below us, we could see a blazing fire in the fire-pit. A few feet from the fire-pit was Fergus, his wrists chained over his head, dangling several feet off the floor. He was crying and struggling, swaying violently in the chains and flinching away from Ailill, who was pacing a slow circle around him. I could see that Ailill had Fergus's cloak thrown over his arm, and every so often as he walked, Ailill would pull a feather out of the cloak and throw it into the fire, laughing as Fergus cried.

"'Leave him alone! Please!" I felt Niall bristle next to me at the sound of Sorcha's voice, coming from below and behind us. Ailill laughed and walked towards us, and I turned to see Sorcha, bound hand and foot and seated in a tall, throne-like chair.

"You can save him this," Ailill crooned, laying the cloak on the table next to another, smaller one. "Consent, and be mine."

"I won't!" Sorcha spat out. Ailill laughed and picked up Fergus's cloak again.

"Perhaps the brother isn't enough to convince you. Perhaps when it's the boy dangling there, crying for you to make it stop, then you'll agree."

"Leave my son alone!" Sorcha's voice was shrill. Next to me, Niall was trembling with rage. He looked at me, and we both looked at Oscar, who nodded once.

Niall needed no other signal. He was on the wing before I could blink, and on the ground before I'd even left my perch. The wooden sword that we'd crafted was in his hand, and he silently charged Ailill. Sorcha gasped out Niall's name, and Ailill turned, just in time for Niall to drive the sword through his heart. Aillil fell like a stone, pulling the sword from Niall's hands. Niall just left it there, quickly freeing his wife and pulling her into his arms.

I ignored the reunion, going instead to Fergus, catching him around the waist and stopping his swinging. Then I ran to where the end of the chain was anchored, fighting with the end until I had worked it loose. It jerked, pulling my arms painfully before I could get control of it and lower Fergus to the ground. Oscar was at his side before I was, and together we helped Fergus to sit.

"Fergus," I said gently. "Fergus, where are Turlach and Cormac?" Fergus shook his head, burying his face in

Oscar's arm, distraught enough that we didn't think we would hear real words from him for hours, perhaps days. I sighed and rubbed his back gently, standing up to see Niall and Sorcha coming towards us. "Turlach?" I asked.

Sorcha shook her head. "I don't know. Ailill told the others to prepare him, but I don't know for what."

"What did he want you for, Sorcha?" Oscar asked, not looking up from Fergus.

"To be his mate," she said, her voice dripping with disgust. "To breed more like him, so that he could conquer Eire." Niall put his arm around her and gently nuzzled her ear. She turned to him and wrapped her arms around his neck, then pulled back slightly. "Cormac. Ailill took his cloak and chained him in one of the out-buildings. We need to find him."

"You'll be joining him soon enough."

Fergus moaned, and I froze, horrified, as Ailill rose up from the floor, drawing the wooden sword from his own bleeding chest. He took the blade in his hands and broke it neatly in two, throwing the ends away.

Oscar stood up, his eyes wide. "You… you should be dead."

"Fool. I am dead." Ailill laughed and opened his arms wide. "That pathetic stick wasn't going to stop me. Slow me down, perhaps. But there is nothing that can stop me. You made me this way. Remember, Father?"

Oscar went white. "Don't call me that."

"You made me, Father. You created me. How proud you must be of your child…"

"You murdered my child," Oscar whispered, just loud enough that I heard him. Before I could move, before any of us could even think to stop him, he charged Ailill, screaming his pain and rage. Sorcha screamed his name, but it was too late—Ailill vanished into red mist as Oscar reached him. Oscar spun, looking frantic and lost as the mist surrounded him. The last thing I saw before the mist swallowed him whole was the look of resignation on his face. Then Ailill was back, smiling as he looked at us.

"So… Which of you is next?"

Niall pushed Sorcha behind him and drew his sword, and I did the same, standing at his shoulder. I knew it would do no good. The spell-crafted sword had only hurt Ailill. He was vulnerable to wood, but the wooden weapons wouldn't kill him. I swallowed hard and stood up straight, facing my death.

And as I looked at him, I saw standing in the shadows the discolored wooden stump that had once been Ailill's prison. The words that Cuanu had repeated to us ran through my head: *Bound into the wood.*

"Bound into the wood," I whispered. Niall glanced at me, then looked back at Ailill. I saw Niall's shoulder rise, ever so slightly—he was listening. "He's bound to the wood," I whispered. "That's why wood can hurt him. But he's bound into *that* piece of wood over there. If we destroy it…" Niall nodded, his eyes narrowing. He glanced up, then smiled at me. I understood. This was mine to do. I wasn't sure how I was going to do it, but it was mine to do.

I launched myself into the air as Ailill came towards us, soaring over his head and landing in the thatch where I couldn't be seen. As I came to rest, I heard the sound of more wings, and saw Diarmuid and Cathal appear next to Niall, both of them bearing bloody swords. Ailill looked at Diarmuid and bowed mockingly.

"It's been a long time," he said. "One might think that you didn't want to become a meal, raven."

195

There was nothing I could do to help them. Nothing except get to that wooden stump and do… something. I still had no idea what I was going to do, and I hoped I'd figure something out soon. As quietly as I could, I flew down to the stump and crouched down behind it, thinking furiously. How was I going to destroy this thing? If I'd had an axe, I could have simply attacked the stump. But that would have taken too long, and made too much noise. I needed… I had no idea what I needed, until I put my hand into my pouch. I didn't know what I was looking for in there, but my fingers closed around a small flask. For a moment, I was confused. What was that, and why was it in my pouch? Then I remembered—the flask of oil! The answer was right here!

I pulled the flask out and uncorked it, pouring the contents over the blood-stained surface of the stump. The wood drank it in greedily, which made me grin. It was old, dry. It would burn beautifully. If I could just get it to the fire-pit.

It took some work to rock the thing up onto its side, but once it was there, it was easy to roll it along the floor. I hid behind it as best as I could, knowing that it was only a matter of time until Ailill saw me. I knew when he did— his roar was loud enough to shake the thatch above me. I flinched, ducked my head, and kept on going. I was almost there…

With one final shove, I pushed the wooden stump that had been Ailill's prison into the fire-pit. The flames licked at the sides, the oil that I had poured onto the wood catching fire quickly. I straightened, breathing heavily, and was almost immediately bowled over by something hard and heavy that hit me in the side. I landed badly, the breath knocked out of me, and looked up to see Ailill, sitting on my chest.

"I'll rip your heart out!" he shouted, and I could see the rows of razor-sharp teeth in his mouth. I grappled with him, trying to throw him off, but he wouldn't move. His skin, where I could touch it, was hot. He grabbed me around the throat with one burning hand, raised the other one… and someone grabbed him from behind and pulled him away. I scrambled to my feet and saw Fergus, howling like a wolf, pulling Ailill away from me. They struggled together at the edge of the fire-pit. Then Fergus set himself and tossed Ailill into the flames like a discarded doll. Ailill screamed, thrashing the flames. He found his footing for a moment, managing to stand and stagger towards the edge of the flames. A sharp whistle pierced the air, and I heard Diarmuid shout "Duck!" I hit the floor, and a long pole whistled through the air over my head, catching Ailill full in the chest and knocking him back down into the flames. He didn't rise again, and the screaming stopped shortly thereafter. I stood and watched the fire burn for a few minutes, then went to stand with my brothers. I stopped next to Fergus, who looked at me, hurt and anger in his wide eyes. "Bad man," he declared. "Very bad man."

I nodded. "Very bad," I agreed. "You did a good job, Fergus."

He smiled. "I did good. Thank you, Petran."

I stepped back and looked around. Turlach. I needed to find Turlach. I didn't even stop to say anything to any of my brothers. I took off running, calling Turlach's name. The bedchamber off the feast-hall was empty, save for a single feather cloak that had been hung on the wall. Turlach's cloak. I took it and made my way outside into the near-darkness. There were a number of other buildings, and I set out to search each one.

I found Turlach in the kitchens. He was on the cook's table, naked and bound, blindfolded, and gagged. His wrists and ankles had been bound and then lashed together behind him, and then his arms and legs had been wrapped in more rope, all pulled tight enough that I could see the deep divots being left in his flesh. The only thing they hadn't done was tie him down to the table. He was lying on his side on a tray large enough to hold a whole boar, and every inch of his skin looked as if it had been scrubbed raw. I realized with horror exactly what Sorcha had meant when she'd told us that Ailill had sent Turlach off to be prepared. If Sorcha had agreed to the travesty of a wedding that Ailill had tried to force her into, my Turlach would have been the wedding feast.

I thought at first he was unconscious, but he must have heard me enter, because he whined and started to struggle weakly. "Turlach, it's me," I called out as I hurried across the room to him, seeing the wound in his thigh that Grainne had spoken of. From the looks of it, it had been a deep cut. Someone—one of Ailill's men, I assumed—had taken the time to burn the wound, and the cauterized area was swollen and red. I ran my hand over Turlach's arm. "I'm here, *a shiorghra*. It's over. The bastard is dead."

He fell still, whimpering slightly as I started to cut him free of the web of ropes and yowling behind the gag when I cut his legs free and he tried to straighten them. Then he started to toss his head; I guessed that he wanted me to remove the blindfold and gag. The blindfold went first, and I saw relief and joy mingled with the pain in his eyes. Gently, I touched his cheek, then cut the cord holding the gag in place. As I pulled the gag from Turlach's mouth, I saw what they had used and had to fight down a wave of laughter that threatened to explode from my chest—the gag was a turnip with a cord driven through it. The mirth was lost as Turlach started coughing; I held him until the spasm passed, jumping up to sit on the table-top next to him.

"… Water…" he managed to croak out.

I got down and found a water barrel in the corner. The water was cold and clear, so I grabbed a cup and filled it, bringing it back to Turlach and helping him to sit up and drink. He drained the cup, coughed again and shifted, pulling against the ropes that still bound his wrists.

"Untie me," he whispered in a rough voice. "Please."

I resumed my place on the table and pulled him into my arms. "Just a minute, *a shiorghra*. I need to convince myself you're all right." I could feel him shivering as he pressed against me, smell in his hair the herbs that they'd used when they'd bathed him. He was alive, alive and in my arms. I cupped his cheek in my hand and raised his head so that I could claim his mouth, kissing him with everything I was or ever could be, letting him know without words how lost I had been without him. He moaned against my mouth, and I pulled back slightly. "Did I hurt you?" I asked.

"If you don't keep doing that, I'm going to hurt you," he answered.

I laughed and pulled him back into my arms. "That can wait, Turlach. Until we're out of this death-pit." I turned him and cut his wrists free, then settled his cloak over his shoulders and pinned it. "You look good wearing your cloak and nothing else."

He laughed weakly. "You say that to all the ravens."

"Only you, *a shiorghra*. Only you."

* * *

At dawn, Cuanu and Maelan arrived with the High King's men. We left them to do whatever they wanted with the rest of Ailill's band, and took wing to Dun-Righ. I took Turlach to the healers, and from there straight to bed, where we both slept the day 'round, waking only when a servant came to our door to summon us to a family meeting. We dressed in silence, and Turlach leaned on me the whole way to the Eogan's feast-hall. His leg ached; the healers had said that the cautery had been badly done, and that Turlach would never again walk without a limp.

We entered the hall to see all six of my remaining brothers seated at a long table, their wives next to them. Cormac and Niamh were playing some noisy game off to the side, but I paid them no mind, leading Turlach to an empty bench and helping him to sit, then talking my place next to him.

"We need to decide what to do now," Diarmuid said without preamble. "Dun-Morrigan is in ruins. Do we rebuild?"

"I would like to. I want to go home," Cathal said. "And Scath needs us. They have to rebuild, too. We can help each other."

Maelan sighed softly and took Caitilin's hand. "We're going to stay here, for a time. Until the baby comes. Cait needs a roof over her head."

Diarmuid nodded. "Understandable," he said, and looked at Grainne. "Do you want to stay here, too?"

"Will you be staying?" she asked.

"Not if we're rebuilding, no."

She smiled and rested her hand on his arm. "Then I'll be with you. Pregnant or not, my place is at your side."

"Pregnant?" Sorcha repeated, her face alight with glee. "You are?"

Grainne laughed. "We knew before, but we didn't want to spoil Petran and Turlach's wedding. So we thought we'd wait a little. Yes."

"Good. Then you and Alis can keep the midwives busy," Cathal added.

Turlach burst out laughing. "I told you!" he proclaimed.

Diarmuid waited until the laughter and chatter had died down, then cleared his throat. "So, are we rebuilding?"

I looked around at my brothers, at the way that each of them was looking at their wives. I could tell they were thinking of their futures. Of the children they would have, of the works they would do together. We needed a place to ourselves. A place apart.

"We need to rebuild. We're not men, not like they are." I nodded towards the door, indicating the other inhabitants of Dun-Righ. "It isn't right that we should live among them, watch them live and die. Watch over them, yes. Do what we can for them, yes. But live among them? No. We need to go home."

Diarmuid looked at me, then looked around the table, at the nodding heads and murmured approval. "So be it," he said. "We rebuild. I'll tell Eogan. He's offered us whatever we need."

"How long will it take?" Cuanu asked.

"By Midsummer, I was told."

* * *

And so it was. Midsummer morning we stood at the gates of the rebuilt Dun-Morrigan. I looked with pride at the new house that had been built for Turlach and me. He stood next to me, grinning broadly.

"What's so amusing," I asked.

"You'll see," was all he would tell me. He limped towards the house, and I followed him inside, closing my eyes to take in the clean smells of fresh thatch, new wood, and beeswax. When I opened my eyes, Turlach was standing in front of me, a box in his arms.

"This is for you," he said.

I took the box and sat down on our bed, looking at Turlach. His expression gave away nothing, so it was a complete shock when I opened the box and found a beautifully made harp inside.

"Turlach!"

"The one you used to sing to me is lost," he said softly. "I was hoping you'd sing to me again with this one?"

I swallowed hard past the lump in my throat and patted the bed next to me. He sat, and I leaned over and kissed his cheek. "I'd be honored to," I whispered into his ear.

"And then, perhaps, we might try out this bed?" he asked in a breathy voice. I chuckled and took his earlobe into my mouth, making him shiver with delight.

"After, hm? Can you wait that long?" I teased him.

"I want to hear you sing to me again."

I smiled and checked the tuning on the harp, unsurprised to find it tuned and ready. Then I closed my eyes and looked for the words:

Love of my heart, thy love,
Love without fear or failing;
Love that knows not death,

Love that grows with breath,
Love that must shortly slay me;
Love that heeds not wealth,
Love that breeds in stealth,
Love that leaves me sorrowing daily;
Love from my heart is thine, and such a love is mine
Is found not twice—but found, is unfailing.

Introduction to
The Ice Raven

The Ice Raven came about because Oscar wanted his story told. Oscar had become something of a favorite character of mine, from the moment he walked onto the page back when Niall's story was the only one I'd told. I liked the snarky, prickly sorcerer. So I decided to tell his story. But his story… well, if you're this far into the book, you know his story doesn't end well.

Sitting down to write what I thought was Oscar's story turned into something of a journey, because it almost immediately turned into Muirenn's story. My prickly, snarky sorcerer might have wanted his story told, but he wasn't about to let me into his head to tell it from his point of view. He wanted his beloved wildling Muirenn front and center, thank you very much.

So here's the story of the wildling Muirenn, and how she caught herself a particularly peculiar Raven boy named Oscar.

The Ice Raven

I am nothing.

Or so I have been told. As a very young girl, too young to know better, my ears were filled with insults and curses. I was unwanted, unloved, and not even my own mother had seen fit to give me more than my miserable life. I had from her not even a name that I could call my own. Not that she could have named me—I doubt that she even had the wits to name herself.

My mother was a child of the forest, mad as mad could be, and she lived like a beast in the great forest of Uragh. My earliest memories are of the forest, and of living wild with my mother. I was, I think now, perhaps seven or eight when I was taken from her. The winter had been bitterly cold, and we'd ventured too close to a village, searching for food. We were seen, and the men of the village hunted us down, trapped us, and took me away. I was brought to live in a village not far from the forest, and I was given into the keeping of the innkeeper, who kept me as his nameless slave. He spoke of teaching me, training me as he would a beast, and under his fists, I lived as a beast, valued only for the work I could do. I rebelled, and tried to return to the forest, to the wild things that had been my home, escaping the inn to make my way the edges of the village and look with longing on the forest in the distance. But the innkeeper came after me and beat me with his own hands until I was half-dead. After that, I learned not to look to the forest, not to leave the shadows of the inn and the stable yard beyond.

And yet, I hungered for more, for something I could not name, could not voice, had I even the words to speak of them. I dreamed. I dreamed of flying, soaring to touch the clouds on wings made of ebony and midnight. I dreamed of freedom and joy, such as I had never known. I dreamed such dreams as would make men weep, and I woke with my own tears soaking the rough ticking of my pallet.

Such, then, was my beginning. I lived in that village for two winters before my freedom found me.

Because of my parentage, I suppose it is to be understood that I have always been a little fae. It came as no surprise, then, when a passing druid took an interest in me, seeing in me something that prompted him to take me from the inn. He never told me what he paid for my freedom, but it was freedom indeed that he gave me, adopting me as his daughter, and showing me for the first time what it was to be truly cared for, truly loved. His name was Gaynor, and it was he who taught me to dress, to speak, to be something more than an enslaved beast. It was he who truly tamed the wild creature that I had been. And it was he who named me at last, calling me Muirenn, which he told me had been his own mother's name.

Thus it was that I came to his house, a tidy little cottage under the elms, outside the village that surrounded the great college of Druids. For five years I lived there, growing from a child to a young woman. As my body blossomed, so too did my mind. Gaynor taught at the college, and as his daughter, I was allowed to attend any of the lessons that I wished. Everything to do with learning fascinated me, who had been deprived of such things for so long. I learned to speak Latin and Greek, and to read and write those languages as well as my own. I learned the songs of the bards, and could sing with a clear voice the deeds of the great heroes and kings. The only classes closed to me were those on magic and sorcery, for it was too soon to say if I held those gifts. Despite that, I lingered near the secret places where the sorcerers gathered, and it was there that I saw him the first time.

I thought that I knew all of the men and women who lived and worked in the college, so when I saw the stranger, I naturally stopped to stare. What caught my eye initially was his magnificent cloak, made all of black feathers. He was tall, taller even than Gaynor, thin as a willow wand, and his features sharp as a blade. As sharp as a blade and as cold, and yet… I saw something else. Something more. Something I knew that I needed, more than life, or breath, or freedom. I could not say what it was, nor could I explore it further, because it was at that moment that Gaynor found me.

"Muirenn!" he growled softly, catching me about the shoulders and guiding me away from the sorcerers, who had gathered in a circle and were talking amongst themselves. "Muirenn, you have no business being here, child!"

"Gaynor, who was that?" I asked, craning my neck to see over my shoulder. "Who was he?"

Gaynor looked back, and his eyes went wide. "He's no one to cross, Muirenn. Now come away, and leave them be."

"Gaynor? Gaynor, are you frightened?" I asked, suddenly alarmed. "Who *is* he?"

"Frightened? Hardly," Gaynor answered. "He is Oscar mac Morrigan. He is the Goddess' own son, and a very powerful man. One of my students, a long time ago." He led me away, and I heard him murmur, so softly that I wasn't certain I was meant to hear, "And the most lonely man in Eire."

* * *

It was at the end of that year, on the morning of the Longest Night, that I woke with a fire in my head that would not be stilled, would not be quenched. The magic that Gaynor had long suspected slept within me had awakened, and he brought me that day to the sorcerers, kissed me on the forehead and bade me be a good girl, and left me to their care. It was they who would have the teaching of me until I was judged ready to stand among them as a full sorceress. I worked harder than I ever had before, even as a slave in the inn, learning the ways and words of power. Before, learning had come easily to me, but no longer. Now, every day was a struggle to learn, to succeed and prove myself worthy to remain, to not be sent in disgrace back to Gaynor's house.

Female students in the college were rare. I was the first in a generation, and thus I was considered an oddity. More so once the other students somehow learned of my history. Overnight, I became an outcast among those who should have been my brothers. Again, I heard the names I thought I'd left behind; they called me Wild Muirenn, Mad Muirenn, and they tormented me with wild tales of my life with the beasts of the forests. None of this was said where the *ollamhs* who taught us could hear. Not that they would have done anything to stop it if they had heard. Rivalries were common among the students, and were thought to help strengthen us against the rigors of the world outside the school.

As I grew older, the stories changed. It was whispered from every corner, from every shadow, that Mad Muirenn was not the maid that she claimed to be. I was a wildling, and I had lain with the wolves, they said, as had my mother before me. I was the child of a wolf, and I had taken mates among the packs that ranged in Uragh. I was not human, I was a beast, and beasts had no place among sorcerers, save only to serve them. What they meant by serve was very clear.

To ward off the increasingly persistent advances of some of my fellow students, I set about making myself as unattractive as possible, and began to affect a wildness that reflected the rumors they told about me. I wore men's clothing, shapeless garments that were often dirty. I allowed my hair to grow wild, and I plaited it with feathers and leaves and sweet-smelling herbs. I kept my own counsel, and I walked alone in the forests often. Faced with what in truth seemed to be a mad child, a wildling, most of the boys left me in peace. The *ollamhs* noted my appearance, but none remarked upon it. It became normal, as such things were considered normal. Mad Muirenn, who went with rushes in her hair and mud on her face, the wildling who would be a sorceress. Even the boys who had once pursued me so ardently came to ignore me. All save one.

I was beginning my final year of studies when my dealings with the other students came to a boil. At the heart of my troubles was Bricriu, a boy a year or so younger than I. He was the oldest son of the *Ard Ollamh,* the chief among all our teachers. Bricriu was the undisputed prince of the college, spoiled and pampered.

Anything that he wanted was handed to him on a platter, and anything he could not have, he wanted. That, somehow, came to include me.

At first, he was solicitous, treating me as if I were a high-born girl, and not one whom he had been tormenting for the past several years. I ignored him and focused on my studies; I had heard that in the spring, the established sorcerers would take on apprentices for advanced training, and I meant to be one of those chosen. I still dreamed of the mysterious Oscar, even though I had seen him only once since that first time. That once had been shortly after I had started at the college; he had come there with a cartload of prisoners, and had spent hours closeted away with the *Ard Ollamh*, only to leave in a temper. He had not returned since, but I'd heard tales of his demands for information. Something about a spell that he was trying to break, although I knew no more than that. I wished him well, regardless.

Despite only having seen Oscar twice, I was still fascinated by him, and I had learned more about him in my time at the college. Learned that he rarely came to the college, never taught there, regarded most of the sorcerers there as worthless. And that he had never once taken an apprentice. In my mind, I would show myself to be better than the others, better than even my teachers. I would show myself to be worth his attentions, and he would take me as his apprentice. After that, my mind meandered into territory in which I had no experience. I knew nothing of men and women. I knew only that when I thought of Oscar, there was a heat inside me, one that felt similar to my magic, yet not the same. I had no idea what it could be, but I wanted it, wanted to understand it, and I knew I could never unlock those secrets without his help.

I should, perhaps, have paid more attention to Bricriu, if only to notice that he had stopped pestering me. But I was lost in my studies, and in my daydreams. I spent long hours with the *ollamhs*, practicing and reading, often until late at night. It was on one such night, late in the winter, that I gave in to my exhaustion and left my scrolls behind to return to my bed. I knew the paths of the college as well as I knew the lines on my own hands, and I was half-asleep as I made the silent, dark walk back to my lonely cottage. Halfway there, I stopped and looked up at the night sky and the stars, hazy from the wards that had recently been layered and relayered over the college grounds. I remember the *ollamhs* warning us not to walk alone outside the walls of the college, remembered them telling us of the creature that now hunted in Eire—a *deamhan aeir*, a nightmare straight out of legend. A chill wind blew along the path, and I shivered and pulled my cloak tighter around my shoulders, hurrying the rest of the way to my cottage, hearing my feet crunching on the snow as I walked. As I made my way to the door, I heard scurrying footsteps behind me. None of the other students lived near me, and there was no reason for anyone else to be abroad this late at night; I turned and frowned, seeing the empty path behind me.

"Is someone there?" I called. The only answer was an owl hooting; I shook my head at my own foolishness and turned, intent on my bed. As I reached my door, I was hit from behind, someone knocking me to the ground before grabbing me and pulling me into my cottage. I may have cried out, but if I did, no one heard. Before I could shout again, he hit me, hard enough that I knew nothing for several minutes. When my head cleared, I found myself sprawled over my bed, a cloth shoved into my mouth, with someone crouching over me, tearing open my *leine* to expose my breasts. I started to struggle, clawing at his face with my nails; he cursed, and I recognized Bricriu's voice. I saw him raise his hand to strike me… then he was gone, pulled off me as if by a giant's hand. I pushed myself up, holding my torn *leine* closed with one hand while pulling the gag from my mouth with the other. And I saw, silhouetted in the door, a tall, thin figure. I scrambled to light my lamp, fumbling over the fire-calling spell, unable to order my thoughts or control my magic enough to do the most basic of spells. I heard a voice, clear and wondrous deep, speaking the words, and the lamp flared to life in my hands. I turned, and saw Oscar standing there, fury writ plain in every line of him. Of Bricriu, I saw no sign.

"Did he hurt you?" Oscar asked.

"… no," I answered softly. "I… he did not hurt me. Thank you. Where… what happened to him?"

"I sent him to his father," Oscar said. "Under a compulsion. He will tell the truth of what he meant to do here. I suppose I should bring you there as well, so that Cathbad knows that this was not some jest." He stepped back from the door and gestured. "After you?"

I stared at him for a moment, then slowly got to my feet, holding my torn *leine* closed with both hands. I felt a brush of feathers on my bare arm as Oscar moved past me, then the warm wool of my cloak settled around my shoulders. He pinned it carefully under my chin and stepped back to look at me. He frowned slightly, cocking his head to one side and just… looking at me.

"Is… is something wrong?" I asked.

"No. Just… why all this?" His gesture took in my matted braids and my dirty cloak and *leine*. "Wildling, you do realize that you're taking the 'all sorcerers are mad' nonsense just a bit too close to heart?"

I blinked, startled, and saw his mocking smile. Saw beyond it to the teasing humor in his startlingly pale eyes. A giggle escaped me; he nodded once, then waved the lamp flame out. "That's better. Come along. Let's go see what happens when we stir up the hornet's nest."

* * *

Oscar must have known what the reaction would be, because the area around Cathbad's rather grand hall did indeed remind me very much of a riled hornet's nest. Oscar ignored all of the bustling and the outrage, putting his arm around my shoulders and guiding me through the press as if the crowd was not even there. He entered the hall without announcing himself, and led me straight up to the head of the hall, where I could see Cathbad and Bricriu. Bricriu looked like a statue, his eyes fixed and staring at some point far in the distance. As we came closer, I heard his voice, flat and emotionless:

"… attacked her. I forced her down and hit her when she screamed, and I gagged her so she could not scream again. I tore her clothing, and I was going to rape her. Then I was going to strangle her and dump her body in the forest for her beasts."

I flinched at hearing plans for my own murder, and Oscar's arm around my shoulders tightened. "So, Cathbad. Do you believe me now when I tell you that the boy is a menace?" he called.

The *Ard Ollamh* stared at Oscar, then sputtered and pointed at him. "You! You did this! You made my boy say these things! Have you not caused enough trouble…?"

"Your boy did those things, and would have done more had I not stopped him," Oscar said coldly. "I've brought the woman with me. Her injuries and her clothing will add to the truth that Bricriu speaks. I charge him with attempted rape, Cathbad, and with intending to commit murder. Will you summon the *Brehons*, or shall I? I should tell you that he will remain in just that state until his words are heard and acknowledged by one of the *Brehon* judges."

Cathbad went pale as death, and he shook his head. "He's my son…"

"And the woman is mine."

Everything stopped. I heard nothing else, saw nothing save for Oscar's proud profile. His? What did he mean?

"The woman is mine," Oscar repeated. "I claim her as my apprentice. Injury done to her is injury done to me. I am within my rights to demand *log nEnech,* or see him sold as a slave…"

"No," I whispered, interrupting him. Oscar glanced down at me, one eyebrow raised in silent inquiry. I shook my head and repeated, "No. Not slavery. The honor fine, yes. Dismissal from the college, if you think that necessary. Not slavery."

He nodded and turned his attention back to Cathbad. "My apprentice has made her wishes known. Before the *Brehons*, I will demand *log nEnech,* and that Bricriu be dismissed from the college of sorcerers. See to it, Cathbad." Without another word, he guided me back out of the hall, leading me down a path and away from the college, towards the cottages where the *ollamhs* lived.

"Where are we going?" I asked.

"I keep a house here, though I rarely stay," he

answered. Never once had he taken his arm from around my shoulders. "You'll be staying with me, as is appropriate for my apprentice."

I stumbled, and he slowed so that I could find my footing again. "You... you were serious?"

"I never make jokes, Wildling," he answered.

"You do!" I blurted. "You were teasing me, not even an hour ago."

I looked up, and in the moonlight I saw the corner of his mouth twitch. "Ah, but that was not a joke. Now, the first thing you will do as my apprentice... what is your name?" When I hesitated, he sighed, leading me into a house. Once inside, he waved his hand once; all of the lamps flared to life, revealing a tidy workspace, and a pair of beds tucked into opposite corners. Only then did he let me go, moving to stand in front of me. "I can't keep calling you Wildling," he pointed out. "Name?"

I looked down at the rushes on the floor and answered, "I... they call me Muirenn."

"Muirenn," he repeated, and the sound of my name from his lips sent shivered up my spine. To my surprise, I felt his hand under my chin, and he raised my face so that I was looking into his eyes. "I understand why you've done all this, but you needn't try to hide behind your hair and your past anymore. No one will try to hurt you now that you're under my wing. So, your first duty as my apprentice is to bathe, Muirenn. Comb out your hair. I wish to see you."

My skin where his hand touched was oddly warm, and I swallowed once before I could answer. "Yes, Master."

"Oscar. Call me by my name."

"Yes, Oscar."

* * *

It being the middle of the night, I had to wait until morning to follow my first instructions. Oscar had pointed to one of the two beds, dowsed the lamps, and thrown himself down on the other bed without another word. I wrapped myself in my cloak and lay down, listening to him breathing in the darkness. What had brought him to the college now? I fell asleep wondering, and woke in the gray hour before dawn with an aching head. Silent as a mouse, I crept out of the cottage and ran to the deserted bath house.

The spells to heat the water were simple ones, and I was soon submerged up to my neck in hot water, attempting to tease bedraggled feathers from my long, matted hair. I had to renew the spells on the water four times before my hair was clean and combed free of tangles and knots. The sun was well over the horizon before I made my way back to the house where I'd left Oscar. He was not there, but my belongings were bundled up on my bed, so I changed into my other *leine* and went looking for my master.

By this hour, the college was awake, full of students and *ollamhs* going to the morning meal or their classes. I did not see Oscar anywhere I looked, and for some reason, everyone I asked stared at me as if they'd never seen me before. I assumed it was because I was far more presentable than I had been in a long time. Unable to find Oscar, and uncertain if he'd eaten, I decided to collect something for the both of us to eat, and to return to the cottage to wait.

I was carrying a basket down the path towards the cottage when I heard the raven calling behind me. I looked over my shoulder to see the bird sitting on a barren branch over my head; as I watched, it launched itself into the air and flew towards me. Before it had covered half the ground between us, the raven shifted, changed, grew, and Oscar fell in next to me, shortening his stride to match mine, his cloak billowing behind him.

"Ah, you thought to get us something to eat. Thank you," he said, looking over the contents of the basket.

"Oh… will you show me how you did that?" I breathed. "Is that something I could do?"

He looked at me, and again I saw amusement in his eyes. "Perhaps. We shall see. You are lovely, Wildling."

His idle complement stopped me in my tracks, abruptly enough that he kept on walking a few steps before he noticed I'd stopped. "What?" I stammered.

He turned to face me. "Looking for compliments, Muirenn?" he asked. "Surely you know that you're a beautiful woman?"

Stunned that he would think so, I shook my head. "No. No one has ever told me that."

He sniffed. "I'm not surprised. We're surrounded by idiots. Come along, Muirenn. We'll eat, and then I will tell you what your next duty will be." He turned and walked into the cottage, and I followed him in a daze. Oscar, perhaps the most powerful sorcerer in all of Eire, possibly in the entire world… thought I was beautiful?

We sat at the table together and ate the food I had brought, and Oscar served me with his own hands, leaving me even more dazzled. I watched him as I ate, trying not to be seen as I studied him, the sharp planes of his face, and his amazing eyes, which seemed to move between blue and silver-gray. He was possibly the most beautiful man I had ever seen.

"You're staring," he murmured. I felt my face grow warm, and dropped my eyes.

"I apologize," I answered. "I just…"

"Curious?" he asked. "Curious about the freak?"

"What?" I gasped.

"That's what they call me," he nodded towards the door, indicating the world outside. "I'm the freak. Or the Ice Raven. Even my own brothers call me that. That one I'm rather fond of, actually. Surely you've heard those?"

"No!" I sputtered, shaking my head. "No, I've never heard that. And I wouldn't call you that. You're no more a freak than…" My voice trailed off. Perhaps that wasn't the best comparison…

"Then you are?" Oscar finished. "Accepted. Both the sentiment, and the compliment. Thank you, Muirenn. So why are you staring?"

"It's just… you're fascinating," I said, deciding on complete honesty. "And… I've dreamed about you, Oscar."

"Have you?" Now he looked intrigued, as if he were studying me. I looked down at my plate and nodded.

"Yes. For years now. I… I hoped you might choose me as your apprentice." I looked at him, then asked, "Why have you never taken an apprentice before?"

He shrugged one shoulder and tore a piece of bread into crumbs. "Who told you that I hadn't?" he asked, not looking up. "Gaynor?"

"Gaynor doesn't speak of you," I answered. "I asked the sorcerers here at the college. I forget who told me."

"Whoever it was, they know nothing," Oscar said. He sat up straight and looked past me, and I turned on my stool to see through the window a pair of *Brehons* coming up to the cottage.

"About Bricriu, I imagine," Oscar said. He stood

219

and walked towards the door, his cloak furling behind him. I rose and followed, standing just behind him, feeling safe in his shadow.

Then my world fell apart.

"Oscar mac Morrigan, you are summoned to answer before the Council," one of them announced as Oscar unbarred the door and opened it.

"Summoned?" Oscar sounded surprised. "For what purpose? What is it that I'm to answer for? Defending my apprentice?"

"No," the *brehon* answered. "For the creation and unleashing of the *deamhan aeir.* You will come with us."

Oscar staggered back a step, bumping into me. "Before the Council? Eogan would not…"

"Cathbad ordered it," the *brehon* interrupted. "You will come with us."

"Cathbad," Oscar breathed, and it was as if he cursed. "Of course. Again…" He stepped back, almost stepping on me as he did so. His eyes met mine, and he took a breath. I saw him hesitate, consider… and then he swept his cloak off his shoulders and held it out to me.

"Keep this safe for me, Muirenn," he said. "Until I return."

I gathered the cloak in my arms and held it to my breast. "Yes, Oscar. Should I… should I come with you?"

He hesitated again, and this time, I could see he was wavering. He wanted me with him, for what reason I knew not. But he shook his head and answered me, "No, Muirenn. Bar the door and allow no one in. No one, do you understand me? And… should anything happen to me, bring that to my brothers. They will know what to do."

A chill ran through me at his words, and I shook my

head to deny even the concept. "Nothing will happen to you!" I said vehemently. For the first time, I saw him smile, a real smile that lit up his face, and I wished that I could see that again. To my surprise, he leaned down and kissed me gently, barely brushing my lips with his.

"I'll be back for you, my wildling," he told me. Then he turned and strode out of the cottage, leaving the *brehons* to scramble after him. I watched them go, then closed the door and barred it as he'd ordered. But I could not stay and wait, alone and ignorant. And he had not ordered me to stay, only to bar the door. I put his cloak of feathers over my shoulders and crawled out the window to follow.

* * *

The Council met in a grove of trees located halfway between the college and the High King's hall of Dun-Righ; I knew where, and I knew that I could make my way there unseen. I crept through the undergrowth, making no more noise than one of the forest beasts, and so came up to the Council grove. There was not enough cover to hide myself and still hear, so I clambered into one of the towering pines and lay along a wide branch, hiding my face with my hair so that I might not be seen.

Below me in the circle, I saw the half-circle of Druids, *Ollamhs* and *Brehons* already gathered, with Cathbad at their heart. I saw, too, that the place at the middle, the one usually taken by the High King himself, was empty. I worried at my lower lip, wondering how they could hold Council without the High King. Unless this was not a proper Council meeting? But then, what was it?

I had somehow arrived before Oscar and his *brehon* guard, and so I was watching as he entered the grove. To my surprise, he stopped just inside the trees, looked up at me, and winked. Then he continued on to the center of the grove, where he stopped, folded his arms over his chest and scowled.

"And what is the meaning of this?" he asked. "Cathbad, this is your doing. Revenge for my revealing your boy's shortcomings? Or simply another stab in the back for old time's sake?"

Cathbad's face went red, never a good sign. "Oscar mac Morrigan, you are summoned before the Council to answer to your peers…"

"Are there any here?" Oscar interrupted. Cathbad turned even more red and continued.

"To answer to your peers on the charges that you, through carelessness and complete disregard for life, have created the… the monster that is preying on the country-side."

Oscar nodded once, clasping his hands behind his back. He paced across the grove, back and forth, then shrugged one shoulder and said clearly, "Yes."

"Yes?" I nearly bit my tongue at the sound of that voice—it was Gaynor! "You admit to this?"

"I admit it. I have already admitted it to the High King and accepted his judgment." Oscar stopped and stood there, tall and proud. "I created the creature, out of my desire for revenge on the mortal man who tortured and imprisoned my youngest brother. I cursed him, and I imprisoned him within the roof-post of a hall that Eogan then ordered burnt. That he is freed now is none of my doing."

"No, you simply created him, created a monster that

lives on mortal flesh and cannot be killed!" Cathbad shrilled. "He admits his guilt, and must be punished! I call for the highest penalty!"

There was a low rumble from the other members of the Council, and I had visions of the great woven wicker prisons that were used on only the vilest of criminals. I had seen one such execution and I still had nightmares about it. That they might do that to Oscar was unthinkable.

"Cathbad, we cannot contradict the will of the High King!" Gaynor called out. Then he asked. "Penalty has already been set, you say? Oscar, what punishment did the High King lay on you?

Oscar raised his chin and said, "I believe he accepted the murder of my brother as punishment enough for my… misjudgment , Gaynor, and he has charged me to destroy the beast, no matter the cost. If he had been summoned to this Council, he could have answered the question himself. Which calls the question. If this is a legitimate Council meeting, then why was he not summoned? Where is the High King, or his representative?"

Gaynor frowned and looked at the rest of the Council, who were starting to murmur uncomfortably. "I do not know, Oscar. Cathbad, when you summoned the Council, was a messenger not sent to Dun-Righ?"

"This is not a matter for the High King," Cathbad said stiffly. "This is a matter for sorcerers. It should be our justice that prevails, not the High King, who knows nothing of these matters. Again, I call for the bonfires!"

Oscar looked at him, sighed deeply, and shook his head. "Cathbad, this grudge you insist on keeping alive is grown very old and very tiresome. Enough of it. I have admitted my guilt, and my shame, to my King. There is no reason for this… farce, unless it is for revenge for something you know well was none of my doing, and all of yours."

Cathbad's face was nearly purple, and he sputtered and stammered until another Druid stepped forward and asked, "Revenge? Cathbad, what does he mean?"

"Enough!" Cathbad shouted.

"Yes, Cathbad. Enough. This is no true Council meeting, and you had no right to call it. However, there is a matter I need to lay before the College, a matter for sorcerers, as Cathbad called it. I call for justice of my own," Oscar interrupted. "Gaynor, Cathbad's son attacked Muirenn last night."

"Muirenn?" Gaynor gasped. "My Muirenn?" He wheeled on Cathbad; in all the years I had lived with Gaynor, I had never before seen him this angry.

"She's fine, Gaynor," Oscar said quickly, laying his hand on Gaynor's arm. "I stopped him, and that is, I think, the heart of this matter." He looked past Gaynor to where Cathbad was pacing, and pitched his voice lower. I could just barely hear him ask, "Gaynor, where is Bricriu?"

"I don't know. I haven't seen him."

"I bespelled him. He's caught in a truth-telling, that will only be released when he tells what he tried to do to Muirenn to one of the *Brehons*. I've demanded an honor-fine and that Bricriu be expelled from the college."

Gaynor hummed, something he did when he was thinking deep thoughts. The sound was carried to me on the wind, as were his words when he said, "That won't sit well with Cathbad."

"I know." Oscar went silent, considering, then looked at Gaynor. "Gaynor, tell the *Brehons* to find Bricriu."

Gaynor nodded, "Of course. And… I'll speak to the

rest of the Council as well. I do not like that Cathbad is attempting to use us to attack you. Calling for the fires, and without the High King's say? This is more than the old grudge, Oscar."

"You know I've always thought it might go this far," Oscar said.

"Yes, I know. But now… if necessary, I'll go to Dun-Righ and speak to Eogan."

"Ward yourself, Gaynor," Oscar warned, making me shiver slightly from the chill in his voice. "Cathbad guards his position like a *leithbrágan* guards his gold. And is likely to turn as violent when threatened."

Gaynor nodded soberly, then quirked an eyebrow and asked, "Will he throw shoes like a *leithbrágan*, do you think?"

Oscar snorted at the jest. "Be careful, my friend."

"I will. But Oscar, you haven't said. Where is my Muirenn?"

Oscar smiled. He looked over his shoulder, towards where I hid in my tree, and called out, "Come down, Wildling."

I felt my face grow warm, and I slowly climbed down the tree and made my way into the grove. Any other day, I would have gone to stand with Gaynor, but today was different. Today, I took my place next to Oscar, taking his cloak from my own shoulders and offering it to him. He took it with a nod, swinging it over his shoulders. Then he looked oddly at me.

"Thought I told you to stay," he murmured.

"You didn't," I answered. "You told me to bar the door."

"So?" I could see his lips twitching, and I couldn't help myself.

225

"I went out the window," I answered. "But the door is barred, just as you ordered."

Oscar's jaw dropped, and the look of sheer amazement on his face sent me into a fit of giggles. Giggles that were, apparently, contagious; Oscar started to laugh, and we laughed together like idiots while a dumbfounded Gaynor just stared at us.

"You," Oscar said accusingly when he could talk again. He pointed his finger at me as he spoke, "You are going to force me to pay attention to what I say, aren't you?" I smiled sweetly at him, and he laughed again, pulling me close and hugging me tightly. "Thank you," he murmured into my hair.

"Oscar…?" I heard Gaynor's voice, the confusion in it. So did Oscar, who let me go, but kept his arm around my shoulders.

"Gaynor," he said pleasantly. "I believe you've met my apprentice?"

"Ah… ah… ah… apprentice?" Gaynor stammered. "Apprentice? You… you've taken an apprentice? *You*?"

Oscar sighed, "Try to keep up, Gaynor? Yes, I've taken Muirenn as my apprentice."

"But… Muirenn?" Gaynor's eyes flickered from Oscar to me, and then back again. "Oscar…"

I felt Oscar stiffen, and I looked up to see his eyes had gone cold. "Gaynor, I cannot believe that you have any doubts about your daughter's abilities. Unless you're like the rest of these idiots, and cannot see beyond the surface, or who think that a woman cannot control magic as well as a man."

"I've never doubted my daughter," Gaynor protested. "I know her worth. I'll admit to being a bit surprised at you, and that you've taken as long as you have. I am pleased, and I give my blessing to you both. You take care of Muirenn." Gaynor smiled, and there was something knowing in that smile that I didn't understand. Nor did I understand Oscar's answer.

"I intend to, Gaynor. I intend to."

* * *

Oscar held me close to his side the entire way back to the cottage, wrapping his cloak around my shoulders to keep me warm. Timidly, I slid one arm around his back, sneaking glances up at him through my lashes to see if he disapproved. To my surprise and delight, he smiled.

"I did mean for you to stay here, Muirenn," he said as we reached the cottage.

"But you didn't want me to," I said softly. "I could see it. You wanted me there."

He didn't say anything, instead using magic to unbar the door and let us into the cottage. Inside, he closed the door again, barred it, then turned to face me. "You're right. I did want you there." He stopped, taking his cloak off and hanging it on a peg near the door. He hesitated there, running his hand over the feathers, then turned again, holding his hand out to me.

His hand was warm, his fingers calloused, and he held tight to my hand as he led to me sit with him on the edge of the bed where he'd slept the night before. For several minutes, all we did was sit there, my hand in his. I was very aware of him, aware of the long length of his thigh pressed against mine, and I turned to look at him, only to find him looking at me. He smiled, a crooked, uneasy smile that made him look endearingly young.

"Amazing. I find that I have no idea what I am doing," he said softly. "I suppose… yes."

227

"Doing about what?" I asked, puzzled. And in answer, Oscar leaned down and kissed me, his free hand cupping the back of my head, his fingers tangling in my hair. His lips were soft against mine, and I closed my eyes in pleasure, pressing against him, as wanton as a cat in heat. It was as if this was what I had been seeking my entire life, and I wanted him to hold me tight and never let me go.

When at last he pulled his lips from mine, I opened my eyes to see him smiling at me. "My lovely Muirenn," he whispered. "I take it you have no objections?"

"Only if you stop," I answered. He laughed, sliding his hand down my neck, tracing his fingers over my collarbone. I caught my breath as his finger brushed over my skin, then twisted, shifting so that I was straddling his legs. Kneeling up, I could look him in the eyes, and I rested my hands on his shoulders.

"Oscar," I murmured, suddenly hesitant. "I've not…"

"I know, my wildling," he said, his hands settling on my waist, long fingers toying with my belt. "My question is, do you want to? With me?"

"I could never want anyone else," I told him, certain then that it was absolutely true. I wasn't prepared for the · look of pure joy in his face, or the way he folded me into his arms and buried his face in my shoulder.

"My Muirenn," he murmured, his voice muffled. "I've known… years I've known. Since I first saw you. You were such a little girl then. Now… you've grown so beautiful."

"What?" I asked. "Oscar, what are you talking about?"

He smiled, brushing my hair back off my face. "What do you know, my wildling? About me?"

"Gaynor says you are the Goddess's son, and that

228

you're powerful. I know you're one of the Princes, and I know you change your shape. You said you were going to show me how." I stopped and thought, and shook my head. "Nothing more, really. Oh, except that Gaynor says that you may be the loneliest man in Eire."

Oscar blinked, looking surprised. "He says that? Truly?"

I nodded. "He said it once. I don't know if he meant for me to hear. But… yes." I studied Oscar for a moment, then cupped his face in my hands. "You don't have to be. Not anymore."

He smiled slightly, and his hands running down my arms. "Ah, Muirenn. Thank you. Now, I should tell you more. I am old, Muirenn. Old enough to be your father. I am older than Cathbad…"

"You are not!" I protested. He waved me silent and continued.

"I am. Only by a few years, but I am. I've seen 41 summers, Muirenn. To one of your years, that makes me an old man. I am also…" he hesitated, and I could tell that he was looking for his next word. "I am not an easy man to live with. My brothers suffer my moods, but no one else does for very long. I would hope that my wife…"

"What?" I squeaked. That drew a laugh from him.

"My wife. As I was saying, I would hope that my wife would also be able to suffer my black moods. Would you, Muirenn?"

I heard my blood roaring in my ears like the river in its flood, and for a moment, I could only gape at him. Then I stammered, "You… you said apprentice!"

His eyes went dark, shuttered against me. "You do not want me?"

"No… yes! I… Oscar, I don't understand… ." I sat

down on his legs, my hands folded in front of me. "We met… yesterday. This morning, really. And yet… oh, Oscar, I've never wanted anyone before the way I want you."

"And you dreamed of me, you said. What else did you dream, my wildling?" he asked me, taking my hands in his.

I thought back to my dreams when I was a child. "Flying," I murmured. "I dreamed of flying, on wings… ." I stopped, turning to stare at the feathered cloak on its peg. "Oscar…"

"You dreamed of your own cloak?" he asked. "Oh, Muirenn. Cathbad and the rest of them, they're all of them morons. They have no idea of the treasure in you, do they? But I do. I know." He wrapped his arms around me and pulled me tight to his chest. "Listen, my wildling, and I will explain to you. There is a magic in me that can only be used once. In truth, it is more like half a magic. The other half exists only in you." His eyes met mine, held them. "I have been waiting for you for my entire life, as you have been waiting for me. What you have dreamed of? I can give that to you. Will you be mine, Muirenn? Knowing that I am yours, for now and forever?"

I knew then what it was that I had seen in him all those years ago. Something in me had recognized the other half that I didn't know I was missing, and had yearned for it, all unknowing. I nodded, feeling tears starting to well and not caring. "Yes," I whispered. "Oh, yes!" And I laced my fingers into his hair and kissed him. He groaned, and his arms around me tightened, then he pulled back.

"I will need my cloak," he told me. I smiled and shook my head.

"When we're done here," I answered, and pushed him backwards. He twisted as he lay back, pulling me with him so that we lay facing each other on the bed, arms and legs tangled together. We lay entwined for what felt like hours, exploring, touching, kissing and talking about things that I could not remember if I tried. His touch was intoxicating, and when he slid his hand up underneath my *leine* to stroke my thigh through my trews, I whimpered and pressed close to him.

"I think we may both be wearing too much," he whispered, tugging at my belt. I nodded and slowly moved away from him so that I could undress, watching him as he stripped his shirt off over his head. The skin beneath was pale and smooth, and I couldn't resist touching him to see how he felt. He gasped as my fingers brushed over his shoulder, then sat very still, his eyes half-closed, as I ran my hands over his chest and stomach, up and down his arms and over his shoulders. I ran my fingers up his neck, and he caught them in his hands and pressed kisses into each of my palms.

"If you keep on doing that, we may never get into bed, my love," he murmured. "May I undress you?" I nodded and let my arms fall to my sides, watching as he slowly untied my belt and let it fall to the floor, then reached under my *leine* and fumbled at the laces of my trews. "Do you always dress like a boy?" he asked as he loosened the laces and slid my trews down.

"It's convenient," I answered, steadying myself with my hands on his shoulders as he helped me step out of my clothes. Clad now only in shoes and my knee-length *leine*, I shivered at the chill in the air.

"I would like to see you in a gown," he said simply, and slid his hands up underneath my *leine*. "And I would like to see you without anything on at all."

"I don't own a gown," I murmured, then gasped as his fingers trailed over hips.

"You will. I'll see you dressed as a princess should be," Oscar told me. "Leave this on for now. I don't want you to freeze." He let my *leine* fall back into place, and stood up, quickly unfastening his own trews and stripping off them and his shoes before going to his knees in front of me. He unlaced my shoes, then ran his hands up my legs, drawing my *leine* up as he rose, stripping it up over my head and letting it fall to the floor. He studied me for a long moment, then muttered the words of a spell and waved one hand carelessly; the air in the cottage lost the bitter chill and slowly began to grow warmer.

"I can't have you freezing, now can I?" he asked me. "Come, my wildling. Come to bed."

I let him take my hand and lay me back down on the bed, watching him as he stretched out next to me. All of his skin was pale as milk, saving his hands and the back of his neck, and it was as soft as willow catkins as I ran my hand over his side. His ribs were far too prominent, and I told him so. He laughed and leaned over to kiss me.

"I sometimes forget to eat," he admitted. "You will have to remind me."

I smiled and let my gaze travel lower, to the one area where I'd been trying not to look. I knew that if I had looked, I would have stared; I had never before seen a man in his pride, and I wasn't certain what to expect. Oscar saw where my gaze traveled, and rolled onto his back so that I could better see him.

"May I…?"

"Of course. But gently, my wildling," he answered me. I nodded and slowly skimmed my hand over his chest, down over his stomach, following the thin line of dark hair to his crotch and his cock. I looked at him quickly; he smiled, then his breath caught sharply as I ran my fingers down his length. I jerked my hand away, and he laughed. "No, no. Muirenn, that was nice. It felt good. Do it again."

I nibbled my lip and touched him again, hearing him gasp as I closed my hand around him. His cock was warm, the skin soft as rose petals, and he was larger than I'd ever expected a man to be.

"I… Oscar, will… will it fit?" I whispered.

He looked surprised at the question. "Muirenn?"

"It's… big…"

"Oh." He looked down, then back at me, laughing a little. "Wildling, I'm flattered that you think so. Yes, it will fit. It may hurt, since this is your first time, but I will be very careful. I promise." He held his arms open, and I lay down next to him, resting my head on his shoulder. "Shall I show you, my love?"

I nodded, and he pushed me onto my back, then leaned down and kissed me. I felt his hand run over my body to cup my breast, toying with my nipple and sending the most incredible sensations rushing all through me. I moaned, and felt him laugh against my mouth. Then his lips moved, trailing over my skin, down my throat to my chest. He kissed each of my breasts, then started to suckle; I arched my back and wrapped my arms around him. The inner heat that I had always felt around him had become a raging fire, and I wanted—needed!—more! I raked my nails down his back, and he gasped, finding my mouth once more and kissing me deeply.

"Wildling, slow down," he murmured. "I don't want to hurt you."

I whimpered, unable to find words, and unsure of

what I could say to him if I did. I didn't know what the next steps were, or what he would be doing. So when his hand slid between my thighs and his fingers brushed against my nether lips, I yelped in surprise.

"Are you…?" he started to say.

"Cold!" I blurted out. "Your hand is cold."

He froze in place, looked at me, and a moment later, we were both giggling again. Oscar brought both his hands to his mouth and made a show of blowing on them, then touched my arm. "Better?"

"Much. I'm sorry…"

"Don't be. I should have thought of that. Now, lay back, wildling." He ran his now-warm fingers down my stomach and back between my thighs. I had no idea what he was doing, but it felt wonderful, and when his mouth returned to my nipples, I lost all control of my wits. I thought it couldn't possibly get better, until he slowly slid his fingers into me. He twisted his hand, and the fires within consumed me; I howled and shook, holding tightly to Oscar as my body reacted to everything that he was doing to me, things I could never have imagined.

When I came back to my senses, Oscar was smiling down at me, his hand damp on my stomach. "I take it you liked that?" he murmured.

"Was that…?"

"Oh, that wasn't all, wildling," he said. He leaned down and kissed me, then shifted, moving to kneel between my knees. He ran his hands up my legs and looked at me, then smiled, suddenly full of mischief. "No, I think we're going to try this another way." He took my hand and pulled me up, then guided me until he was flat on his back, and I was once again straddling his hips. "Now, you're in control, my wildling."

"But what do I do?"

He smiled up at me, running his hands up and down my thighs. "I'll help you. Rise up a bit." I felt his hand sliding under me as I moved, then felt… something… pressing against me.

"Oh…" I said softly.

"Just lower yourself down, Muirenn. As fast or as slow as you wish. Take your time."

I nodded and slowly pressed down against him, feeling the most amazingly pleasurable pressure as he filled me. He slid his hand free as I moved, resting it on my hip, subtle support and comfort as I moaned and gasped and spread my knees wider so that I could feel even more of his cock inside me. There was a moment, a sharpness that made me gasp in surprise, but it passed quickly, and the pleasure returned; when I looked down at Oscar, his eyes were closed, his face slack, and I saw him bite down on his lip as my hips finally came to rest against his.

"… now…" he whispered. "Now, move. Whatever… whatever feels good… oh, Muirenn, you feel so good…"

I didn't answer, unable to string more than three letters together, let along words. The only thing I could manage was "Oh." So that was what I said as I started to move, feeling him moving with me, inside me, setting off flames of pleasure the likes of which I had never know. "Oh… oh… oh…"

His hands on my hips shifted, trailing up, fondling my breasts and my nipples, then taking my hands in his, lacing his fingers with mine as I rode him. His breathing was growing faster, and I could feel him struggling to stay still. I shook my head and managed to say, "… move…"

It was all I needed to say. He thrust his hips up,

driving into me, making something that was already wonderful somehow even better. I could feel something building inside me, something similar to what Oscar had done to me before, but somehow... more. I heard him gasping and moaning under me, responded with my own cries, felt them adding fuel to the flames within me. A small voice in the back of my mind whispered that anyone who ventured into this part of the college would surely know what we were doing, but I dismissed it—I didn't care. All that mattered was here, now, and what we were doing to each other.

He thrust up again, throwing me off-balance, and we tumbled to the side; I wrapped my leg over his hip and kept on moving with him, in time with his rocking. His mouth found mine, and his kiss was what I needed to complete the spell that he'd cast over my body. I clung to him tightly as I came, crying my pleasure to the world and hearing Oscar's harsh cries in answer. When he fell still, we lay there for a moment, spent, and I noticed that it was again cold in the cottage. Oscar noticed it, too; he looked puzzled for a moment, raising his head and looking around. Then he laughed.

"Lost the spell," he murmured, and reached down to drag a blanket up over us. We curled together under the warm wool, and I listened to Oscar's steady heartbeat under my ear, as happy as I'd ever been.

"We'll go to Dun-Morrigan in the morning," Oscar said, his voice heavy with sleep. "It's too late in the day to fly tonight."

I tipped my head so that I could look at him. "Fly?"

He laughed, low and sleepy. "A surprise, my love. You have to wait until morning. Then I'll show you."

I nodded, closing my eyes and listening to him

breathe. A question floated to the surface, and I murmured, "Oscar?"

"Hm?"

"Why does Cathbad hate you so much?"

"Who says that, wildling?" he asked, sounding suddenly much more alert. "There is no love lost between us, surely. But I do not hate him…"

"I didn't say that," I said, turning so that my chin rested in his chest. "I know you don't hate him. I asked why he hates you."

Oscar sniffed, then asked, "How is it that you can see through me so clearly?"

"Oscar?"

"No one else can do this, you know. Not even my brothers. No one else sees me so truly. I wonder… I'll have to ask Diarmuid. Or Niall. My brothers," he said, in answer to my unspoken question. "I have eight…" He stopped and closed his eyes, and then said quietly. "Seven."

I slid my arm around him and held him tightly. "What was his name?"

"Ronan," Oscar said. "He was a *filidh*, a poet of some renown. He was… a bit of an ass, most of the time. He loved to argue, loved to poke at people until they couldn't see for their rage. It amused him. He was abrasive, and annoying, and I loved him. And because of me, because of my… arrogance, he's dead." I heard Oscar's breath catch, and looked up to see tears sliding down his face. I pulled him into my arms and held him as he wept. When finally he drew away, I could see the pain in his face, and the guilt.

"I heard you, when you spoke to the Council," I said. "I heard you tell of the creature, that you created it. Why?"

Oscar lay back on the bed, pulling me closer and tracing arcane patterns on my shoulder with his fingertips. "There was a witch, playing a power game. She claimed as her father Eochaid, the High King that was, and thought to challenge Eogan for the throne. She and her brother captured and tortured my youngest brother. They kidnapped his mate, and let us all think she was dead for two years." He looked at me, and his voice gentled as he stroked my cheek. "We mate once, Muirenn. Once, and for a lifetime. For two years, we thought Niall would die from his loss. Then they took him prisoner, and because of what they did to him, he has no voice today. The witch was killed when we rescued Niall, but the witch's brother…" he paused, then shook his head. "I should have just killed him. But I was angry, and I wanted revenge for Niall, for everything they'd done to him. I made the *deamhan aeir,* and I imprisoned him in the roof support in the ruin where they'd kept Niall chained like a beast. When Eogan ordered the hall burned, I celebrated."

"But he was released. How?"

"His mother," Oscar told me. "A blood witch. She found the post and saved it, somehow. I still don't know how she knew, or how she broke my spells. And the curséd thing killed her, so I'll never know. She released it, and was its first victim."

I sighed, rubbed my cheek against his chest. "Oscar, it wasn't your fault."

"I should never have cursed him. I should have just killed him."

"I know," I murmured. "But regrets won't stop the thing. They will only stop you. You will find a way to kill it. I know you will. And I'll help you, however I can." I promised, settling myself again on his shoulder. "Now, tell me about Cathbad."

He barked with laughter. "Are you always this single-minded?" he asked.

"Stubborn is what the *ollahms* called me."

"Not a bad trait in a sorceress, no matter what you call it," Oscar said. "So… Cathbad. I have had very few failures in my lifetime, Muirenn. So when they happen, they tend to be… disastrous. Cathbad was my first, and he resents me greatly for it."

"Cathbad?" I puzzled at what he might mean, then gasped. "Was he your apprentice?"

"I thought to make him my apprentice, yes. And he is the reason that I have never taken one. Until now." His arm around me tightened. "Because of who I am—what I am—you must understand that I came to my magic very young, and I had my earliest training at my mother's hands. I came to the college when I was a boy of 10, already half-trained. I was a full sorcerer before I was 14."

I raised myself up on my elbow so I could look at him. "Fourteen?"

"There's something to be said for training at the hands of a Goddess," he answered with a smirk.

"I imagine so," I answered tartly, then leaned down and kissed him. Then I straddled his hips and lay down over him, resting my chin on my folded hands on his chest. He looked at me and laughed.

"Comfortable?" he asked.

"I was going to ask you the same question."

"You weigh hardly anything, wildling. This is distracting, though."

I made a face at him. "I want to look at you. I like looking at you."

He ran the backs of his fingers over my cheek, then clasped his hands behind my back. "Very well, then. That, I think, is why Gaynor called me lonely. He was right, you know. It's hard, to be so different from everyone. To be considered by many to be a freak for simply being who you were born…"

"I'd know nothing about that," I murmured. Oscar smiled.

"Just so, my wildling. When I was younger, I tried to… associate, with those who would be my peers. So, when I was 20, I taught here at the college. Cathbad was a student here then. He was 18, and thought he was the most powerful sorcerer to ever walk the wide world."

"No, that would be you."

"Thank you, my wildling. He did appear to have promise, I will give him that. I taught him what I knew, helped him polish what he was capable of doing. But he thought he could do more, be more. He thought I was keeping information from him, keeping him back because I did not want him to succeed. When I offered to make him my apprentice, he spat in my face."

"He didn't!"

"He did. And he accused me of conspiring with the rest of the Council to hold him back. He swore that he would prove himself better than the rest of us. He attempted…" Oscar stopped and grimaced. "I haven't thought of this in 20 years."

"Liar," I murmured. His eyes went wide, and he stared at me for a moment before snorting.

"Very well. I think on it often. I wonder how I could have been so wrong about someone. But I have never told anyone about this. The rest of the Council who saw the aftermath… they're all dead now. I'm the only one left who Cathbad can point to and blame for his misfortunes."

"But he's the *Ard Ollahm*!"

"He was married once before he married Bricriu's mother. His wife then… pretty little thing. Her name was Maire, and she was the last woman before you to be a student here at the college. I taught her, too." Oscar stared up at the ceiling. "She was so talented. I was fond of her. But for some reason I can't imagine, she loved Cathbad. They'd been married a year or so when Cathbad decided to attempt some magics that were… far beyond him. He lost control of the magic, and it went wild."

I shivered; I'd heard too many stories of wild magic and what could happen. "Did it kill her?"

Oscar shook his head. "She would have been lucky if it had. No, she went mad. The healers tried to save what was left of her wits, but she escaped them. Vanished into the forest and was never seen again. No one knew that she was carrying Cathbad's child when she disappeared." His eyes met mine, and I knew then what he was saying.

"Me? She was my mother?"

Oscar nodded. "In all likelihood, wildling. I find it very hard to believe that there was more than one madwoman living in Uragh, let alone another who could have passed the gift of magic to you in your blood." He ran one finger over my brow. "You have her eyes, wildling."

I closed my eyes and rested my forehead on his chest. "Cathbad knows?"

"He'd be an idiot not to have made the connection. Which probably means that he's denying it with every breath he takes." Oscar rubbed my back gently. "I managed to save his life, and dispel the magic. But he never forgave me for not saving Maire, and he blamed me for not teaching him properly. He charged me with her murder before the Council."

"But…"

"Oh, the Council laughed at him. The healers swore to them that Maire lived—this was before she escaped their care—and the other sorcerers swore that the failure had been Cathbad's alone. Regardless, he blames me. I left the college not long after, returned to Dun-Morrigan. I was tired of petty mortals and their games, and I knew that I would never truly belong there. I also knew that if Cathbad kept cherishing his hate, that he would turn on me. Rather than challenge him and destroy him, I left."

"If Cathbad is such a poor sorcerer, how did he become *Ard Ollahm*?" I asked.

Oscar snorted. "He married again six months later, and his second wife was the daughter of the previous *Ard Ollahm*. I think she somehow persuaded her father to name Cathbad his successor. I wasn't here, so I don't actually know, but it's the only reason I can imagine that he became *Ard Ollahm*." He sighed and closed his eyes. "Enough, Muirenn. I'm tired of talking. I don't often talk this much, and I'm not used to it."

"I like the sound of your voice," I told him.

"I'll talk to you," he assured me. "I don't care to waste my time on idiots who won't understand me."

I laughed and rested my head on his chest, my eyes closed, the better to listen to his heartbeat and his slow, regular breathing. His arms around me grew heavy, relaxed, and I slowly joined him in sleep.

* * *

I woke up slowly, dreaming of Oscar's hands moving on my body and waking to find that it was true. In the dim light of the half-moon, I saw him smile at me, and I slid up his body and kissed him.

"In the morning, my love," he whispered. "In the morning, we'll seal the bond between us, and you'll be my wife. We'll be happy."

I squirmed against him, feeling his erection against my bottom. "Do you want children?" I asked.

"As many as you want to have, wildling. Our own sorcerer's college, if you want," he agreed. "Children with your eyes, your spirit. Muirenn, nothing would make me happier."

I laughed, kissing him again, feeling his arms around me. He rolled, pushing me down onto the bed, and I spread my legs for him, moaning into his mouth as he kissed me fiercely. There was no preamble this time, no teasing. He slid into me, slowly starting to thrust as I whimpered and moved with him. He somehow knew I was tender from our earlier lovemaking, and he was careful, gentle as he brought me to climax again and again before reaching his own shuddering peak, then collapsed over me, panting hard. I could see his hair hanging down into his eyes, and I reached up and brushed it back; he turned his head and kissed my hand, then shifted to lay next to me. He pinned me to the bed with his arm over my chest and his leg over both of mine, then laughed quietly in my ear.

"Look what I've caught," he murmured.

"Indeed, look what we've caught."

Oscar froze at the sound of Cathbad's voice, and started to turn. His back was to the door, and his body between me and Cathbad, so I saw nothing. But I felt the magic swell, felt the force of it as whatever spell Cathbad used struck Oscar from behind; Oscar cried out in pain and collapsed over me, trapping me under the weight of his body. I could feel his breath on my neck, knew he still lived. But he would not wake, no matter how hard I shook him or called his name. Desperate, I tried to remember the words of a spell—any spell!—that would let me defend the both of us. I was still trying when I heard Cathbad speak again.

"Take him," he ordered. Oscar's limp body was lifted off of me, and I saw men in dark cloaks and hoods, who carried him between them out of the cottage. And there was Cathbad, carrying a lit lamp and looking down at me with contempt.

"Poor child," he said, his voice dripping with sarcasm. "It would have been best for you if you'd died with her in the forest."

"No…" I closed my eyes and used the first spell I could think of, the one to call fire to the lamps. I threw it as hard as I could, and heard Cathbad yell in shock and pain as his *leine* and cloak caught fire. I scrambled to get off the bed and past him, thinking only of Oscar.

"Bitch!" he snarled. Behind me, I felt his magic swell again. I didn't even have time to scream before the spell caught me and sent me hurtling into the dark.

* * *

I woke in pain, to find myself curled up against the wall of the cottage, where I'd apparently landed, and very much surprised that I was alive. The cottage was empty, and I whimpered as I slowly got to my feet. Everything hurt, and Oscar… Where was Oscar? I looked around, and the first thing I saw was his cloak, hanging on the peg.

I had to find him. I stumbled outside into the snow, using great handfuls of it to scrub my face until my mind had cleared enough that I could think. They wouldn't have taken him into the college. Cathbad wouldn't risk his position by having anyone know he'd attacked another sorcerer. They'd have gone into the forest.

And no one living knew Uragh the way that I did.

I rose and went back into the cottage, dressing myself as warmly as I could, and tying clothes for Oscar into a bundle that I'd leave in a safe place. I took my knife and tied my belt around my waist, stuffed my hair down the back of my *leine,* and started for the door. As I reached the threshold, I stopped. The cloak. It was hardly practical, but something about the cloak called to me. I swung it over my shoulders and was away before I could give myself time to think. Outside, I looked around again, and sniffed in disgust. The idiots hadn't even bothered to try and hide their trail. Moving as silently as I could, I breathed a prayer to Flidais, the Lady of the Forest, and followed their clear-laid path into Uragh.

They must have thought me dead, to have left such a clear path. For the trail they'd left was so clear that a new-born wolf pup could have followed it, and they left no sentries, no watchers of any kind. But the trail was also hours old; the birds flew without fear around it, telling me that there was only myself about. I paused for a moment, listening to the birds, tasting the winds. Then I ran.

They'd gone deep into Uragh, the better to hide their deeds. I found them in a small clearing surrounded by short, scrubby pines, the better to hide them from anyone in the forest. The better to hide me from them. I concealed the bundle and the cloak in the crook of a tree, then crawled through the undergrowth to see into the clearing. The first thing I saw was a large bonfire blazing at the center of the clearing. Beyond that was Oscar, still naked and kneeling in the snow, his arms stretched out wide and bound to two young trees. He was gagged, and I could clearly see bruises on his pale skin, even across the clearing. I bit down on my lip to keep myself in control, and drew back into the undergrowth, looking for the others.

Cathbad chose that moment to pace in front of me, and I caught the scent of scorched wool and linen. I fought the urge to laugh and kept watching, seeing two other men. I knew both of them—Ros and Ninean, two minor sorcerers who were part of Cathbad's coterie. I wondered how he'd gotten them to do his bidding. Then I wondered how I was going to get past them. Oscar wasn't going to be able to help me. Bound and gagged, he couldn't use the words and gestures that were necessary for the greater magics. Could I get to him, cut him free? No. And even if I could, he'd been beaten and left exposed to the cold for hours. He was in no shape to do any magic. This was for me to do.

I slowly wormed my way back out of the undergrowth and took cover close enough to the clearing that I could still hear. How could I fight them? How could I defeat three sorcerers, all on my own? After a moment, I kicked myself. How do I defeat three sorcerers? The same way I would eat a horse all by myself: one bite at a time. I would have to separate them. Quietly, I moved out from under cover and started my hunt.

The first was almost too easy; Ninean came out of the clearing and stalked into the trees, calling back over his shoulder that he needed to piss. I caught him with a sleeping spell that I'd been taught by an old midwife, and left him lying under a bush, his trews around his knees and his wrists bound behind him with his own belt. I took to the trees then, and I waited. Sure enough, no more than

10 minutes later, Ros came looking for his partner. He had barely any time to react to seeing Ninean before my spell hit him, and I left him in much the same position. Once they both woke, they'd be able to help each other get free. By then, Oscar and I would be gone.

Now, for Cathbad. I made my way back to the clearing, and I could hear Cathbad's voice as I got closer. I couldn't quite make out what he was saying, though, as I slowly circled the clearing, then made my way through the underbrush near where I thought I had seen Oscar. Once I could see clearly, I saw what the bonfire had hidden from my vantage point across the clearing.

Cathbad had arranged Oscar for burning. There was kindling and dried grasses and leaves piled several hands deep all around Oscar's legs, and I could smell on the wind the scents of the ritual oils that were used in the great bonfires. When I looked closer, I could see the gleam of them on Oscar's skin, and that his hair was dripping with them. Acting on impulse, I called to him, mimicking the call of a raven. He jerked, looking around, tugging on the thongs that bound his wrists.

"Looking for help, freak?" Cathbad taunted. "There's no help for you, Oscar. Now, you'll pay for what you've done. You'll pay for my Maire's death…"

"He didn't kill her," I called out, my voice ringing through the clearing. "You did. You killed her, and you would have killed me… Father." I stepped out into the open, seeing the look of shock on Cathbad's face; he must have thought me dead. Which meant that Oscar had thought me dead, too—no wonder my calling had startled him so!

"No!" Cathbad shouted. "No… he did it. He kept the knowledge from me, he held me back… it was his fault

247

that magic went wild." I saw his hands move, and I reacted, raising a wall of magic that shielded Oscar and me from Cathbad's poorly thrown magical fires. I held the wall, my mind racing. He was off-balance, losing his wits. If he kept on this way, he would lose control of all of his magic, and there was no way I could protect us both, free Oscar and get us to safety in a storm of wild magic. I looked to the side, quickly, to see Oscar staring at me, his eyes wide. He shook his head, then jerked it back towards the forest. Clearly, he wanted me to run.

"I'm not leaving you," I told him. "I only just found you, I'm not giving you up that easily."

He groaned, his eyes turning back towards Cathbad. I saw his face go pale, and turned to see Cathbad gesturing wildly, chanting words I'd never heard before. Oscar grunted, and I could hear the alarm in his muffled voice. What could Cathbad be doing that would frighten Oscar?

Something he'd done before, and badly.

"Oh, no," I breathed. "He's going to kill us all." I threw myself at Oscar, grabbing my knife and sawing at the thongs that bound his left wrist. The knife was dull, and the thongs refused to part; I could feel Cathbad's magic building, growing, taking on life…

An idea sparked, and I forced myself not to think about it, not to weigh the options or consider what would happen if I failed. It was our only chance. I met Oscar's eyes, saw the fear there, and knew it was for me; he knew what I was going to do. I leaned in and kissed him quickly.

"I love you," I whispered. I left the knife with him and stepped out from behind the shielding wall. Behind me, I could hear Oscar's muffled voice. He might have been calling my name, but I wasn't sure. I ignored him, ignored everything but the swell of magic. I tested it, tasted it, probed gingerly at it… and found a way into the stream. I grabbed onto the magic with both hands and all my will, and I ripped it away from Cathbad. I thought I heard him scream, but I paid him no mind; the magic howled like a *bean-sídhe* as it swirled around me, fighting my attempts to control it, calling to my own power to join the storm, to sweep through the forests and devour anything it could find, anything at all that would feed its unquenchable hunger. Starting with Oscar.

Not the forest. Not my forest, I screamed back at the magic. Not my forest, and not my mate!

I fought the magic for what felt like hours, days, years, wrestling with it the way one might wrestle with a giant snake. Finally, hours, days, years into the battle, I found the heart of the storm, found the place where I could drain the power out and let it flow into the sleeping earth beneath me. Finally, the storm faded away, leaving behind nothing in its wake.

And in the nothing that followed, I fell into nothing, and knew no more.

* * *

I woke cold and wet, shivering, and with the oddest sound in my ears. A strange gargling. No, a strangled sobbing. I rolled onto my back and looked up at the circle of blue far away. I knew it was the sky, but my entire world pitched and rolled like a small boat on storm-tossed waters, and for a moment, up was down, and everything in between was a memory. Then the world abruptly decided to properly assert itself, and up stayed up. But the damage had been done; I rolled onto my knees and threw up bile until my stomach ached from it. Then I forced myself to crawl away from the stench, lay down on my side and wondered again what the sound that I was hearing could be.

In a moment, everything came rushing back. I groaned as I made myself move, pushing myself up onto my knees again and looking around. The first thing I saw was Cathbad: his body lay near the remains of the bonfire, unmoving in the snow, his eyes wide and staring. Good riddance, I thought, and turned to see Oscar, struggling against his bonds, the thongs cutting into his wrists enough that blood ran down his arms, and his skin nearly blue from the cold. I forced myself to stand, and staggered like a drunkard towards him, kicking kindling out of the way so that I could kneel in front of him. This close, I could see the frozen tracks of his tears on his face. I fumbled at the gag with hands that didn't want to obey me, finally managing to pull it free. He coughed, gasped, and was about to say something when I caught his face in my hands and kissed him as hard as I could. Then I rested my face on his shoulder and cried.

That was how Gaynor and his druids found us. They'd felt the magic battle, and had followed the trails of magic to the clearing. What had happened was only too clear, and they set out to take care of the living, leaving the forest to take care of the dead. I managed to tell them where I'd hidden Oscar's clothes and his cloak, and where I'd left Ros and Ninean, then I let them bundle me into a blanket and settle me under a tree where I could ignore the rest. Until Oscar staggered over to sit with me. They hadn't returned with his clothes or cloak yet, so he was wrapped solely in a blanket and his dignity.

"Little idiot," he said, his voice harsh and gravelly. "Do you have any idea what that could have done to you?"

"Killed me," I answered. "Left me without a mind, like my mother. I knew that, Oscar."

"And yet…"

"It would have killed you first," I interrupted him. "It would have killed you, and it would have taken your magic and it would have gotten stronger. It would have gone to the college and gotten stronger still…"

"You don't know…"

"I do. I was… I was inside it, Oscar. It was…" I frowned, worrying at the edge of the blanket with my nails, trying to put my thoughts into something that might have resembled order, if you were being generous. "It was everything that Cathbad was, Oscar. He was dead from the moment he cast the spell. That storm, that was… him, all of his magic, all of his ambition, all of his anger, all of his hatred for you, for the other sorcerers." I closed my eyes and shivered. "I wasn't going to let it take you from me."

"I thought you were dead," he said quietly. I turned and saw that he was looking at me, saw the stricken look in his eyes. "I thought… I'd finally found my mate, the one who would never look at me as if I were a freak, who wanted to be with me. And she was dead. Because of me. I couldn't… I couldn't bear it, Muirenn. The thought… that I might not have you… I was ready to die."

"Oscar…"

He looked away, staring at the snow. "I never understood before… never knew… how the bond would be. How it would make me feel." He snorted, shrugging one shoulder before saying, "I never knew what it was to feel this much. Muirenn… promise me that you will never do that again." He looked at me again, his eyes hard as flints. "Promise me!"

"I promise…"

"No." He shook his head, then reached out and cupped the back of my head in his hand. "You do not understand, Muirenn. I. Could. Not. Bear. Losing. You. Swear to me that you won't ever try something like that again."

"Of course," I said, wrapping my hand gently around the bandages on his wrists. "What will you have me swear it on? On our bond? On my love for you?"

"On your cloak," Oscar answered. "The one I'm going to give to you."

He left me then to puzzle out that remark, as the men who had gone searching for the hidden bundle had returned. When Oscar came back, he was dressed, and his feather cloak again graced his shoulders.

"Muirenn, I asked you before, and you said yes. Is your answer still the same? Will you marry me?" he asked, standing over me. He held his hand out, and I took it and let him help me to my feet.

"Yes, Oscar," I answered.

He smiled, and it was as if his entire demeanor changed. Gone was the arrogance, the annoyance at everyone around him who simply could not see the things that he could. Now, there was only happiness, joy that he would no longer be alone. He leaned down and kissed me, and I felt a strange magic wrap around me, filling me with warmth and light and love. I felt a prickling in my shoulders, heard Gaynor's gasp of surprise. And when Oscar let me go, I found that I, too, wore a magnificent cloak of midnight feathers.

"Well?" Oscar prompted. I laughed, delighted with the cloak and with all that it meant for me, for us.

"I swear it, Oscar. On my own cloak, I swear it. I will never leave you."

* * *

They took us back to the college on litters, and the healers saw to both of us. After hot baths and a hot meal, we both of us slept the rest of the day and all through the night. I woke in darkness, hearing from outside the windows the chorus of birds singing to summon the dawn, and knew that sleep would not claim me again this night. I curled up against Oscar, my head on his shoulder, listening to his soft breathing, and had a sudden need to see him. To assure myself that he was here, and hale.

I couldn't get out of the bed to fetch a candle without waking Oscar, so I propped myself up on my elbow and conjured a tiny, flickering light, setting it hovering over the bed. In the dim light, the bruises on Oscar's face faded in the shadows. He slept like an exhausted child, all outspread limbs, one arm thrown over his head in the true abandon of deep sleep. He looked younger than the years he claimed, and fragile enough to shatter at a harsh word. Without warning, I felt a sudden rush of tears.

I must have made a sound, because Oscar jerked, coming awake all at once, searching for the source. I couldn't even hide my tears from him, not when the light still shone. He blinked, alarm turning quickly to concern. "Muirenn? *A ghrá geal,* what's wrong?"

The sweetness of the endearment and the depth of the concern in his still sleep-filled voice undid me the way nothing else ever had. He gathered me to his chest and held me as I sobbed, his hands moving in small circles on my back. I couldn't speak, could barely breathe, and I clung to him as if my entire life depended on having him there, in my arms. Because I knew that it did, and I'd come so close to having it torn from me forever. We'd come so close to dying, the both of us. So close to losing the one thing that we'd both been searching for, and I couldn't bear even the thought of being without him.

Finally, eventually, I could breathe again, albeit with every breath accompanied by a shudder that make my entire body shake. I sniffled, then wiped my fingers against Oscar's soggy chest.

"I've gotten you all wet," I murmured, my voice still thick. He chuckled, a wondrous sound with my head so close to his chest.

"I'll dry, my wildling," he said, and pulled me closer. "Better now?"

"I think so."

"What upset you so?" He kissed my forehead, then my lips, and in the growing light of dawn, I could see the worry clear in his eyes.

I tried to smile at him, to reassure him. I couldn't. I reached up and ran my fingers lightly over his cheek. "I came so close to losing you," I said. "I understand now, what you meant. You said you couldn't bear it to lose me. I can't imagine living without you. And I almost lost you, before I ever had a chance to even know that."

Oscar sighed. He smiled, running one hand down my side. "It's over now," he said. "You saved me. You saved us, and so many others. Tomorrow, I will take you home, and we'll have the rest of our lives together." He frowned slightly. "That will be a very long time. Did I mention that?"

"Mention what?"

He smiled more broadly. "That in addition to the power of the change, being my mate gives you my lifespan. And I am immortal. As you are now, my Muirenn."

"You mean that?" I gasped. "But—"

"We can die. You did save my life, Muirenn. But we won't age." He ran his hand back up my body. "You'll always be young. Always beautiful."

"And always yours," I whispered, and kissed him. He returned the kiss with ardor, pressing me back onto the bed. I moaned against his mouth, welcoming his touch, his cock, running my hands over his skin and up his back as he rose and shifted against me, slowly filling me until his body was sealed against mine. Braced over me, his hands on either side of my head, he stopped, looking down at me. For an infinite time, we stayed that way, our bodies joined, our eyes only on each other, breathing in unison. Then he lowered himself down to kiss me again, and he started moving. It felt like a blessing, like a most solemn ritual, like an invocation of powers that not even the greatest sorcerers of song had ever wielded. I clung to him, scoring his back with my nails as I crested and crashed like a wave against rock, over and over until his voice raised with him and we fell together into ecstasy.

Warm in his arms, feeling him curled around my body, I watched as the light warmed and brightened around us. His breath was soft and gentle against my neck, and I thought him asleep until he kissed my nape.

"We should bathe and eat," he murmured. "If we want to fly today."

As his words, a thought occurred to me. "Do ravens mate on the wing?"

He chuckled. "You're thinking of eagles, my love."

I smiled, twisting so that I was facing him. "Can ravens mate on the wing?"

He looked thoughtful, then shook his head. "No. That's not our way." He looked quizzically at me. "Why? Were you wanting to try it?"

"Maybe," I demurred, and he laughed.

"Perhaps. Perhaps one day. But for today, our flying is for going home."

We bathed, playing like children in the bathhouse until others arrived, wanting their turn. Then we broke our fast with Gaynor, who kissed me, told me he loved me, and wished me well. Then he glowered at Oscar and threatened him with a plague of fleas if anything should ever happen to me. Oscar laughed, clearly delighted to be treated so familiarly, then surprised Gaynor by hugging him warmly. Finally, we left the College, and I took wing for the first time as a raven, racing Oscar and the wind through the skies, hearing his laughter echoed in my own. We were going east, he told me. East, towards the highest peaks. Towards home.

It was nearing sunset when we finally circled down to land just outside the wall of a baile built into the side of the highest mountain. Oscar landed first, then caught me as I shed my feathers and landed.

"Well?" he asked. "Was it everything your dreams led you to believe?"

I laughed, hugging him tightly. "And more. Oh, when can we fly again?"

"Tomorrow, my wildling. Now…" He turned, and I looked past him to see a man standing at the gate. His resemblance to Oscar was strong, save only that his eyes were gold, and his hair was streaked with gray. His arm was injured, and he had it in a sling.

"Well, this is a surprise," he called out. "Oscar?"

"My older brother Diarmuid," Oscar murmured. "Diarmuid, my wife, Muirenn. Also, my apprentice."

Diarmuid stopped in his tracks, looked at me, then looked back at Oscar. "Which surprises me more, the wife or the apprentice? I'm not certain. Welcome to Dun-Morrigan, little sister."

"Thank you," I said softly, hanging back. Oscar looked down at me, then wrapped his arm around my shoulders and smiled.

"Come inside, the both of you. There's food ready, if you're hungry. And the others will be curious. And… Oscar?" Diarmuid asked as we all started through the gates. "Why do you look as though you've been in a fight?"

Oscar looked down at me, then back at his brother. He smiled and asked, "How's the wing?"

"Ah. Of course. Why do I even bother to ask? Grainne says I should be able to start trying to use it again soon. Ah… you won't tell me what happened, but I will ask this. Do you need to speak to her as a healer?"

"Thank you, but no. I'm fine," Oscar answered, and his arm around me tightened. "Better than fine."

* * *

I came into our house to find Oscar bent over his worktable, muttering to himself. I waited until he stopped before approaching; I didn't want to disturb what he was working on by startling him.

"Any news?" I asked.

"None so far," he answered. He turned, and I saw the dark shadows under his eyes, the hollows in his face.

257

How many meals had he worked through? How many times in the two months that we'd been wed had I brought him a bowl or a plate, only to find them untouched and cold hours later? I'd lost count.

"How are you, wildling?" he asked, his voice softening. "The message, that unsettled you far more than it should have." He held his arms open, and I gladly moved into his embrace, resting my head on his chest. For the moment, we were at peace.

"You'll find a way," I murmured.

"I will. I promise you that. I will," Oscar murmured into my hair. "And then…"

"Then, we'll be safe," I said, looking up at him and smiling. "The three of us will be safe."

He frowned, just for a moment. Then his jaw dropped slowly. "Muirenn…?"

"I missed my courses again this month. I'm pregnant." I squeaked as he scooped me up in his arms and spun me around, laughing. Then he put me down on my feet and kissed me, holding my face between his hands as if I were the most precious thing in the world.

He let me go, sitting down hard on his stool, then drawing me into his lap. "Oh, my Muirenn. Thank you. That… that was what I needed to hear." He rested his hand on my stomach. "A boy or a girl, do you think?"

"We'll know in seven months. But does it matter?"

He smiled. "No. Not at all. Maire, if it's a girl?"

"I would like that. And what for a boy?"

He leaned his head against mine, and I felt him sigh. "You choose, for a boy."

"Oscar," I answered immediately. He looked at me quizzically, then realized I wasn't calling his name.

"After me?"

"Why not? After the best man I know."

He kissed me again, and his hands started roaming. We were a few short steps from our bed when the crystals in his distance-communication spell chimed. He groaned, his hands falling still on my hips.

"Why did I ever think that thing was a good idea?" he muttered, making me giggle as he went to activate the spell. The giggle, the ardor, that all faded as we listened to the report from Dun-Righ. Another attack by Ailill, but this time, someone had fought back and had driven off the beast. More, they had somehow hurt Ailill, something that had never been done before. I looked at Oscar, and knew that this was the end. We knew now what could kill the thing.

"That's it," he whispered as the spelled crystals fell silent. "The answer. The weapon. How stupid I am! I should have known… it was in the blasted spell that made him! I'm an idiot, wildling! I have to tell them. I have to tell the others."

"They're in the hall. Petran finally claimed Turlach this morning."

"Did he really? It's about time!" Oscar ran his fingers through his hair, laughed once, then pulled me back into his arms and kissed me. "Stay warm for me, my wildling. I'll be back."

I smiled up at him and let him go. "I'll be waiting."

He grabbed his cloak and ran for the door, stopping only a moment to turn back to me and say, "I love you, Muirenn."

"I love you, too," I answered as he ran out the door. I wasn't sure if he heard me, but it didn't matter. We had all the time in the world.

Excerpt from
The White Raven: Morrigan's Heir

Chapter One

The *urla* in Dun Righ was the pride of High Queen Aideen. The ornamental lawn of smooth, even grass was usually kept immaculate, unmarred by weeds or blight. Today, however, there was a definite path being carved in the turf—the marks of a single man pacing back and forth through grass still kissed by frost. Diarmuid knew he might be courting the queen's wrath, but he simply could not stand still.

Six years. It had been six years since he'd married Grainne. Four times, her womb had quickened. Four times, the babe had died long before it had ever drawn breath. But this time, he'd dared to hope. At five months, Grainne had still been well, glowing in her joy. It had been the longest she'd ever carried a child, the first time she'd ever felt the babe move within her, and her hopes were high. High enough that she'd insisted on accompanying Diarmuid to the celebration of the birth of the High King's daughter. She would be fine, she assured Diarmuid. And so, they'd come to Dun Righ.

Only she hadn't been fine. She'd awakened him in the middle of the night in tears. She was bleeding. Frantic, he'd called for healers. Gormlaith, the queen's midwife, assured him that she would do all in her power to make certain that Grainne bore a healthy babe. Diarmuid had let her words wash over him—he'd heard the same too many times before. He'd sent the others back to Dun Morrigan, silently assuming that he and Grainne would be joining them before too long.

That had been three months ago. Gormlaith had proven her words over and over, until this morning at dawn had come the servant with word from the midwife—Grainne was in labor. That had been hours ago, and Diarmuid had been forbidden to see his wife since then. So, he waited, and paced, watching the cold winter sun crawl toward the horizon as he silently traced the ruins of his despair into a narrow strip of frost-tipped grass on the High Queen's *urla*.

"Diarmuid."

The voice was familiar and unexpected. Diarmuid spun, shocked.

"Petran!" he looked at his brother, not quite believing what he was seeing. "What are you doing here?"

"Came to check on you. We miss you at home," Petran answered. "And honestly, I can count moons with the best of them. I know it'll be soon." He looked around. "Where's Grainne? What are you doing out here alone when everyone else is in the feast hall?"

"Is it that late?"

Petran nodded. "Diarmuid, what's going on? You look like you haven't slept. What's wrong? Where's Grainne?"

Diarmuid blinked. Where had his wits gone? "Because I haven't slept. Are you alone?" Diarmuid looked around, half expecting to see the other sons of the Morrigan and their families appearing from the darkening sky.

"No. Turlach and Sorcha came with me. Sorcha

wanted to see Cormac." Petran's smile faded, and he grabbed Diarmuid's arm. "You didn't answer me. Where's Grainne?"

Diarmuid turned to look at the house that he'd been doing his best to ignore. "There. They told me I can't see her. Not until—"

"She's giving birth?" Petran interrupted. "That's good, isn't it?"

Diarmuid turned back to Petran. He swallowed, meeting his brother's eyes. "You'll take care of them? The rest of the flock? If—"

Petran's jaw dropped. He looked horrified. He opened his mouth to protest, but Diarmuid shook his head and kept speaking, "You're the next oldest now. It's for you to do, if—"

"Don't *say* that!" Petran snapped. "She'll be fine! And the babe will be fine." He looked past Diarmuid, then stepped closer and pulled him into a tight embrace. "We've lost too many brothers. No more. You're not leaving us. And neither is she."

Diarmuid closed his eyes and rested his forehead on his brother's shoulder. "I never should have sent you home."

"No, you should have come with us," Petran murmured.

Diarmuid shook his head and straightened. "No. No, it was good that we stayed. Gormlaith… Petran, if I didn't know better, I'd swear that she's Brigid in disguise. I don't think Myrna could have done this."

Petran nodded. "Or she would have, with the others. How long has it been?"

Diarmuid closed his eyes and took a long breath. "Since before dawn."

265

"And you've been here, killing the grass, since then?" Petran whistled. "Right. You need to get warm. You need a drink, something hot to eat, and someone else to take the watch for a bit. Tell Turlach where I am, will you?"

Diarmuid nodded past Petran. "You can tell him. And we'll all wait. I'm not leaving." He smiled at his brother's mate, who was limping toward them through the growing shadows.

"There you are," Turlach called. "What are we doing out here?"

"Waiting," Petran answered. "Where's Sorcha?"

Turlach shook his head. "On a tear." He glanced over his shoulder, then pitched his voice low. "I think we'll be taking Cormac home with us when we go. I know you think that the Queen is a lovely woman, and I know you think it's good for him to be part of the boys troop here—"

"He needs to learn to live alongside the mortals," Diarmuid said. "And it's good for him to be in a new place. The change—"

"Oh, I know that," Turlach agreed. "But he's learning more than that. Someone has put some funny ideas in the boy's head, and the healing we were hoping for doesn't seem to be happening here. Sorcha isn't happy, and I think the fostering ends tonight."

Diarmuid stared at Turlach. "Ideas? What sort of ideas?"

Turlach raised both hands. "Nothing I'll say aloud. But do you remember when we were coming to Dun Righ for the wedding? I told you about the girls that you'd find here? The ones that wanted a high-born husband?"

Diarmuid frowned, but he nodded. "That was a time ago. I do remember."

"Aideen was one of those. And I think she might be realizing that the high-born husband that she got isn't the one that she wanted. She isn't happy, and she's souring. And she's realizing that any sons of yours might have more claim to the throne than hers."

Diarmuid sniffed. "Hardly. There's not many that know that Eogan and I share a sire, and I've no claim nor desire to be High King." His eyes narrowed. "Turlach, are you telling me that the *Queen* is ill-wishing my child?"

Turlach coughed. "I never heard her say it, nor can I prove anything. But just now, I heard words from Cormac's mouth that I would never think to hear. Not from one that bore feathers. And he's been here long enough to pick up some habits that have made Sorcha ready to pull hair out by the roots, and she's not too picky about whose. Which is why I'm here and not there. I know better than to be between two she-cats when they fight, and one of them our Sorcha."

Diarmuid studied him for a moment, then looked up at the clouds painted scarlet and gray by the setting sun. "Spending the year here was supposed to help him. That's what Grainne thought. That new surroundings, new people, would bring him out of his pain. We'll bring the boy home. Niall will be glad of it. It's time Cormac started training with his father."

"True," Petran said. "He's grown taller. He'll be a big man, Cormac will. His namesake was a big man, too."

"Sorcha's father?" Turlach asked. Diarmuid nodded.

"Cormac probably massed the same as you both together," he said. "And none of it fat. But he was a merry man, for all of it."

"Our Cormac will be a merry one, too," Petran

assured him. "We'll bring him home. He's been through a time of it, but we'll find a way to gentle him again. You'll see."

"It's simpler at home, on our mountain." Diarmuid turned back toward the house he'd been trying to ignore. "I want my son to see our mountain. My daughter."

A hand closed over his shoulder, and he turned to see Petran. "They'll be fine, Diarmuid. They'll both be fine."

Diarmuid nodded, looking back toward the house. It was far enough from the *urla* that he couldn't hear what was happening inside—that was why he'd chosen to wait here and not any closer. The waiting was torturous, but hearing Grainne calling for him had been worse.

"What are you all doing out here?"

Diarmuid smiled and turned toward the red-haired woman approaching them. "Sorcha. Waiting."

"Waiting?" Sorcha repeated. Her eyes widened. "Grainne's having the baby? What are you doing here?"

Diarmuid nodded toward the house. "Gormlaith wouldn't let me stay."

"Wouldn't—and you *listened*?" Sorcha gaped at him, then grabbed his arm and started to drag him toward the house. "Men!"

"What did I do wrong?" Diarmuid asked. "She told me I couldn't stay!"

"And what did Grainne want?" Sorcha asked. "You don't listen to the midwife for this. You listen to your wife, Diarmuid. Now you're going in there."

"But—"

She stopped and turned toward him. "Who knows more about this? You or me?"

"You do, but—"

"You were there when the pair of you started this road, no?"

Diarmuid blinked at her, realized what she was saying, then gasped, "Sorcha!"

She folded her arms over her chest. "You should be there at the end of the road, too. Myrna had Niall in for all of our children. You should be there for yours."

Diarmuid tried to think of an argument, but his brains seemed to be frozen. Silent, he nodded, and followed Sorcha back up to the door.

"I'll go in. Wait a moment," Sorcha said. She opened the door and slipped inside, leaving Diarmuid outside to fidget uncomfortably. He could hear voices inside, indistinct, and wondered what was happening. When Sorcha would come back, and if he'd be banished to the *urla* once more.

The door opened, and Sorcha looked out. She smiled. "Come inside. Grainne's been waiting for you."

* * *

At dawn, Petran sent Turlach back to Dun Morrigan to summon the others. Either they'd be here to welcome their oldest brother's child… or they'd be here to support Diarmuid and Grainne as they had before. Petran wasn't sure which it would be. He hoped not the latter. Not again. Alone, he wandered into the feast hall, thinking he might find a servant to bring him something to eat before he returned to his vigil. He wasn't expecting to find anyone but servants awake, so hearing voices made him stop and step back into shadows. He drew his cloak of feathers around himself, preparing to shift and fly.

"You're not going to be important anymore, Mama

says!" a high voice exclaimed. 'And that's why you're not going to be allowed to stay here. You can't sit at my table or share my lessons or be my foster brother anymore, because you're not important. Nobody is going to care about you anymore."

"I am so important! My father is the High King's own smith, and that's important!"

Petran moved through the shadows until he was behind a pillar and could see the two boys. One was his nephew, 11 year-old Cormac. The other, the one who was loudly declaring to his porridge that Cormac was no longer worthy, was the High King's seven-year-old son, Diarmuid. They were alone, which struck Petran as strange. Where were the rest of the boys being fostered at court? Or the man tasked with teaching them? Petran wasn't sure who that was, but these boys should have been breaking their fast with him and learning their morning lessons.

"You're not a smith, and you won't be for years and years. You're only here because you're Uncle Diarmuid's heir. Mama says that when Uncle Diarmuid's son is born, you won't be his heir anymore." The boy sniffed, then gestured with his spoon. "You go back to being a nobody that no one cares about."

Cormac frowned down at his own bowl. Then he raised his head. "Aunt Grainne's lost four babies. This baby is going to die, too, and good riddance."

"Cormac!" Petran snapped, stepping out into view. Cormac went white, staggering to his feet.

"Uncle Petran!"

"Shame on you," Petran growled. "Is this what fostering has taught you?" He heard giggling and turned on the younger boy. "And you! Don't think I won't be speaking to your father about this!" He turned back to

270

Cormac. "Go to your mother, boy. And you'll tell her exactly what you just said, or I will, and it will be that much worse for you." He waited until Cormac had fled before turning to the other boy. "Your father is where?"

"Still abed," Diarmuid answered insolently.

"Then it looks like we'll be waking him," Petran said. "Up and march."

An hour later, Petran was fighting a headache, and to keep from swearing aloud as he crossed the *urla* toward the guesthouses. Eogan had been abed, all right. With Aideen, and she'd taken exception to Petran dragging her precious boy in by the ear. He hadn't realized that a woman could be quite that shrill—certainly none of his brothers' wives ever were. But Eogan had made her be still once Petran told him the conversation he'd overheard. There would be some shaking up in the high king's household, Petran was certain.

Now to see about his own kin—he whistled as he came to the door of the closest house, then peered inside. Empty. He hadn't seen Sorcha in the hall, nor had he seen Cormac since he'd sent the boy to find his mother. Not in the hall, not in the guesthouse. There was one other place he could check; he turned and started off toward the other guesthouse, the one where Diarmuid and Grainne were staying. The place where they were waiting. As he got closer, he heard it.

The wail of a baby's cry.

He stopped, his heart in his throat. He wasn't hearing things. That was a baby. And the sound was coming from in front of him. He staggered into a run, stopping only when he saw the door open. Sorcha came out, closing the door behind her. She saw him and smiled. She looked tired, but very pleased.

271

"And?" Petran demanded.

"And we're to send for the others," she answered. "Diarmuid wants to present the baby to them all."

"Already done," Petran said. "I sent Turlach an hour ago. *And*?"

Sorcha's smile broadened. "A boy." She glanced over her shoulder, and her smiled faded slightly.

"What?" Petran demanded. "What's wrong?"

"Nothing," Sorcha answered. "Just… no, nothing."

"Sorcha!"

"You'll see him when the others do," Sorcha said. "Now be still. Grainne needs to sleep."

"Looks as if you do, too," Petran said. He put his arm around Sorcha's shoulders. "Come on. Have you seen your boy?"

"Cormac? No. I've been here since before dawn. Why?"

Petran considered it. Then he shook his head. He'd tell her later. "Nothing. Come on. You need to sleep."

* * *

Petran was watching the skies from the *urla*, tracking the flock of ravens as they approached. Silently, he counted. Who had come? Who had stayed? The younger children had stayed behind, surely. They weren't ready for the all-day flight from Dun Morrigan. Who had stayed with them?

Turlach was the first to shed feathers, landing with a lightness that disguised his lame leg. He landed close enough to Petran that all the harper needed to do was close his arms to embrace his mate. The others shed their cloaks of feather around him, revealing that only the men had come, and then not even all of them.

"Fergus stayed behind?"

"Fergus stayed with the women, to help keep an eye on the littles," Cuanu answered. "What's the news, Petran?"

Petran grinned. "The news is that we're all to meet Diarmuid's son in the hall." He stressed the word, and saw smiles appear. "I haven't seen him yet. The only one who has is Sorcha."

Niall touched Petran's arm and arched a brow. Petran shook his head. "I haven't seen her since midday. I think she's been off with Grainne, teaching her to care for the baby. Don't be surprised if she wants another one after this, Niall."

Niall laughed silently, shaking his head. Petran grinned and gathered his brothers with a wave. "Come on. Eogan is waiting for us."

He waited, watching as they moved past him toward the hall. Cuanu was the next oldest after him, ever since his twin Ronan had died. Unmated still, and it looked as if he would always be so. Cathal and Maelan followed him, and silent Niall trailing after.

"What's wrong," Turlach murmured.

"I don't know," Petran answered, keeping his voice low. "Sorcha's been very closed mouth about the babe. And I've not been allowed to see him."

"We'll see him now," Turlach said. He tucked his arm into Petran's. "Lead on, love. I'm tired."

Petran nodded and followed his brothers into the hall. Inside, the High King greeted them all, pouring mead with his own hands. The Queen was there, but her smile was brittle. Petran met her eyes, and she looked away before making a muffled excuse and leaving the hall.

"Something wrong with the Queen?" Cuanu asked Petran.

Petran considered, then shook his head. "She's had something stuck in her craw these past few days."

Cuanu looked puzzled. He arched a brow, glanced the way the Queen had gone, then narrowed his eyes at Petran. "Truly?"

"Something of the sort, yes," Petran answered mildly, ignoring Turlach's snickering.

"Strange." Cuanu moved away, and Turlach shifted closer.

"Does she now?" he whispered.

"I caught her boy and Cormac, and I perhaps heard what you heard, or worse," Petran whispered back. "And I brought it to Eogan. The queen will be taking the winter with her own kin, for her health. And we might have young Diarmuid to foster."

Turlach nodded. "That will be good for him. He'll learn."

Petran grinned. "He will, won't he?"

A quick flurry of movement, and Petran turned to see Niall heading toward the door. The reason was obvious—Sorcha had come into the hall. She kissed him, then drew him off to the side. A moment later, Diarmuid appeared in the door. He looked more tired than Petran could remember seeing him, but there was a light to him that was new. On his right arm was Grainne, still pale, leaning on her mate for support. And in the crook of Diarmuid's left arm...

"Oh, he's a tiny one!" Maelan said from behind Petran.

"Not surprising," Cathal added. "He's a month early."

"He cried well," Petran said. "Heard him from a good distance away."

"Good. Good lungs on him, then." Cathal said.

Diarmuid cleared his throat, and everyone fell silent. He glanced at Grainne, who smiled and nodded. Then he looked back at his brothers. "Brothers, come and meet our son."

Petran moved closer along with the others. From where he stood, the baby looked like a bundle of blankets. Then Diarmuid moved a fold of cloth, and Petran stopped. So did everyone else.

"Diarmuid?" Eogan finally broke the silence. "Are… are his feathers *white*?"

Diarmuid had been looking lovingly down at the baby in his arms. He glanced up, then back down. "Yes. So is his hair. What little he has."

"A white raven?" Petran murmured. "Is that because he was early, do you think? Will he get darker?"

"I don't know," Diarmuid answered. "Mother didn't answer when I asked her. It doesn't matter, Petran."

"Is he broken?" The voice was high, piping, and Cormac came closer, repeating himself. Petran hadn't even realized he was there. "Is he broken, like Fergus?"

"He is not," Grainne snapped. "He is perfect, and he is healthy." She reached out and rested her hand on the baby's chest. "He'll grow to be a fine man."

"Has there ever been a white raven before?" Maelan asked. "Cuanu, do you know?"

Cuanu scowled. Then he shook his head. "Not that I know of. Perhaps. If it happens now, it's likely happened before. I can find out, if you think it matters."

"It doesn't," Diarmuid said. "Not to us." He looked up, drew himself up to his full height, and announced, "I,

Diarmuid, son of the Morrigan, called the Raven King, acknowledge this child as my son and heir." He glanced down again, and his smile softened his face. "His name is Lorcan."

Glossary

Acushla—an endearment. Literally "My pulse"

A Ri—A term of respect. Literally "My King"

A run mo chroi—an endearment. Literally "O love of my heart."

a shiorghra—an endearment. Literally, "My forever love."

Baile—A hold or keep with a wall. It is from the word baile that we get the word bailey, meaning the inner portion of a castle. Literally "home"

Deamhan aeir—A malevolent spirit in Celtic mythology. May have been associated with vultures or carrion-eaters. Literally "Demon of the Air"

Dun—An ancient Celtic stronghold or fortress, usually of some importance. May or may not have been a ring-fort.

Fianna—The warrior band led by Fionn Mac Cumhaill, a legendary Celtic hero.

Fidchell—an ancient Celtic game of strategy, similar to chess

Hurling—An ancient Celtic team game, similar to rugby, soccer and field hockey, played with sticks called *hurleys* and a ball. The object of the game is to knock the ball between the other team's goalposts. The ball is moved by kicking, slapping with an open hand, or using the hurley.

Scath na Fiach dubh—the full name of Scath, the fictional village located near Dun-Morrigan. Literally "Shadow of the Raven."

Urla—an ornamental lawn found inside a baile.

Petran's song to Turlach is adapted from two songs found in the book *The Love Songs of Connacht*, collected and translated by Douglas Hyde, and published in 1904.

The Need-fire chant is adapted from two songs found in the book *Carmina Gadelica*, collected and translated by Alexander Carmichael, and published in 1900.

About the Author

Elizabeth Schechter has been called one of the top erotica and alternative sexuality writers in the world. Her writing credits include the award-winning steampunk erotic romance *House of Sable Locks*, the Celtic fantasy *Princes of Air,* and 2021 VIVIAN finalist *Written in Water*, the first book of the *Heir to the Firstborn* serial

She was born in New York at some point in the past. She is officially old enough to know better, but refuses to grow up. She lives in Central Florida with her husband and son.

Elizabeth can be found online at
http://elizabethschechterwrites.com,

or on Facebook at
https://www.facebook.com/Elizabeth.A.Schechter.

You can also find her on Patreon, at
https://www.patreon.com/EASchechter.

Subscribe to Elizabeth's newsletter at
https://www.subscribepage.com/k4u7k2

If You Like This Title, You Might Like Books in the SoulShares Series by Rory Ni Coileain:

Hard as Stone:
Book One of the SoulShares Series

Gale Force:
Book Two of the SoulShares Series

Deep Plunge:
Book Three of the SoulShares Series

Firestorm:
Book Four of the SoulShares Series

Blowing Smoke:
Book Five of the SoulShares Series

Mantled in Mist:
Book Six of the SoulShares Series

Undertow:
Book Seven of the SoulShares Series

Stone Cold:
Books Eight in the SoulShares Series

Back Door to Purgatory:
Book Nine in the SoulShares Series

Other Riverdale Avenue Books
You Might Like

The Siren and the Sword:
Book One of the Magic University Series
By Cecilia Tan

The Tower and the Tears:
Book Two of the Magic University Series
By Cecilia Tan

The Incubus and the Angel:
Book Three of the Magic University Series
By Cecilia Tan

The Prophecy and the Poet:
Book Four of the Magic University Series
By Cecilia Tan

Spellbinding:
Tales From Magic University
Edited by Cecilia Tan

www.ingramcontent.com/pod-product-compliance
Lightning Source LLC
Chambersburg PA
CBHW020948260626
4716 9CB00000 6B/1878

* 9 7 8 1 6 2 6 0 1 6 3 1 6 *